MCGURK STOOD ON THE EDGE OF THE TRENCH.

Now he had the fighting room he needed. He snorted through both nostrils like a wild bull and glowered at the Japanese soldiers rushing toward him, murder and destruction in their eyes. He heard rifle fire and grenade explosions all around him, and was aware other GIs were climbing out of their holes too. He raised his rifle and bayonet high in the air and screamed: *"Come on! Here I am!"*

Lowering his rifle, he aimed the tip of his bayonet at the Japanese men and charged...

D1530228

Suicide River

by
John Mackie

A JOVE BOOK

Excepting basic historical events, places, and personages, this series of books is fictional, and anything that appears otherwise is coincidental and unintentional.

The principal characters are imaginary, although they might remind veterans of specific men whom they knew. The Twenty-third Infantry Regiment, in which the characters serve, is used fictitiously—it doesn't represent the real historical Twenty-third Infantry, which has distinguished itself in so many battles from the Civil War to Vietnam—but it could have been any American line regiment that fought and bled during World War II.

These novels are dedicated to the men who were there. May their deeds and gallantry never be forgotten.

SUICIDE RIVER

A Jove Book/published by arrangement with
the author

PRINTING HISTORY
Jove edition/September 1985

ISBN: 0-515-08342-9

Jove books are published by The Berkley Publishing Group,
200 Madison Avenue, New York, N.Y. 10016. The words
"A JOVE BOOK" and the "J" with sunburst are trademarks
belonging to Jove Publications, Inc.

PRINTED IN THE UNITED STATES OF AMERICA

ONE . . .

It was night in the jungle, and the full moon bathed the trees and bushes in a spectral glow. The young Japanese officer walked along the path confidently, because he was far behind his lines and didn't think American soldiers were about. He carried his pack on his back and a Nambu pistol in its holster attached to his belt. His cap perched low over his eyes; his knee-high boots were highly polished. He was a staff officer, on his way to the headquarters of Colonel Yukio Katsumata.

Birds sang in the trees and crickets chirped all around the young Japanese officer. He was tall and emaciated, because rations weren't plentiful for Japanese soldiers on New Guinea. It was July 2, 1944, and they'd been taking a beating on the hot, steamy island since 1942, but still had plenty of fight left in them. A major offensive was being planned by General Adachi, to retake the Tadji airfields and expel the Americans from the territory around Aitape.

The young officer was in a good mood. He wanted to whistle a tune, but that wasn't proper in a war zone where so many Japanese soldiers were suffering from inadequate rations and medical supplies. The young officer felt excellent because he believed General Adachi's big offensive would succeed. He knew General Adachi had been working on it for weeks, and the general had a brilliant tactical mind. It would be wonderful if the offensive succeeded, because the Imperial Japanese Eighteenth Army on New Guinea badly needed a victory to boost morale and improve its strategic situation in the Aitape area.

If a major victory was won, the young officer hoped he'd get a promotion and perhaps a furlough back to Japan. He was from Tokyo and wanted very much to see his family again, especially his younger sister, whom he adored. He also wanted

1

to go to the Ginza at night and spend time with geisha girls, drinking sake, smoking cigarettes, and getting laid. The young officer was only twenty-two years old and got awfully lonely sometimes. It'd be fabulous if he could hold a beautiful woman for a while, and have her hold him. He imagined himself rolling around on a tatami mat with a geisha girl whose face was painted white, her hair shining like a net full of diamonds. Slowly he'd take off her clothes and fondle her soft skin. An erection grew in his pants when he thought of the pleasures he'd enjoy if ever he returned to Tokyo again.

He became so involved with his vision of glamorous geisha girls that he was barely aware of mosquitoes biting his neck and arms. A faint rustle in the bushes in front of him hardly registered in his turbulent mind. The narrow path wound through the jungle in front of him and eerie shadows were cast by the pale moonlight, but the young lieutenant saw only a tiny room in a geisha house off the Ginza, and he made wild passionate love to the prettiest geisha he'd ever seen.

Something metallic flashed for a split second in the moonlight, and then *chung!*—an American Army–issue Ka-bar knife slammed blade-first into his chest. The young Japanese officer stopped dead in his tracks. He dropped to his knees, and two American soldiers burst out of the bushes beside him, one grabbing his arm, another grabbing a leg; they dragged him into the thick tangled vegetation. The first American soldier returned to the path and messed up all traces of the dragging. Then he joined the other American soldier in the bushes.

The first American soldier was Pfc. Frankie La Barbara from New York City. "He got anything on him?" he asked.

Lieutenant Dale Breckenridge from Richmond, Virginia, searched the young Japanese officer's pockets, as blood oozed from the wound made by the knife.

"Nothing yet," said Lieutenant Breckenridge, turning the Japanese officer onto his side.

Lieutenant Breckenridge opened the pack on the back of the dead man and found a leather case inside. "What's this?" he asked.

He opened the flap of the leather case and saw a sheaf of papers. He thumbed through the pages, and they were covered with typed Japanese characters. "Looks like something important," he said, answering his own question.

He took off his pack and opened it, stuffing the Japanese leather case inside. The bushes swished behind them and Private Clement R. Bisbee appeared, a smile on his baby face.

"Gimme my knife," he said.

"Take it yourself," replied Lieutenant Breckenridge.

Bisbee bent over the dead Japanese officer and turned him onto his back, pulling out his Ka-bar knife. Blood welled after it, and Bisbee wiped the knife on the pant leg of the dead Japanese officer. Bisbee had been a roustabout with a carnival before the war, and taken lessons from the knife thrower. His ambition had been to become a knife thrower himself, but the Japs bombed Pearl Harbor and he was drafted into the U.S. Army.

The bushes rustled again and Private Victor Yabalonka, the former longshoreman from San Francisco, appeared, followed by Pfc. Billie Jones, known as the Reverend Billie Jones because he'd been an itinerant preacher in Georgia before the war. Last came Private Joshua McGurk from Skunk Hollow, Maine. McGurk was seven feet tall and weighed three hundred pounds. He was the giant of the recon platoon, but had the brain of a flea.

Lieutenant Breckenridge closed his pack and put his arms through the straps. He was six feet four inches tall and weighed 250 pounds, with a few old acne scars on his cheeks. Before the war he'd been first-team fullback for the University of Virginia, but a bullet had punctured his left leg two weeks ago and now he walked with a limp. He raised his head and listened to the jungle around him. He and his men were on a reconnaissance far behind enemy lines, and they had to be careful. One wrong move and everybody was dead.

Lieutenant Breckenridge wondered what to do next. All his men except one looked at him expectantly, hoping he'd end the reconnaissance and return to their lines on the other side of the Driniumor River. The one man who didn't look at him was Private Bisbee, because he was down on his hands and knees, going through the pockets of the dead Japanese officer. Bisbee was a pathological thief and couldn't help himself. He knew the other men despised him for what he was doing, but they could go fuck themselves. Bisbee wasn't sensitive about what other people thought of him.

He yanked out the Japanese officer's wallet and opened it

3

up. The first thing he saw was a picture of a young girl, around fourteen years old. Bisbee tossed the picture over his shoulder and searched through the wallet for loot. He found Japanese money, and there was no place to spend it, but that didn't stop Bisbee. A smile spread over his baby face as he stuffed the money into his back pocket. The wallet contained nothing else except cards, so he tossed them over his shoulder and opened the Japanese officer's mouth, looking for gold teeth. His smile broadened when he spotted one in back on the bottom, and he reached into his rear pocket for his pliers.

"Look at this guy," Frankie La Barbara said disgustedly. "What a fucking scumbag—stealing from the dead!"

"Up your ass," Bisbee said. "You wanna do the same thing yourself, but you ain't got the fucking guts."

Frankie snarled and bared his teeth. He had swarthy Mediterranean features and his nose was bent and broken in numerous places along its once-noble length due to hand-to-hand combat with Japanese soldiers and other GIs. "Say that again," Frankie said, balling up his fists.

Lieutenant Breckenridge turned at him. "Cut it out!"

"Whataya looking at me for?" Frankie replied. "Why don't you say something to that fucking thief down there?"

"Shut up," Lieutenant Breckenridge said. "You two can fight it out when we get out of here."

Frankie looked down at Bisbee. "I'm gonna kick your ass," he said.

"That's what you think," Bisbee replied.

Private McGurk jerked his head three inches to the right and twitched his nose. "I hear something," he said.

"Hit it," Lieutenant Breckenridge said softly.

The men dropped silently to the ground, holding their Thompson submachine guns ready to fire. At first they heard nothing except ordinary jungle sounds—the chirps of insects and the hoot of an owl—but then they heard footsteps and bodies brushing past leaves and branches. Lieutenant Breckenridge looked at McGurk and realized that the big imbecile had sharp ears. Throughout the patrol McGurk had heard ominous sounds before anyone else. Lieutenant Breckenridge looked at McGurk with new respect, and McGurk turned to Lieutenant Breckenridge and grinned like a happy little puppy. *What a strange son of a bitch*, Lieutenant Breckenridge thought.

4

The sounds drew closer, and the GIs heard them more distinctly. A group of soldiers was headed their way along the trail, and they had to be Japanese. The trail was only eight feet away, on the other side of the bushes, but it was night and the bushes were thick. The Japanese soldiers should pass by without noticing the GIs lying there.

Lieutenant Breckenridge looked at his watch. It was three o'clock in the morning. They'd been out since 2300 hours roaming around behind enemy lines, an ordinary reconnaissance to gather information. So far they'd seen troop movement and supplies being hand-carried forward. They'd killed the young Japanese officer and taken the papers in his pack. They'd learned that a road on their maps didn't exist in reality. Lieutenant Breckenridge figured that was enough for one night. There was no sense pushing things. It'd start getting light in another hour and a half anyway. When the coast was clear they'd start moving back.

The Japanese soldiers turned the bend and came into view through the tangled leaves and branches. The GIs lowered their heads and held their breath. Each hoped none of the others would sneeze or make a wrong move. Some of the men on patrol were new to the recon platoon, and the old-timers didn't trust them yet. Their hearts beat faster and their mouths got drier. The Japanese soldiers probably wouldn't spot them, but you could never be sure. Private Bisbee gripped the blade of his Ka-bar knife in his right hand. Bisbee was certain he could pierce the throat of a Japanese soldier with his knife, because he wasn't far away. The Japanese soldier wouldn't even know what hit him.

The Japanese soldiers came closer. The GIs could see them clearly now, and counted eight of them. An officer with knee-high boots led the way, his samurai sword swinging back and forth in its scabbard attacked to his belt. The Japanese soldiers came abreast of the GIs and marched by, not looking to the left or right, never suspecting six GIs were so close. The GIs watched them pass, hoping they wouldn't stop suddenly, or that one of the Japs wouldn't see something he shouldn't.

The last Jap in the column stopped, dropped to one knee, and retied his shoelaces. He made the bow slowly and deliberately, because it was difficult to see in the moonlight. He finished tying the knot on his right shoe, checked the one on

5

his left shoe, and then, as he stood up, saw something glint in the moonlight to his left.

It was the blade of the Ka-bar knife in Bisbee's hand, but Bisbee and the other GIs didn't know that. All they could see was the Japanese soldier staring suspiciously in their direction. They wondered what he was looking at. The Japanese soldier leaned closer to them, a quizzical expression on his face, and they knew he'd seen something he shouldn't. Lieutenant Breckenridge turned to Bisbee and gave him a meaningful look. Bisbee raised himself up quickly, drew back his arm, and threw the knife.

The Japanese soldier saw Bisbee's movements and jerked to the side. The knife sailed past him, and he heard it whistle through the air. He shouted at the top of his lungs, and Frankie La Barbara charged out of the bushes, his own Ka-bar knife blade-up in his right hand, thrusting it into the Japanese soldier's belly. The Japanese soldier raised his arms to protect himself, and Frankie's knife ripped his wrists and hands. The Japanese soldier screamed, and the other Japanese soldiers who'd just passed by hollered something in reply. Frankie raised his Ka-bar knife, slashing the Japanese soldier's throat and jugular vein. A torrent of blood gushed out. Frankie heard Japanese soldiers running toward him on the path. Turning around, he jumped back into the bushes, the Ka-bar knife in his right hand dripping blood.

Lieutenant Breckenridge jumped to his feet. "Let's get out of here!" he said.

He turned around and plunged into the thickest, most tangled part of the jungle, and the other GIs followed him, leaving behind the body of the dead Japanese soldier on the path, and the body of the dead Japanese officer in the bushes. The Japanese soldiers on the path came to the body of their fallen comrade and were shocked to see him dead because they hadn't imagined American soldiers could be this far behind their lines. They heard a commotion in the jungle straight ahead and their officer told them to open fire. They raised their Arisaka rifles and worked the bolts, but just then Thompson submachine guns blazed in the jungle, and .45-caliber bullets cut them apart.

The GIs from the recon platoon shot down the Japanese soldiers on the path, and the Japanese soldiers who weren't hit by bullets dropped to their bellies. The firing stopped and the screams and moans of the wounded could be heard.

In the jungle, Lieutenant Breckenridge raised himself up and turned around. "Follow me!" he said.

He raised his submachine gun and charged into the jungle with all the speed and power that had made him an outstanding fullback for the University of Virginia football team. His men followed him and the recon platoon rampaged through the foliage like wild horses, wanting to put as much distance between them and the path as possible, because they knew more Japanese soldiers would be coming soon to find out what all the commotion was about.

Not more than one thousand yards away, Colonel Yukio Katsumata was awakened out of a deep sleep by the shooting and shouting. He snapped to a sitting position and reached for his Nambu pistol on the little stand beside the tatami mat where he'd lain. Blinking his eyes, his long mustaches twitching, he realized the firing wasn't that close and represented no physical threat to him. "Officer of the Day!" he screamed.

A sallow sad-faced officer leapt through the tent flap and saluted. "Yes sir!" He was Lieutenant Masaji Fujiwara, assigned to the intelligence staff of Colonel Katsumata's regiment.

"What's going on out there !" Colonel Katsumata demanded.

"I don't know, sir!"

"Find out!"

"Yes sir!"

Lieutenant Fujiwara bounded out of the tent. Colonel Katsumata reached for the pack of cigarettes beside him and lit one with his lighter. *That shooting was very close,* he thought. *I'll have to beef up security around here.* He wanted to go back to sleep, but knew he couldn't until he found out what was going on. He pushed away his mosquito netting, and immediately the swarms of mosquitoes in his tent attacked him, sticking their needles into his flesh. Cursing, his long mustaches dangling an inch below his chin, he pulled on his uniform pants and put on his shirt, then waddled across the room to his desk, lighting the kerosene lamp with his cigarette lighter and sitting down. He placed his Nambu pistol on the desk beside him and puffed his cigarette, scowling as he waited for Lieutenant Fujiwara's report.

• • •

Approximately two miles away, Lieutenant General Hatazo Adachi perked up his ears at the sound of gunfire in the distance. He was sitting at his desk, working on the master plan for his grand offensive, and wondered what was going on. The gunfire sounded close, on his side of the Driniumor. "Officer of the Day!" he shouted.

The officer of the day, Lieutenant Tomoyoki Arazaki, poked his head past the tent flap. "Yes sir?"

"Find out what's going on out there!"

"Yes sir."

Lieutenant Arazaki's head disappeared. General Adachi returned his attention to the documents and maps on his desk. His big offensive against the Americans was scheduled to begin on the night of July 9, only seven days away, and he still had much to do. He wanted to make sure of all the plans himself, down to the smallest detail, because he could leave nothing to chance. He'd become commander of the Eighteenth Army in November 1942 and had been pushed all over eastern New Guinea by the Americans ever since, but now the time had come to stop. He and the Eighteenth Army were going to make their last stand, fighting to the finish, and winner take all.

General Adachi's Army deployed as he sat at his desk. Supplies were hand-carried to the front because he lacked transport, and if he had transport he wouldn't have gasoline, because the American Navy controlled the seas. American airplanes controlled the air. General Adachi's situation was desperate. His great offensive was doomed on paper, but still he thought he could bring it off because he believed Japan had God on her side. Like most Japanese officers, General Adachi was unable to admit defeat. He believed fighting to the death was the only honorable way out.

The Japanese Eighteenth Army on New Guinea was like a cornered wild animal, and there was nothing more dangerous than a cornered wild animal except maybe a cornered Japanese general with his reputation on the line.

General Adachi was fifty-four years old, of average height and build, and his thin mustache gave him the appearance of a Hispanic. He desperately wanted a victory, just as a gambler who's lost his shirt desperately wants his horse to come in. General Adachi knew his reputation had lost its luster on New

8

Guinea. He also knew the Imperial Army was being pushed back steadily all across the South Pacific by American and Australian soldiers. If he could win a victory it would be wonderful for his career, and a terrific morale builder for the Imperial Army. Imperial General Headquarters in Tokyo would have to take notice. Even the Emperor himself would hear about it. General Adachi would become a hero, although that wasn't the main reason he wanted to defeat the Americans.

The main reason he wanted to defeat the Americans was he wanted to defeat the Americans. He was a Japanese Army officer and his function in life was to win battles for the Emperor. The Americans had humiliated the Emperor with their various trade and naval treaties of the thirties, and finally pushed Japan to war. The Americans had to be punished for what they did, and General Adachi viewed himself as an instrument of the Emperor's justice.

He had to defeat the Americans, or at least inflict upon them a seriously crippling blow. His basic strategy consisted of a feint, another feint, and then his main blow, delivered with unswerving ferocity. The first feint would be against the middle of the American line. The second feint would strike the Americans on their left flank, which abutted the Pacific Ocean. Then the main blow would follow the first feint, against the center of the American line. General Adachi hoped to split the American forces in two, and then capitalize on their confusion by pushing forward quickly to the Tadji airfields, destroying all enemy aircraft in sight.

If General Adachi could capture the Tadji airfields, he'd feel he'd won the battle. But General Adachi was more ambitious than that. He wanted all the fruits of victory. After taking the Tadji airfields, he intended to press on to Aitape itself, attack the American headquarters there, capture the American high command in the vicinity, and make them prisoners of war.

He was certain all American resistance in the area would collapse if he could do that. Then a truly great victory would be his. The American advance in the South Pacific would be stopped. He and his men would become heroes to the Japanese people, and he wanted his men to have that recognition, because they'd sacrificed and suffered so much.

The maps blurred in front of General Adachi's eyes. He'd

9

been working all night, and now he had to get some rest. He knew he'd be no good to his men if he was too fatigued to think clearly. He removed his glasses and rubbed his eyes, then stood behind his desk, stretching and yawning. The sound of rushing footsteps came to his ears from the outer tent, and Lieutenant Arazaki entered his office, halting his forward movement and standing at attention in front of the tent flap.

General Adachi ended his stretch and sat back in his chair, reaching for a cigarette. "Well?" he said.

"Bad news I'm afraid, sir," Lieutenant Arazaki said. He was a tall, slender young man with a clean-shaven face and large ears. "An American patrol has somehow infiltrated this area. They've killed five of our soldiers, wounded three, but worst of all they've killed Lieutenant Kaneko and stolen the orders he was carrying to Colonel Katsumata's headquarters."

General Adachi was disturbed by what he'd just heard, but Japanese officers weren't supposed to show their emotions. The orders Lieutenant Kaneko had been carrying to Colonel Katsumata comprised the fundamental battle plan for Colonel Katsumata's regiment in the upcoming offensive. If the Americans were able to translate the orders and figure them out, they'd know the attack would come on the night of July 9. The element of surprise would be lost, but the Americans still wouldn't know the full attack plans. All they'd know was what the Katsumata Regiment's orders were on that night, and those orders could be altered.

"The Americans are still on the loose back here?" General Adachi asked.

"I'm afraid they are, sir."

"I assume they're being pursued?"

"Yes sir."

"Good. In the morning I want a full report on the final disposition of this matter. I want those Americans stopped first of all, and secondly, wake up Major Honda and tell him I expect to have his suggestions for improved security on my desk no later than 0800 hours. Is that clear?"

"Yes sir."

"Dismissed."

Lieutenant Arazaki turned and marched out of the office. General Adachi relaxed in his chair, puffing his cigarette, wondering how an American patrol could have penetrated so deeply

10

into the Japanese lines. *Our security must be lax,* General Adachi thought. *Measures will be taken tomorrow to make certain there are no more repetitions of this disgraceful situation.*

General Adachi stubbed out his cigarette in the ashtray. Wearily he rose from his chair and shuffled across the room, heading for his tatami mat and a few hours of much-needed sleep.

Corporal Charles Bannon from Pecos, Texas, lay on his back and stared at stars twinkling in the sky. He heard random bursts of gunfire in the distance and occasional explosions, typical sounds of a night on the front lines. Under ordinary circumstances Bannon would've slept through the night without a murmur or tremor, but the front lines no longer were ordinary circumstances for Bannon. He'd been away from the front for four months, languishing in Army hospitals, taking a thirty-day furlough back in the States, and he'd lost his front-line instincts. He was jittery and tense, still feeling pain from his old wounds, and not at all sure he'd be alive a week from then.

Bannon had a steel plate in his head and wore a long, jagged, thin scar on his face. His insides were stitched together because he'd been bayoneted during hand-to-hand fighting on Bougainville. He'd been a cowboy in Texas before the war, but that had been long ago and far away. Now he was an old soldier back at the front. He'd returned last night, too late to say hello to his old pals because they were all out on a patrol.

He knew some of his old pals were dead and many had been wounded. Last night he'd been told that his old platoon sergeant, John Butsko, had been wounded only a week ago and was at the division medical headquarters, recuperating. Bannon intended to visit him in the morning, if he could get away.

He heard the rattle of an automatic weapon firing in the distance, and a few seconds later another automatic weapon started up. Then he heard an explosion, random shots fired from rifles, and more automatic weapons. Bannon sat up and turned toward the direction of the fighting, which was far behind enemy lines. He wondered what was going on, and was glad he wasn't there. He wasn't sure of how well he could handle a firefight now. His wounds had been painful and he'd suffered much. He still got headaches from the steel plate in

11

his skull, and his guts still hurt dully deep inside him. He wasn't a hundred percent healed yet, but there he was back at the front, at his own request.

He was back because he'd felt guilty about taking it easy while his buddies were fighting, but that was only one of the reasons he'd requested the return to his old unit. The other reason was the nagging fear that he'd become a coward. Bannon was a Texan, and Texans deplore cowards. Bannon hated himself, because he suspected he'd lost his courage sometime during the fighting on Bougainville. That last fight, when he and the others had been surrounded, outnumbered, and fighting for their lives, had been a nightmare. Blood from the cut on his face had got into his eyes and he'd barely been able to see. He'd fought like a wild man, and then he'd been bayoneted. He'd fallen to the ground, but hadn't passed out for a long time. The pain had been incredible and there'd been no escape from it. It had been a gruesome experience which he never wanted to go through again.

But he knew he might very well go through it again, possibly even tomorrow, and the prospect of it scared him. He didn't think he could handle that degree of pain again. He was afraid he'd turn tail and run if the Japs ever came at him, and he despised the fear inside him, but there was nothing he could do about it. It was there and that was that. Somehow he'd have to overcome it. Somehow he'd have to become a man again. He didn't want to spend the rest of his life thinking he was a coward.

He sighed and fell back onto his back again, looking up at the starry heavens. Maybe tomorrow he'd find out what he was made of. He hoped he'd be able to handle whatever came up. He prayed he'd be able to overcome his fears and doubts.

From the distance, as background music for his thoughts, he heard explosions and the sounds of automatic weapons. *I wonder what's going on out there?* he asked himself.

Lieutenant Breckenridge held back the trigger on his Thompson submachine gun, and the deadly weapon bucked and stuttered in his hands. He aimed it high in the air and leveled a stream of hot lead at a Japanese soldier standing on a hill at the edge of the glen where the recon platoon had got itself trapped. The Japanese soldier was silhouetted against the moon, and Lieutenant Breckenridge saw him lose his footing and drop out of sight. Another Japanese soldier appeared on the hill where the first one had been, and Lieutenant Breckenridge squeezed the trigger of his submachine gun again, shooting that Japanese soldier off the hill.

All around Lieutenant Breckenridge his men fired their submachine guns at the swarms of Japs who'd managed to surround them in the jungle. Every time the Japs attempted to charge, the GIs held them off with barrages of withering submachine gunfire. The GIs threw hand grenades and stayed in motion, so the Japs wouldn't be able to zero in on them. It was dark in the jungle and the GIs had cover and concealment on their side.

Frankie La Barbara lay behind a bush, pointing his submachine gun around its side. He'd seen something move out there a few seconds ago, and was waiting for it to move again. Something jiggled, and he waited for a clearer look at what it was. It moved again and he thought, *Fuck it,* pulling the trigger of his submachine gun.

The gun barked viciously and Frankie saw the Japanese soldier pitch forward onto his face. Frankie turned around so he could retreat several yards, and saw Private Bisbee behind him, pointing his submachine gun at him. Frankie dropped onto his stomach and aimed his submachine gun at Private Bisbee. Both men stared at each other for a few awkward seconds.

"Go ahead!" Frankie shouted. "I dare you!"

"You go ahead!" Private Bisbee replied.

The Reverend Billie Jones happened to be standing near Bisbee, firing his submachine gun at a Jap trying to climb a tree, and he kicked Bisbee in the ass.

"Cut it out you two!" he hollered.

A Japanese bullet exploded into the ground to the right of the Reverend Billie Jones's foot. Two Japanese soldiers charged out of the bushes near Frankie La Barbara, screaming at the tops of their lungs, but Private Victor Yabalonka happened to be standing there with his Thompson submachine gun, and he mowed them down. Three Japs lunged out of the jungle on the other side of the clearing and Private McGurk pulled the trigger of his submachine gun, killing one of them, wounding another, and then his submachine gun said *click!*

13

It was empty, and the third Jap kept charging. He was a gaunt, scraggly son of a bitch, and McGurk dug in his heels and waited for him. The Japanese soldier drew closer and lunged with his rifle and bayonet. McGurk parried the blow easily and slammed the Japanese soldier in the face with the butt of his submachine gun.

The side of the Japanese soldier's head crumpled under the power of the blow, and he was thrown to the ground. *Pow*—a Japanese bullet passed so close to McGurk's face he could feel its heat. McGurk loaded a fresh clip into his submachine gun and sprayed the jungle in front of him.

A Japanese hand grenade sailed through the air and landed on the ground near Frankie La Barbara. He scooped it up and hurled it back at the Japs, then dropped to his stomach on the ground. *"Grenade!"* he hollered.

The other GIs dived to the jungle floor. The grenade exploded in midair, ripping apart the Japs who were in that vicinity. A Japanese bullet tore up the ground in front of Lieutenant Breckenridge. He flinched and fired his submachine gun in the direction from which he thought the bullet had come, while trying to figure out what to do next. He knew he and his patrol were surrounded. There was no clear path to freedom, so he and the others would have to make their own path.

"Listen to me!" he yelled. "When I say the word, follow me out of here! Don't stop until I say stop, and shoot anybody who gets in your way! Check your weapons and get ready!"

The men made sure their submachines had plenty of ammunition for the breakout. They had to get moving before more Japs arrived, because they couldn't fight off the entire Japanese Army.

"Anybody not ready?" Lieutenant Breckenridge asked, as bullets whistled over his head.

Nobody said anything, and that was good enough for Lieutenant Breckenridge. "Keep those guns firing," he said, "and follow me!"

The men from the recon platoon pulled the triggers of their submachine guns and sent hot lead flying into the jungle all around them. They swung their submachine guns from side to side so they could pepper as much of the jungle as they could, and then Lieutenant Breckenridge jumped to his feet and charged into the jungle, his big boots pounding on the ground.

14

"Follow me!" he bellowed.

The men rose up and ran after him, firing their submachine guns straight ahead. Lieutenant Breckenridge was the first one to hit the bushes, and he hurled himself through them the way he used to hurl himself through the line of the opposing team when he had the football and they told him to run for it.

But the opposing teams didn't have guns, and the Japs did. A bullet whizzed past Lieutenant Breckenridge's shoulder, and another nicked the fabric of his shirt. He ran forward as quickly as he could, swinging his submachine gun from side to side while keeping the trigger depressed, and his men followed, tearing the shit out of the jungle. The Japanese soldiers on that side of the clearing couldn't withstand the firepower, but they didn't retreat either. Bullets flew at them like angry gnats, and it was difficult for them to take careful aim. The GIs rolled right over them, shooting them in their heads, kicking them in their faces, stepping on their bodies, and rushing toward safety.

The GIs broke through the Japs on that side of the clearing and kept going, speeding through the jungle as quickly as they could, while behind them the Japanese soldiers still alive tried to figure out what the hell was going on. A few fired wildly at the retreating GIs, but the GIs disappeared rapidly into the jungle, and in a matter of minutes they were long gone.

TWO . . .

The sound of a typewriter clacking awoke Colonel "Hollerin'" Bob Hutchins, the commanding officer of the Twenty-third Infantry Regiment. He opened his eyes, wrinkled his nose, and raised his arm so he could look at his watch. It was 0700 hours, and his regiment had reveille at 0600 hours. His men already had eaten their breakfasts and were at work, while he still was all sprawled out in his sack.

He ran his tongue over his teeth and his mouth tasted as if a Japanese soldier had shit inside it. Groaning, he reached underneath his cot and groped around until he found his combat boots. Reaching inside one of the boots, he pulled out his flask full of white lightning, the booze concocted in his mess hall by one of his cooks. It was based on a recipe by the legendary Sergeant Snider, a former moonshiner who'd been wounded and shipped back to the States.

Colonel Hutchins unscrewed the cap and raised the mouth of the flask to his lips. He took a long draft, his Adam's apple bouncing up and down, and exhaled loudly as he screwed the top back on the flask. The white lightning burned its way down his throat and into his stomach, stimulating his mind, waking him up somewhat. Then he reached down into his other boot and pulled out a package of Luckies. He placed one between his lips, lit it with his trusty old Zippo, and inhaled the rich strong smoke into his lungs. That woke him up more. He was able to sit and swing his legs around to the floor. He looked at his office, the portable desk against the far wall, the chair behind the desk, and the two chairs in front of it, and he groaned, because it was another day at the front.

He puffed his cigarette and stood up, wearing only his baggy skivvie shorts and a few bandages here and there. His big fat stomach hung over the waistband of his skivvie shorts, and he

16

had skinny legs underneath a flaccid flat ass. His graying brown hair was cut at crew length and was sparse on the top of his head. Staggering, his cigarette hanging out of the corner of his mouth, he made his way to the tent flap and pushed it to the side.

Sergeant Koch, the regiment's sergeant major, sat behind his desk and studied the morning's correspondence and communiqués. Opposite Sergeant Koch, Pfc. Levinson, the regimental clerk, pounded his Remington typewriter. Colonel Hutchins cleared his throat. Sergeant Koch and Pfc. Levinson spun around and faced him.

"Get me some coffee," Colonel Hutchins croaked.

Sergeant Koch turned to Pfc. Levinson. "Get the colonel some coffee."

Pfc. Levinson jumped out of his chair as if he had a rocket up his ass, and ran out of the command post tent.

"Did the patrol get back all right?" Colonel Hutchins asked.

"It's not back yet," Sergeant Koch replied.

Colonel Hutchins felt a sinking sensation in his stomach, because the patrol should've been back by then. "Let me know when they get back."

"Yes sir."

Colonel Hutchins returned to his cot and picked his clothing off the chair beside it. He dressed himself, pausing to puff his cigarette and sip his white lightning. Pfc. Levinson arrived with a canteen mug full of hot black coffee.

"Put it on my desk," Colonel Hutchins said.

Pfc. Levinson placed the coffee on the colonel's desk and ran out of the office. Colonel Hutchins sat behind his desk and raised the canteen cup to his lips. The coffee tasted like kerosene, and Colonel Hutchins always wondered why Army coffee never tasted like regular civilian coffee. It was one of the great mysteries of his life, because he'd been told that Army coffee was identical to civilian coffee, and was brewed the exact same way.

Army cooks'd fuck anything up, he thought as he sipped the coffee. *The whole army's fucked up. So's the world.* Colonel Hutchins muttered and grumbled to himself as he tried to wake up and face the day. He wondered what had happened to his patrol from the recon platoon. If they weren't back yet, something bad must have happened to them.

Shit, he thought. *Those bastards had better get back here*

17

soon. I don't have time to put together a whole new recon platoon.

American troops in the Aitape vicinity were code-named the *Persecution Task Force*, and were under the command of Major General Charles P. Hall. As the sun rose in the morning sky, the Persecution Task Force came to life. Trucks rumbled over the bumpy dirt roads, carrying men and supplies. Artillerymen zeroed in their big guns and prepared for action. Smoke rose into the sky from mess halls; clerks tapped typewriters; and infantry soldiers dug holes, cleaned weapons, and cursed their miserable lot.

At the Eighty-first Division Medical Headquarters, Master Sergeant John Butsko from McKeesport, Pennsylvania, tried to stand up next to his cot. He'd been shot in the left leg three days ago when he wasn't completely recovered from a shot in that same leg sustained on bloody Bougainville. The original wound had been so bad the doctors wanted to amputate, but Butsko had fought them successfully and managed to stop the operation.

Butsko was six feet tall and built like a tank. He had scars all over his body and a few on his face, which was the face of a killer. His arms, chest, and back were as hairy as a gorilla, and his thick spiky black hair was crew-cut. He was going nuts in the hospital, because he wasn't the kind of man who could lie around on his ass all day.

He was pleased to discover that he actually could stand up on his leg. Then he tried to take a step and nearly fell on his ass. His left leg simply wouldn't hold up all of his weight. He sat on his cot and reached for his pack of Camels, lighting one up. All around him other wounded soldiers lay on cots, smoking cigarettes, reading *Yank, Life,* and other magazines nurses had given them.

Son of a bitch, Butsko thought. He was angry because he couldn't walk around, and he needed his mobility. A soldier without mobility was as good as dead, and just because he was in the hospital tent, that didn't mean he was safe. Japanese infiltrators could slit his throat while he was asleep at night. A strong Japanese attack could put the hospital behind Japanese lines. A soldier had to be mobile if he wanted to stay alive.

His leg felt stronger than yesterday. Maybe in a few days

he could walk on it. He was a strong man with powerful recuperative powers. If the Japs left him alone for a few days, he was sure he'd be all right.

A nurse entered the tent, and Butsko recognized her instantly. She was Lieutenant Betty Crawford, whom he knew from the Army hospital on New Caledonia, where he'd been shipped after being shot in the stomach on shitty Guadalcanal. He'd managed to screw her the night before he returned to Guadalcanal, and hadn't seen her again until a few days ago at the Eighty-first Division Medical Headquarters. He wanted to get her alone someplace, and knew she wanted him to get her alone someplace, but he couldn't walk, and that made romance difficult.

He watched her strolling through the tent, chatting with soldiers, but knew damn well she was there to see him. She was trying to be subtle about it, as if anybody would suspect that such a beautiful young nurse, as sweet and nice as the girl next door, could ever fall for nasty, grouchy old Sergeant Butsko.

Finally she approached his cot, and he looked up at her, puffing his cigarette. Their eyes met and lust simmered in the air between them. Sweet young blondes turned him on, and she'd always had a weakness for tough guys.

"Good morning, Sergeant Butsko," she said.

"Morning, Nurse Crawford," he replied. "How's it going?"

"Very well, thank you. How's it going with you?"

"It's not going at all. I can't walk on my fucking leg."

"Watch your language, Sergeant Butsko."

"Sorry, Nurse Crawford. Guess I forgot where I was for a moment there."

"I put in a requisition for a pair of crutches for you, Sergeant Butsko, and I should have them later on today. That should help you get around, don't you think?"

He saw the twinkle in her eye and was amazed by how proper she appeared on the outside, and how passionate and even raunchy she was beneath that facade. She was doing her best to make him mobile, so they could go off into the bushes someplace and fuck like wild animals.

"Should help a lot, Nurse Crawford," he said.

"Perhaps we can have some walking lessons this afternoon."

"That'd be real nice, Nurse Crawford."

"See you later, Sergeant Butsko."

"Yes ma'am."

She turned around and walked away. She wore combat boots and baggy Army fatigues that disguised the shape of her body, but he knew how curvaceous it was. He'd held her in his arms in that hotel room in New Caledonia and fucked the jelly out of her beans. She had a great figure, a real corn-fed country girl, and she loved to make love. Butsko got horny just thinking about it. She left the tent and Butsko hoped those crutches would arrive soon, so he could take a walk with her someplace.

He saw a tall lanky soldier walking toward him. *It can't be!* Butsko said to himself. The soldier had sandy hair and carried his helmet under his left arm. It was Bannon, and Butsko hadn't seen him since that bad night on Bougainville when most of the old recon platoon was wiped out.

Bannon grinned from ear to ear as he held his hand down to Butsko. "How ya doing, Big Sergeant," he said.

Butsko shook his hand. "Not too bad," he replied. "When'd you get back?"

"Last night."

"How is everybody?"

"I don't know. They were all out on a patrol, and they still weren't back when I left to come over here."

Butsko looked at his watch. "Not back yet? They should've been back by now. Maybe their luck ran out back there."

"I hope not," Bannon said.

"I hope not, too." Butsko looked at the cot beside him. "Have a seat."

"It's stuffy in here," Bannon said. "Let's go for a walk."

"I can't walk," Butsko said.

Bannon raised his eyebrows and looked down at Butsko's bandaged leg. "What happened to you?"

"I got shot in the leg."

"How bad is it?"

"Not that bad, but I can't walk around yet. They're getting me a pair of crutches this afternoon."

"Think a cane might help?"

"If I had one it would."

Bannon stood and pulled his Ka-bar knife out of its scabbard. "I'll go out and cut you one."

"Good deal," Butsko said.

Bannon walked toward the tent flap to go outside, and Butsko puffed his cigarette, watching him go. Bannon always had been one of his favorites in the old recon platoon. The Texan was smart, crafty, and a born leader of men. He'd even been able to keep that maniac Frankie La Barbara under control. Bannon usually stayed calm in hot circumstances and was able to make sensible decisions when the other guys were blowing their corks. Butsko was glad to see him again, particularly since Bannon was cutting him a cane that would enable him to take a walk in the woods with Nurse Betty Crawford.

Colonel Hutchins cleaned himself with a washcloth and a basin full of tepid water, and shaved his ugly face. Then he had his morning coffee and two slices of GI issue bread, plus some scrambled powdered eggs. Finally he sat behind his desk and looked over the morning's correspondence, reports, communiqués, orders, and other trash that filled his IN basket every morning. He looked through the papers quickly, initialing some, signing others, not giving a shit about them either way because he was a combat commander and knew the only thing that really mattered in a war was killing as many Japs as possible.

Sergeant Koch poked his buzzardlike head into the office. "Sir?"

"What is it?"

"Some new replacements have just arrived. Would you like to see them?"

"How many?"

"Ninety-four."

A faint smile creased Colonel Hutchins's face for the first time that morning. "I'll be right out."

"Yes sir."

Sergeant Koch withdrew his head. Colonel Hutchins stood behind his desk and put on his steel pot. He strapped his cartridge belt around his considerable girth, and attached to his cartridge belt was a holster containing his Army-issue Colt .45 and a clip full of bullets. He checked himself in his tin mirror and was satisfied with his appearance. He looked like a gruesome old wardog, and that's the way he wanted his replacements to see him.

I'll give 'em my standard pep talk, he thought, stomping

out of his office. He had to make the new men realize they were in for rough days ahead, but not too rough because he didn't want to discourage them right off the bat. He passed through his outer office and the desks of Sergeant Koch and Pfc. Levinson, then stepped outside.

It was another bright hot day on New Guinea. The sun hung in the sky like a frying pan and insects buzzed everywhere. The jungle smelled like rotting vegetation, and in front of his command post tent were four ranks of new replacements wearing fresh green fatigues, looking bewildered, probably tired and sick after their ocean voyage. Sergeant Donnelly from Headquarters Company had marched them here and made himself ramrod straight, hollering: *"Attention!"*

The replacements snapped to attention and Colonel Hutchins advanced toward them, his helmet low over his eyes, looking mean as hell. His green uniform was faded and torn in a few places, and he knew he looked like a fat old man to them, but they'd find out all about that soon enough. *"At ease!"* Colonel Hutchins shouted.

The men kicked out their left feet and clasped their hands behind their backs. Some were tall and some were short. Some were on the hefty side and some were on the skinny side. Their faces were maps of Ireland, Italy, Poland, England, and various other European countries. They came from all over America, from all walks of life; some had enlisted, some had been drafted. They'd had sixteen weeks of basic training, a trip on a boat, and now they were at the front on New Guinea.

Colonel Hutchins threw back his shoulders, sucked in his chest, and hollered, *"Good morning, men!"*

"Good morning, sir!" they replied.

"Can't hear you!" he told them.

"Good morning, sir!" they shouted louder.

"Still can't hear you!"

"Good morning, sir!" they screamed at the tops of their lungs.

"You sound like a bunch of cunts! Let's hear it one more time!"

"Good morning, sir!"

Their voices reverberated across the Headquarters Company area, making tent poles tremble and scaring birds roosting in the trees. Soldiers looked in the direction of the sound to see what was going on. Mess gear rattled in the mess hall, and the voices even carried to the other side of the Driniumor River, where Japanese sentries wrinkled their foreheads and wondered what the hell was going on.

"That's better," said Colonel Hutchins. "You're supposed to be men and I expect you to sound like men, not a bunch of goddamned cunts. Is that clear?"

"Yes sir!"

"Good." Colonel Hutchins placed his fists on his hips and looked them over. "My name's Hutchins," he said, "Colonel Robert Hutchins, and I'm the commanding officer of this regiment. That means I'm your boss from now on, and when I tell you to shit, I want you to say how much, what color, and where. I don't take any guff and if any one of you thinks you can give me some we can go in back of this tent here and have it out right now. Anybody wanna try that?"

Nobody moved a muscle, and that's what Colonel Hutchins expected. He knew none of them would dare step out of line. They were too intimidated by the whole Army system. It had ground them down and fucked them over until they'd become American Fighting Men.

"Very fine," Colonel Hutchins said. "I'm glad there ain't no dopes among you. I don't want no dopes in this regiment, because this is the greatest regiment in the Army. This is the fighting Twenty-third Infantry, and in this war we've seen action on Guadalcanal, New Georgia, Bougainville, and now we're here in the asshole of the world, New Guinea. Your mommas never told you about New Guinea, did they?"

There was silence for a few seconds.

"I thought I just asked you fuckheads a question!" Colonel Hutchins said.

"No sir!" the men replied.

Colonel Hutchins cupped his right hand next to his ear. "Can't hear you," he said.

"No sir!" the men hollered, and once again mess gear rattled in mess halls and tent poles trembled in the ground.

"That's better," Colonel Hutchins said. "For a moment there I thought I had a bunch of Red Cross girls in front of me. Now where was I? Oh yeah—I was gonna tell you about this island of ours. Well, it ain't gonna be a vacation, gentlemen. We got scorpions, snakes, and every bug you ever dreamed of, including some even the scientists never heard of before. And if you think it's hot right now, this is only morning. This is the *cold* part of the day. It'll probably get up to a hundred degrees in the shade this afternoon, because it gets up to that every afternoon unless it rains, and when it rains you're gonna wish the sun was out, because when it rains on this rotten fucking island, it really rains. The ground turns into the consistency of rat shit. Does everybody here know what rat shit is like?"

"Yes sir!"

Colonel Hutchins stuck his little finger in his ear and wiggled it around. "There go them fucking Red Cross girls again."

"Yes sir!"

"Well that's what it gets like here," Colonel Hutchins continued, "rat shit. But if all we had to worry about was rat shit and the weather, we'd be okay, because there's one more problem we got here that's the worst of all, and that's the Japs. Now all you men know what Japs are, don't you?"

"Yes sir!"

"That's bullshit," Colonel Hutchins told them. "You don't know what Japs are because you never faced them in battle, and let me tell you, gentlemen, that real war is a damned sight different from what they taught you in basic training. War is hell, somebody famous said, but I think it's worse than hell. How can anything be worse than hell? you might wonder. Well you're gonna find out in a little while, maybe even today. Now where was I? Oh yeah, I was gonna tell you what Japs are like. Well first of all, Japs are the ugliest sons of bitches you ever seen in your life. Most of them are runts and look something like monkeys, except they ain't as smart or as decent as monkeys. They got this sick-looking yellow skin, and some of them are even a pale-green color like a fucking lizard. What a Jap doesn't have in brains, he makes up for in sneakiness. You got to stay alert here on the front lines, gentlemen, otherwise a Jap will crawl beside you and cut your fucking throat. You won't hear him coming. He won't say 'hello' and 'how are you.' He'll just rip out your jugular vein and that'll be the end of you. So keep your eyes open. Don't ever fall asleep unless your buddy is awake, because Japs love to cut throats at night. Any questions?"

"No sir!"

Colonel Hutchins scratched his nose. "Now there's one last

24

thing I wanna tell you about Japs," he said. "They're scrappy little sons of bitches and all they wanna do is die for their Emperor. It's up to you to be decent American soldiers and help them out. Whenever you see a Jap, I expect you to kill him. If he's far away, shoot him, and if he's right in front of you, stick him with your bayonet before he sticks you. If he's in a pillbox you'll cook him with a flame thrower or blow him up with a hand grenade. There's all kinds of ways to kill Japs and I don't have time to go into all of them here, but you'll learn them all, provided you don't let one of the scummy little bastards kill you first. There's one important thing you gotta understand, and if you don't remember anything else I say here today, you gotta understand this one. Japs are tough. They like to fight. You can even say they're fanatics. They keep fighting even when you think they should be dead. So when you kill your Jap, make sure he's dead. Shoot him an extra time for good measure. Run your bayonet across his throat once more so he won't get up again. And whatever you do, don't expect a Jap to play fair. A Jap'll never give you an even break. Japs don't play fair. Japs play dirty, and if you wanna kill a Jap, you gotta play even dirtier. It's okay to kick Japs in the balls. There ain't no Army regulations against that. It's okay to gouge out their eyeballs. You can shoot 'em in the back when they're running away, although Japs usually don't run away. You can do anything at all that you want, as long as you kill the sons of bitches. Is that clear?"

"Yes sir!"

"Is there any man here who's afraid of Japs?"

"No sir!"

"What regiment are you in?"

"The Twenty-third Regiment!"

"Who commands the Twenty-third Regiment?"

"Colonel Robert Hutchins!"

"What's the best regiment in the whole entire United States Army!"

"The Twenty-third Regiment!"

"Take a break in place!" Colonel Hutchins said. "Light 'em if you got 'em! The sergeant major'll be out in a little while with your assignments!"

Colonel Hutchins turned and walked away, pleased with his performance. They'd all kept their eyes on him while he'd been talking; he'd had them in the palm of his hand. He walked to his tent, thinking about the white lightning, when he noticed a shadow approaching out of the corner his left eye. He looked in that direction and saw a barrel-chested soldier approaching, his hand held in front of him.

"Permit me to introduce myself," the barrel-chested soldier said in an upper-class patrician accent, his big meaty hand dangling in the air. "My name's Worthington, Private Randolph Worthington from Connecticut, sir. I used to do a lot of hunting before the war, and I'm a crack shot. If you need a crack shot for any special purpose, sir, I'm your man."

Colonel Hutchins looked him up and down, amazed at the man's audacity. Colonel Hutchins stared at Private Worthington's hand as if it were a piece of shit or a dead rat. Didn't Worthington know that full bird colonels didn't shake hands with privates? Worthington got the message, and withdrew his hand.

"Forgive my boldness, sir," he said, "but a crack shot like me is hard to find, and you may have a special use for me."

"What did you use to hunt?" Colonel Hutchins asked.

Worthington had a jaw like a fist and a confident, almost cocky manner. "I've hunted just about everything all over the world, sir, but I've spent most of my time in Africa. I've shot elephants, lions, leopards—you name it."

Colonel Hutchins turned so he could face Worthington more directly. "If you ever talk to me again without going through the chain of command first, *I'm* going to shoot *you*," he said evenly. "Do you get my drift."

"Yes sir."

"Get back with the others."

"Yes sir."

Private Worthington saluted smartly, executed a neat about-face, and marched back to the assembly of replacements. Colonel Hutchins decided to put Worthington into the recon platoon. Worthington had made a good impression on him. The man evidently had guts. He might be a good leader someday.

"Look at them guys!" one of the recruits said.

Colonel Hutchins's attention was drawn toward the recruits. They all were looking to their right, and he turned in that direction also.

Staggering toward him out of the jungle was a raggedy,

26

bloody group of GIs with camouflage paint on their faces and hands, their faces frozen into expressions of fatigue. Colonel Hutchins recognized them instantly. It was the patrol he'd sent out last night from the recon platoon, led by Lieutenant Breckenridge, limping slightly on his left foot.

"Well I'll be goddamned," Colonel Hutchins said. "Look what the cat just dragged in."

The men from the recon platoon shuffled and hunched toward Colonel Hutchins, and he could see they'd had a bad time. A few wore bloody bandages, and all had that haunted glow in their eyes. The closer they got, the worse they looked. Lieutenant Breckenridge came to attention in front of Colonel Hutchins and saluted, as the new replacements looked on with their mouths hanging open.

"Patrol from the recon platoon returning, sir."

"You look like shit, Breckenridge."

"It's been a rough night, sir."

"Got anything interesting for me?"

"I think so, sir."

"You don't need medical attention, do you?"

"I don't, but a few of my men could use a medic."

"You come with me." Colonel Hutchins looked at the other men from the recon platoon. "Those of you who need medical attention, get your asses over to the medics. The rest of you are dismissed."

Colonel Hutchins turned around and walked toward his command post tent. Lieutenant Breckenridge followed him, and the rest of the recon platoon broke up, some heading toward the medics, the rest veering toward the recon platoon bivouac. The replacements stared at the beat-up bloody soldiers, and the reality of the situation sank into their minds. The replacements wore clean new uniforms and didn't have any scratches on them, but they knew they'd look like these soldiers after a few days, if they weren't dead by then.

Colonel Hutchins entered the outer office of his tent and stopped at the desk of Master Sergeant Koch.

"Sergeant," he said, "there's a man out there named Worthington. I want him assigned to the recon platoon."

"Yes sir."

Colonel Hutchins strolled into his office and sat behind the desk. He took his flask of white lightning out of the top drawer.

27

"Have a seat," he said to Lieutenant Breckenridge.

Lieutenant Breckenridge took off his pack and collapsed onto a seat in front of colonel Hutchins's desk. Colonel Hutchins raised the flask to his mouth and gulped some down, then screwed the lid back on and tossed the flask to Lieutenant Breckenridge.

"Help yourself," Colonel Hutchins said.

Lieutenant Breckenridge unscrewed the cap, threw his head back, and gurgled down the white lightning. There were times in the jungle when he thought he'd never make it back to safety, but he'd done it somehow, and it was good to be back.

"When I said help yourself, I didn't say drink it all," Colonel Hutchins told him.

Lieutenant Breckenridge replaced the cap on the flask, threw it back to Colonel Hutchins, and wiped his mouth with the back of his hand. "That's fine stuff," he said.

"You bet your ass," Colonel Hutchins replied, dropping the flask into the top drawer of his desk and slamming it shut. "What happened on the patrol?"

Lieutenant Breckenridge leaned back in the chair and cleared his throat. "First of all, there's a lot of troop movement on the other side on the river and a lot of supplies being carried around."

"The Japs are up to something," Colonel Hutchins concluded. "What you're telling me confirms other reports that've been coming in. The big question is when that asshole up at division is going to do something about it?"

Colonel Hutchins was referring to Major General Clyde Hawkins, commanding officer of the Eighty-first Division, of which the Twenty-third Regiment was a part. Colonel Hutchins didn't like General Hawkins and everybody knew it. They argued constantly, and on one occasion Colonel Hutchins had accused General Hawkins of not having any guts.

"I don't know what he's gonna do about it," Lieutenant Breckenridge replied. "I'm so tired I can't even think straight. Can I get on with my report?"

"You goddamned well better. I ain't got all day."

"That road you wanted me to check out isn't there. We spent half the night looking for it, and couldn't find a trace of it. Either the jungle has grown over it, or it was never there in the first place."

"Our maps are based on the maps the Dutch drew up. They

had the road on their maps."

"It's not there now. I looked for it and I can assure you that it doesn't exist anymore."

"Anything else?" Colonel Hutchins asked.

"This." Lieutenant Breckenridge opened his pack and withdrew the papers he'd taken from the young Japanese officer Private Bisbee had killed. He tossed the papers onto Colonel Hutchins's desk.

Colonel Hutchins picked up the papers. "Where'd you get this stuff?"

"Private Bisbee killed a Jap officer, and we found it in his pack."

"Looks important," said Colonel Hutchins.

"Might be his laundry list."

"It's on official paper. I'll give you a laundry list right in your head." Colonel Hutchins raised his chin an inch and shouted, "Sergeant Koch—get your ass in here!"

"Yes sir!" replied Sergeant Koch in the outer office.

A few seconds later Sergeant Koch entered Colonel Hutchins's inner office. "Yes sir?"

"Find Lieutenant Harper and tell him I wanna see him right away. Tell him I want him to hand-deliver something to General Hawkins. Get going."

"Yes sir."

Sergeant Koch spun around and ran out of the office. Colonel Hutchins looked at the pages covered with Japanese characters.

"I imagine General Hawkins'll have to forward this stuff to Persecution Headquarters. They got somebody there who can read Jap."

"I don't have anything more to report," Lieutenant Breckenridge said. "Can I go sack out now?"

"You mean you're still here?" Colonel Hutchins asked.

Sergeant Butsko hobbled out of the medical tent, leaning heavily on Bannon and the cane Bannon had cut for him out of a thick, knobby branch. Bannon had included an offshoot of the branch for a handgrip, and the cane bore a slight resemblance to an Irish shillelagh. Nurses, doctors, orderlies, and other wounded GIs couldn't help noticing the battle-scarred, brutal-looking sergeant making his way toward an open clearing.

"Lemme get to that tree over there," Butsko wheezed, hopping up and down every time he took a step. "Goddamn—I'm moving right along, ain't I?" As soon as the words were out of Butsko's mouth he lost his footing and collapsed onto the ground.

"Yep, you're really moving right along," Bannon said, bending over to help Butsko up. "You've just about got that cane whipped."

"Don't be a wise guy," Butsko snarled, getting to his feet again.

He looked around and noticed everyone staring at him. He wanted to crown them all with his cane, but couldn't move. He was a cripple. Butsko thought he'd rather be dead than a cripple. He took another halting step, heading toward the tree, and everything went fine so he stepped out again.

"Just take it slow, Sarge," Bannon said. "You got all day."

"Maybe you got all day, but I ain't got all day," Butsko replied.

They made their way toward the tree and finally reached it. Butsko sat down heavily and laid the cane beside him on the ground, leaning his back against the trunk of the tree. Bannon dropped down next to Butsko and both men took out their packs of cigarettes, lighting up. They looked around them at wounded men lying on the ground, and the medical personnel coming and going. They were near a dusty dirt road, where trucks and jeeps rolled back and forth. Butsko relaxed, letting the tree hold the full weight of his massive upper body. He puffed his cigarette and felt weird, because he'd received morphine shots for the wounds in his leg.

"How're you doing, Sarge?" Bannon asked.

"I'm doing just fine," Butsko replied. "It's good to be alive. I wish the fucking war was over, but there ain't nothing I can do about that. How're you doing?"

"Not bad," Bannon said. "Sometimes I hurt inside, but the doctors said I'm fit for duty, so here I am."

"How long you been away?"

"About four months."

"They should give you a couple more months to rest up."

"I'm sure they wouldn't've sent me back here if I wasn't okay."

"What makes you so sure?"

"The doctors know what they're doing, don't they?"

"I don't know—do they? The bastards wanted to cut off my leg on Bougainville, and I fought them on it. Finally they admitted they made a mistake. They got my X rays mixed up with the X rays of some other poor chump. So don't ever rely on doctors. They're assholes just like everybody else. In fact, sometimes I think they're worse assholes than everybody else."

"If I feel bad I'll go on sick call," Bannon said.

"Good luck."

Both men sat and puffed their cigarettes. They'd known each other since Guadalcanal, which had been Bannon's baptism of fire. Butsko's baptism of fire had come long before that. He'd joined the Army in 1935, during the Depression, because he couldn't get a job. He'd been on the Philippines when the Japs bombed Pearl Harbor, and had fought under General Jonathan Wainwright in the terrible losing fight on Bataan. He was a survivor of the infamous Bataan Death March, and escaped from a Jap prisoner-of-war camp in northern Luzon.

"How was your furlough, kid?" Butsko asked.

"Real nice," Bannon replied.

"Get any pussy?"

"Jesus Christ, Sarge."

Butsko turned to Bannon and raised his eyebrows. "What's the matter with you, cowboy?"

"It's awful the way you talk about women, Sarge. They're all not bad. In fact, some of them are awfully nice."

"Oh shit," Butsko said, "don't tell me you're in love again. Who's the unlucky bitch this time?"

"She's not a bitch. She's a very decent young woman."

Butsko snorted. "Don't make me laugh."

"You don't have to believe me if you don't want to."

"They're all bitches," Butsko said. "Take it from me—I know. If they're not nagging in one way, they're nagging in another way. All women nag. Anyway, who is this *decent young woman* you've been plunking?"

"You'll never guess,' Bannon said.

"Okay, I'll never guess," Butsko replied. "Why don't'cha just tell me and get it over with so's I can have some cheap thrills in my old age."

Bannon puffed his cigarette and twitched his nose. "Homer Gladley's kid sister."

Butsko was astounded. He regained his composure and

31

glanced sideways at Bannon. Private Homer Gladley had been killed on Bougainville, and he'd been one of the most popular members of the recon platoon. He was a big farm boy from Nebraska who went berserk whenever he saw a Jap.

"We're engaged to get married," Bannon said shyly.

"But you're already married to that native girl on Guadalcanal—what's her name?"

"I don't remember," Bannon said. "That one didn't count anyway, because we were married by a witch doctor, and not by a chaplain or a justice of the peace. She couldn't even speak English, and I sure as hell couldn't speak what she spoke."

"How'd you meet Homer Gladley's sister?" Butsko asked.

"Waal," Bannon replied, "it was like this. I went back home to Texas to see my old girlfriend Ginger—you remember Ginger—I believe I told you about Ginger."

"Yeah, you told me about Ginger," Butsko said. "She sounded like a real hot piece of ass."

"Yeah, well Ginger's a little too hot for her own good," Bannon continued, "and when I got home she was shacking up with another guy."

Butsko interrupted him. "You can't trust them hot bitches," he said. "They'll fuck anything. I know because my wife's a hot bitch, and I can't trust her any farther than I could throw this entire goddamn fucking island."

Bannon smiled, because he'd met Butsko's wife once in Honolulu. "Yeah, but Dolly's okay. I'm sure she's worth the trouble."

"Sometimes I wonder about that," Butsko said, "but anyway, what happened when you found Ginger with that other guy?"

"Whataya think happened?"

"You beat the piss out of him."

"Right."

"And then somebody called the cops."

"Ginger called the cops."

"She didn't!"

"Oh yes she did."

"Why that rotten bitch!"

"Waal, she thought I was gonna kill her."

"Were you gonna kill her?"

"As a matter of fact I was."

"She deserved it."

"She damn sure did, but I held myself back at the last moment and decided maybe I'd better get out of town. To make a long story short, I went to the bus station, and the sheriff caught up with me there. He wanted to arrest me, but a crowd of people wouldn't let him because I was a wounded soldier and all that shit, so the sheriff let me go on the condition I'd get out of town and never come back. I didn't know exactly where to go, but somehow I started thinking of good old Homer—don't ask me why—and I thought it might be a good idea to visit his folks and tell them what a great guy he was and that he was brave and he died fighting for his country."

"And to freeload a little," Butsko said.

"Right," Bannon replied.

"And maybe get into his sister's pants?"

"I didn't even know he had a sister. That part came later."

"Don't lie," Butsko said. "You knew he had a sister. Even I knew he had a sister."

"I knew he came from a big family with a lot of brothers and sisters, but I didn't know he had *this particular sister*."

Butsko grinned lewdly. "She's that pretty, huh?"

Bannon nodded. "She's a real good-looker, Sarge."

"She dumb like Homer was?"

"No. She's kind of smart, in fact."

"Then what does she see in you?"

"You'd have to ask her."

"I'd love to ask her. What does she look like?"

"Waal, she's kind of big, like Homer."

"That big?" Butsko asked.

"No, not that big," Bannon replied, "but she's just about as big as me."

"That's pretty big," Butsko admitted, because Bannon was a six-footer and then some. "What else?"

"She's a blonde," Bannon said, "a real healthy girl, up at the crack of dawn milking cows, cooking and baking all day long, sometimes working out in the fields with the men, strong as an ox and pretty as a picture." Bannon smiled happily. "We're gonna get married, Sarge. I gave her a ring."

"What do her folks say about all this?"

"They thought it was a good idea."

"They all must be dumb like Homer."

"No, they're not as dumb as Homer. They just know a good thing when they see it."

"How'd you get into her pants?" Butsko asked.

"C'mon Sarge. That's a personal question."

"Did you tell her you'd marry her so's you could get into her pants?"

"I'd never do anything like that!" Bannon declared.

Butsko looked at Bannon's indignant face for a few seconds. "No, I don't suppose you would," he said. "You'd probably have to convince yourself first that you were really in love with her and really wanted to marry her."

"But I *do* really love her and I *do* really want to marry her."

"Sure you do."

"I do!"

Butsko waved his hand in the air. "Don't gimme that shit," he said. "I know you like a book."

"You don't know about anything," Bannon replied. "You got a dirty mind, that's all."

"That's all you got too, but the difference between you and me is that you don't admit it."

Bannon scowled as he took out his package of cigarettes. He held out the pack to Butsko, who shook his head, and then Bannon placed one between his lips, lighting it with his Zippo. He puffed the cigarette, thinking about what Butsko had said. It disturbed him for two reasons: One, it was insulting; and two, it might be true. Bannon knew Butsko often was right about those things. He used to think Butsko knew him better than he knew himself. Butsko had the ability to cut through all the bullshit and see the truth, however unpleasant it was. Bannon suspected Butsko might be right again, and it wasn't pleasant to contemplate. Did he really give Priscilla Gladley a ring just so he could get into her pants? Was he really a rotten son of a bitch deep down?

He noticed a blond nurse walking toward him and Sergeant Butsko. She carried a stack of mail in her hands, and was a pretty apple-cheeked young woman with pert breasts showing underneath her baggy Army fatigues.

"How did you get out here?" she asked Butsko.

Butsko held up his cane. "My buddy here made this for me."

"Wasn't that nice of him." Lieutenant Betty Crawford looked at Bannon. "What's your name?" she asked.

34

Bannon shot to his feet. "Corporal Charles Bannon, ma'am."

"It's not necessary to stand."

"I'd get up too," Butsko told her, "but I can't."

"You wouldn't even if you could," she replied.

"I would too," Butsko insisted.

She held out a letter. "This is for you," she said to Butsko. "I believe it's from your wife."

Butsko looked at the return address. "I believe you're right."

"Enjoy your letter," she said, a hint of jealousy in her voice as she turned and walked away.

"Wait a minute!"

She just kept walking, not paying any attention to him, handing out mail to the other men sitting and lying around the clearing.

Bannon turned to Butsko and winked. "You're fucking her, ain't'cha?"

Butsko knitted his eyebrows together. "What makes you think that?"

"I can tell," Bannon said.

"Bullshit!" Butsko replied.

"Where'd you put it to her—out in the woods?"

"What're you talking about?" Butsko said. "I couldn't even walk before you gave me that cane."

"That's right too," Bannon said. Bannon was chagrined, because he thought he'd caught Butsko at some hanky-panky. He was sure he'd sensed something between Butsko and that nurse, but evidently he'd been wrong. How could Butsko screw her in the woods if he couldn't even walk? It didn't occur to Bannon that Butsko might've run into Lieutenant Betty Crawford at another Army facility somewhere along the line.

"You think you're smart, but you don't know shit, cowboy," Butsko said.

Bannon shrugged. "You can't win 'em all," he replied.

THREE . . .

The jeep screeched to a halt in front of the command post tent of the Eighty-first Division. Pfc. Nick Bombasino from South Philly sat behind the wheel, and Lieutenant Harper, Colonel Hutchins's aide-de-camp, jumped down from the passenger seat and walked swiftly to the tent. He pushed the flap aside and entered, finding himself in front of Master Sergeant Abner Somerall, the division's sergeant major, sitting behind his desk. Lieutenant Harper raised the briefcase in his right hand.

"I've got something here for General Hawkins," he said.

Sergeant Somerall held out his hand.

"No, it's for General Hawkins personally," Lieutenant Harper said, "and it's important."

"The general's busy right now," Sergeant Somerall said dryly. He loved to push young officers around and keep them waiting. "You'll have to take a seat someplace and wait."

"I'm not going to wait," Lieutenant Harper said. "Colonel Hutchins told me to deliver it to General Hawkins right away because it was important. Do you know what the word *important* means, Sergeant Somerall?"

Sergeant Somerall frowned. He knew what the word *important* meant, but he also knew General Hawkins was in conference with General Sully and Colonel Jessup, and didn't want to be disturbed. However, Sergeant Somerall didn't want to cross Colonel Hutchins. Everybody was afraid of Colonel Hutchins because he was a crazy drunk and liable to do anything. Once he even threatened to shoot General Hawkins. Even General Hawkins treated Colonel Hutchins with a certain kind of grudging respect, although both of them hated each other.

Sergeant Somerall lifted his phone and presed the button. Lieutenant Harper heard Sergeant Somerall mumbling into the

36

mouthpiece. Sergeant Somerall was a master at speaking on telephones so quietly you couldn't hear what he was saying even if you were standing beside him.

Sergeant Somerall hung up the telephone and looked up at Lieutenant Harper. "You can go in, but it'd better be important."

Lieutenant Harper didn't bother to answer. He walked into the next section of the tent, full of clerks tapping typewriters and officers pushing papers around on their desks, then turned left and pushed aside the flap leading to another tent.

He was in the office of General Clyde Hawkins, commanding officer of the Eighty-first Division, but Lieutenant Harper wasn't particularly intimidated. He'd heard Colonel Hutchins speak disparagingly of General Hawkins too many times to be in awe of the general. The other two officers in front of the desk didn't mean shit to Lieutenant Harper either. Lieutenant Harper didn't bother taking off his aviator sunglasses. He wore his straight black hair long and his uniform was tailored to his average build. He walked up to General Hawkins's desk and saluted. "Lieutenant Harper reporting, sir!"

General Hawkins was a handsome man of forty with a blond mustache and wavy blond hair on his head. He was a West Pointer, the son of a general and the grandson of another general. He looked up at Lieutenant Harper with an expression of disapproval on his face.

"The sun too bright in here for you Harper?" he asked.

"No sir."

"Then take off the glasses."

"Yes sir." Lieutenant Harper removed his precious sunglasses and held them in his left hand.

"Don't you believe in haircuts in the Twenty-third Regiment?"

"Yes sir."

"Get one."

"Yes sir."

"What've you got so important that you had to interrupt this meeting?" General Hawkins asked.

Lieutenant Harper opened his briefcase and pulled out the papers Lieutenant Breckenridge had brought in from his patrol. He laid the papers on the desk in front of General Hawkins. "There you go, sir," Lieutenant Harper said.

General Hawkins looked at the papers covered with columns of Japanese characters. "What the hell is this?"

"A patrol from our reconnaissance platoon just brought it back, sir. They took if from the body of a dead Japanese officer who evidently was a courier."

General Hawkins perused the papers. "Looks like it might be something important."

"Colonel Hutchins thinks so too, sir, even though some members of the recon platoon might need haircuts."

General Hawkins looked up at Lieutenant Harper. "Are you trying to be a wise guy, young Lieutenant?"

"Who sir? Me sir? No sir. Not me, sir."

A muscle in General Hawkins's jaw twitched. "Get out of here," he said.

"Yes sir. Right away sir." Lieutenant Harper saluted, performed a snappy about-face, and fled from the office. General Sully and Colonel Jessup leaned over the desk and looked at the captured documents.

"This appears to be official Japanese Army correspondence," Colonel Jessup said.

"It should be taken to Persecution Headquarters right away," General Sully replied.

"I'll take it myself," General Hawkins said, because he wanted to get the glory. Then he stood behind his desk and paused, losing his nerve. "But maybe it's not important," he mused aloud. "Maybe it's just a supply requisition, or Japanese morning reports."

"Doesn't matter," Colonel Jessup said. "Everything can have intelligence value."

"That's true," General Hawkins agreed. "I think I'd better go ahead with my original plan and deliver these papers to Persecution Headquarters forthwith. This meeting is dismissed until later today. I'll notify the both of you as to its exact time."

General Sully and Colonel Jessup saluted and departed from the office. General Hawkins took his tin mirror out of the top drawer in his desk and looked at himself to make sure his appearance was okay. He knew how important appearance was in military matters. If a man looked like a leader, people tended to treat him like a leader. But there were always exceptions to that rule. Colonel Hutchins didn't look like a leader. He looked like an old drunk, which he was. If it weren't for the Army and the war, Colonel Hutchins probably would be lying in the gutter of a skid row in one of America's cities, General Hawkins believed. He put on his helmet and lifted the receiver of the telephone on his desk. "Have my jeep brought around immediately!" he hollered.

He smoothed the front of his shirt, made sure his fatigue pants were bloused neatly around the tops of his combat boots, and placed the captured Japanese documents into his battered canvas briefcase. He stood erect, squared his shoulders, and marched out of his office, passing through the outer office full of clerks and junior staff officers, who snapped to attention, and finally through Sergeant Somerall's office.

General Hawkins stepped outside, and his jeep wasn't there. "Where's my jeep!" he hollered.

"It'll be here in a few minutes!" Sergeant Somerall replied from inside the tent.

General Hawkins glanced at his watch, then stamped his feet impatiently on the ground. He couldn't wait to deliver the captured documents to General Hall, and receive the accolades he was certain would be his.

Private First Class Frankie La Barbara opened his eyes. He saw shafts of sunlight coming down at him through openings among the leaves on the trees. He glanced at his watch; it was nearly 1200 hours. He'd awakened because he had to take a piss, and decided the sooner he got it over with, the sooner he could go back to sleep.

Frankie groaned as he rolled onto his stomach and raised himself to his hands and knees. Looking around, he saw the other men in the recon platoon sleeping soundly all across the clearing. A man he'd never seen before was sitting on a log reading a magazine.

"Who the hell are you?" Frankie asked as he stood up.

The man was startled by Frankie's voice. He jumped to his feet and advanced meaningfully toward Frankie, holding out his right hand. "How do you do," he said. "I'm Private Randolph Worthington and I've been assigned to the recon platoon. Am I in the right place?"

Frankie gazed with contempt at the replacement's new green uniform, and didn't bother to shake the proffered hand. "Yeah, you're in the right place."

"I'm supposed to report to Lieutenant Breckenridge. Where's he?"

"How the hell am I supposed to know?"

Frankie turned abruptly away from Private Worthington and shuffled off to the latrine. Dismayed, Private Worthington sat back on his log and picked up his magazine. All he wanted to do was report to his new commanding officer and settle into his new unit, but somehow he couldn't do that. Everybody was asleep, snoring all around him. He recognized these men as the same ones who'd showed up ragged and bloody after the orientation lecture by Colonel Hutchins, which Private Worthington considered marvelous theater and even rather inspiring. Private Worthington liked Colonel Hutchins even though Colonel Hutchins had refused to shake his hand. Rebuffs didn't bother Worthington. All he could do was behave properly himself, and if other people didn't behave properly, that was their problem.

Meanwhile, Frankie La Barbara pissed into the latrine. It was a big trench six feet long, three feet wide, eight feet deep, half-full of shit and piss. Thick clouds of big fat flies swarmed around his head, brushing past his eyes, lips, and ears. He raised his hand and tried to wave them away, but they wouldn't leave him alone. The latrine stank horribly. The hot humid climate made the shit and piss cook and steam in the hole. Finally Frankie finished draining his vein. He buttoned up his pants and returned to the clearing assigned to the recon platoon.

Frankie was in a bad mood whenever he woke up in the morning, but he was in a particularly bad mood that morning. He'd only slept for a few hours, and a cut on his left bicep hurt as if a bee had stung him there. He was hungry, thirsty, and mildly constipated. He had a stomach ache and a headache. His old pal Morris Shilansky had fallen ill with blood poisoning and had been shipped back to the States. Frankie was sure Shilansky would go to New York and try to screw his wife, because Frankie'd told Shilansky how horny his wife used to get. Shilansky had drooled over pictures Frankie showed him of her.

Frankie thought everything was going against him, and then his eyes fell on the reclining figure of Private Clement R. Bisbee, the pathological thief and ex-carnie with whom he'd quarreled during the night. Frankie walked up to Bisbee and

40

kicked him squarely in the ass. "On your feet—cocksucker!" Frankie screamed.

Bisbee opened his eyes and jumped to his feet, looking around to see who'd kicked him, and his eyes fell on Frankie La Barbara. "You!" Bisbee said.

"Well I ain't your mother," Frankie replied, raising his dukes. "You and me got a little matter to settle, don't we?"

Bisbee raised his dukes too and shook his head to wake himself up. "We damn sure do," he said.

"Then let's go!" Frankie said.

On the other side of the clearing, the Reverend Billie Jones raised his head. "Shaddup over there!" he hollered.

"Fuck you!" replied Frankie La Barbara.

The Reverend Billie Jones looked around and saw Frankie La Barbara and Private Bisbee squaring off against each other. The other men in the recon platoon also had been awakened by the commotion, and they raised themselves up from the ground, rubbing their eyes. They needed their sleep, but they'd much rather watch a good fight.

Lieutenant Breckenridge gazed through hooded eyes at Frankie and Bisbee stalking around each other, their fists raised in the air. He knew he should stop them, but was curious to find out which one would win. He, too, liked to watch a good fight, and believed men should fight it out if they had complaints against each other. It was better than keeping the hatred inside and letting it fester until somebody went berserk and shot somebody else someday. Lieutenant Breckenridge didn't care if his men shot each other, but he didn't want to do all the paperwork. It was simpler when they just tried to beat each other to death.

Frankie and Bisbee circled each other slowly, sizing each other up, looking for openings and potential weak spots. Frankie was six feet tall, tipping the scales at 185 pounds, and he towered over Bisbee, who was five-nine and weighed 155 pounds. It was a tall light heavyweight against a middleweight, and the light heavyweight could be expected to win, but that was by no means a certainty. Sometimes smaller men can beat the shit out of bigger men because smaller men have superior speed and maneuverability, and often hit just as hard.

"I'm gonna fucking kill you," Frankie said to Bisbee.

"Your mother eats shit," Bisbee said.

This made Frankie angrier, and a red flush came over his face. He was a maniac, always too emotional for his own good. Bisbee, on the other hand, was as cool as an ice cube in an eskimo's igloo. He was the kind of psychopath whose mind functioned like a machine. To beat Frankie he'd have to dazzle him with footwork, make him miss, work his body, and wear him down. Bisbee was an orphan and had been fighting since he was five years old. His years with carnivals had been full of brawls. He didn't have a mark on his innocent baby face. He knew what to do and how to do it.

The men from the recon platoon, yawning, burping, and farting, made a circle around the two combatants, because they didn't want to miss a punch. Private Randolph Worthington was among them, appalled that nobody was attempting to stop the fight. Turning his head around, he saw Lieutenant Breckenridge still lying on the ground, facing away from the action. It seemed to Worthington that Lieutenant Breckenridge should try to stop the fight. Worthington was on the verge of walking over to Lieutenant Breckenridge and telling him to stop it, but that wouldn't be proper; privates didn't tell lieutenants what to do.

Bisbee got up on his toes and started dancing. He shifted his weight from side to side and feinted with a few punches at Frankie La Barbara's head, but Frankie didn't get faked out. Frankie stalked Bisbee, trying to cut him off and put him up against a tree so he could work on his baby face and fuck it up a little.

Worthington couldn't stand it anymore. Fighting among soldiers was far beneath the high standards he'd set for military life. He simply couldn't let the fight go on, and if nobody was going to stop it, by God he would. "Now see here!" he said, stepping forward. "Break it up!"

Worthington raised his hands and walked in between Frankie and Bisbee, reaching out to push them apart. Frankie lashed out with a left hook, catching Worthington flush on the jaw, and Worthington heard bells and birds. The next thing he knew he was on his knees, shaking his head, trying to figure out what had hit him.

"Mind your fucking business," Private Yabalonka said. "Let 'em have it out."

Frankie and Bisbee stepped away from Worthington and continued to circle each other. Bisbee darted from side to side on the balls of his feet while Frankie measured Bisbee for a knockout punch. Frankie pawed the air with his left hand, and Bisbee raised his fists a few inches every time Frankie pawed the air. A few times their fists touched. Neither one had thrown a good solid punch yet, except the one that put Private Worthington down.

"Both of them's scared of each other," said Private McGurk.

"This is the dullest fight I ever saw in my life," said Private Roy Cowdell, a recent addition to the recon platoon.

Frankie's vanity was piqued by that last remark. You could say anything about him you wanted, but not that he was dull or ugly. He decided the time had come to turn the fight into a fight. Bisbee dodged suddenly to the left, so Frankie stepped in that direction to cut him off, throwing a left jab to Bisbee's head.

Bisbee ducked easily under the jab and punched Frankie on his left side, just under his rib cage. Then he punched Frankie on his right side under his rib cage. Frankie lowered his elbows to protect that part of his body, and Bisbee hooked up to Frankie's head, slugging him on the left ear, and Frankie heard horns blowing.

Bisbee jumped back, grinning, dancing from side to side. As far as he was concerned, that was the way the fight was going to go. Frankie would charge him and Bisbee would work his body. When Frankie lowered his guard Bisbee would head-hunt. It was the strategy that had enabled Bisbee to kick the shit out of many men bigger than he.

But those men weren't Frankie La Barbara, and Frankie rubbed his left ear because the horns still blared inside it. Frankie was from New York's Little Italy and had worked for the mob, twisting arms and breaking legs. You didn't get a job like that if you weren't tough.

Frankie narrowed his eyes and examined Bisbee. The fight was going to be more difficult than Frankie thought. Bisbee was a fighter—that was clear now. The son of a bitch could use his fists as well as his Ka-bar knife.

Frankie stepped toward Bisbee and threw another left jab at Bisbee's head, but pulled it back quickly; it was a feint. Bisbee ducked and came in under it, because he fell for the feint, and Frankie hit him with an uppercut on the tip of his chin.

Bisbee didn't even see the punch coming. The punch

straightened him up and sent him sprawling backwards. Frankie went after him to finish him off and maybe stomp on his baby face a bit, when Bisbee suddenly lurched forward and held on to Frankie's arms. Frankie raised his big hand, covered Bisbee's face with it, and pushed hard.

Bisbee fell backwards again. He tripped on a rock and dropped onto his ass. Frankie grinned as he stepped forward to do a tapdance on Bisbee's head. The others would have new respect for him, because the only kind of man they really respected was the one who could kick ass. Now Bisbee would know better than to talk back to him again, because Frankie La Barbara was nobody to fuck with.

Frankie stood over Bisbee and raised his right foot for the first stomp. Frankie wore size-eleven combat boots and knew they'd really do a job on Bisbee's baby face. With a haughty smile, Frankie pushed that big boot down.

Bisbee rolled out of the way at the last moment and picked up a branch lying near his hand. He got to his feet groggily. Frankie charged and Bisbee hit Frankie over the head with the branch.

Frankie saw stars. He took two steps to the left and then two steps to the right. Bisbee bent over, picked up a rock, and threw it at Frankie, bouncing it off Frankie's head. This time Frankie saw the entire solar system, all the planets, moons, and quarks. Frankie staggered from side to side and Bisbee attacked, swinging the long thick branch in his hand, whacking Frankie over the head again, and this time the branch broke in two.

Frankie dropped to his knees. The branch opened a gash on his scalp and blood dripped down his forehead. He blinked and tried to get his bearings. Bisbee reared back his foot and shot it forward, to kick Frankie in the face, but Frankie raised his hands at the last moment and caught the foot, holding it tightly.

Bisbee lost his balance and fell on his back. Frankie dived on him, grabbing him by the throat, pressing his thumbs against Bisbee's Adam's apple, squeezing with all his strength. Bisbee clasped his fists together and shot them up between Frankie's hands, breaking Frankie's hold, and then Bisbee bucked like a wild mustang, raising Frankie up a few inches, which was enough to permit Bisbee to squirm out from underneath Frankie and jump to his feet before Frankie knew what was happening.

Frankie looked up to see a size-nine-and-a-half boot flying toward his head. Frankie dodged to the side, but wasn't fast enough. The boot smacked him on his nose, which already was broken, and Frankie screamed bloody blue murder.

Frankie jumped to his feet and touched his fingers to his nose. He looked at his fingers and saw blood on them. Frankie got very pissed off. He bared his teeth and wrinkled his forehead. He pointed a bloody finger at Bisbee and screamed, "I'm gonna kill you!"

Bisbee smiled like a cherub on a painting by Michelangelo and said, "C'mon you big ugly son of a bitch."

Frankie let out a roar like a wild bull elephant and charged Private Bisbee. Frankie waved his fists in the air because he didn't know which one to throw first, and Bisbee, the ex-carnie, dodged to the side and stuck out his leg, tripping Frankie.

Frankie lost his footing and pitched forward onto his face. He held out his hands to save his nose from getting mashed on the ground, and Bisbee jumped with both feet onto his back, knocking the wind out of him, and then kicked him in the head.

Frankie was hurt but by no means out of the ball game. He raised himself up even as Bisbee was standing on his back, and Bisbee slid off to the ground. Frankie turned around and charged Bisbee again, and Bisbee threw his own best uppercut, connecting with Frankie's jaw, but it didn't stop Frankie. Frankie was on an angry, bloody rampage now, and only a bullet would stop him. The uppercut didn't even faze him, he was so goddamned mad. He grabbed Bisbee by the front of his shirt with his left fist and reared back his right fist as Bisbee kicked and tried to get loose, pummeling Frankie about the head and shoulders, his feet striking Frankie's shins and knees, and Frankie drove his right fist forward with all his strength, smashing Bisbee in the face. Bisbee's head snapped back, but Frankie didn't let him fall to the ground. Frankie drew back his fist again and punched Bisbee in the mouth another time, splitting his lower lip, mashing in his gums, knocking a few teeth loose.

Bisbee was out cold, but that didn't stop Frankie La Barbara. He grabbed Bisbee's shirt with both his hands, raised him higher in the air, and threw him across the clearing. Bisbee hit a tree and bounced off it, collapsing onto the ground. Frankie ran toward him and jumped in the air, so he could land with both feet on Bisbee's head, when suddenly out of nowhere a freight train smacked into him and threw him to the ground.

It felt like a freight train, but it wasn't a freight train. It was Lieutenant Breckenridge, and he held Frankie's arms pinned to his sides as they lay on the ground together.

"That's enough!" Lieutenant Breckenridge said.

Lieutenant Breckenridge turned Frankie loose and stood up. Frankie pulled himself together and got to his feet also. He looked at the lieutenant and was mad enough to take him on too, but something held him back. Lieutenant Breckenridge had kicked his ass in the past and Frankie didn't feel like going up against him again. He'd bide his time and maybe give it a try some other day.

Lieutenant Breckenridge took a deep breath. "We're supposed to be fighting the Japs, not each other!" he said. "Let's knock this shit off!" Lieutenant Breckenridge looked at the Reverend Billie Jones. "Get a medic for Bisbee, but before you do that check and make sure he's not dead, because you might have to get somebody from a graves registration unit instead."

Lieutenant Breckenridge turned and walked away, and Private Randolph Worthington's jaw hung open, because he'd seen many barracks brawls during his brief duty with the U.S. Army, but never anything like this one.

The Reverend Billie Jones walked to the supine figure of Private Clement R. Bisbee, bent over, and saw blood welling out of Bisbee's mouth. He also saw Bisbee's chest rising and falling, which meant he was alive. The next step was to get a medic, because the recon platoon's last medic, Corporal Lamm, had been shot a few days ago. The Reverend Billie Jones adjusted his submachine gun on his shoulder and headed toward Headquarters Company, because that's where all the medics were.

General Charles P. Hall, commanding officer of the Persecution Task Force, was on the beach, holding his head high, as military and civilian photographers snapped his picture. He struck a series of heroic poses, turning his head from side to side, trying to look good for the troops and the folks back home.

A crowd of soldiers and officers stood in the background,

watching the photo session. In this crowd was Major General Clyde Hawkins, carrying his briefcase, anxiously waiting for an opportunity to speak with General Hall and give him the captured Japanese documents.

Finally General Hall raised his right hand and smiled cordially. "That's all for today, boys," he said, "I've got work to do."

He turned away from the photographers and walked toward his jeep. A shadow crossed his path, and he looked up to see General Hawkins standing there.

"I've got to speak with you immediately about a matter of the utmost importance," General Hawkins said.

"What is it?" General Hall asked.

"Captured enemy documents."

"Where did you get them?"

"One of my patrols came back with them, and they're official Japanese Army correspondence, from what I can see."

"Lemme have a look at them."

"Yes sir."

They walked together toward the jeep and General Hawkins opened his briefcase on the back seat. He pulled out the documents and showed them to General Hall. The photographers continued to snap more pictures. General Hall held the papers up to the bright sunlight.

"Hmmmm," he said. "Very interesting. We'd better get this to Major Rainey."

Major Rainey was a Persecution Task Force intelligence officer who was fluent in Japanese. He'd been an international representative for General Electric in the Far East before the war and had spent considerable time in Japan selling toasters, vacuum cleaners, and various other electrical appliances to Japanese wholesalers and retail outlets.

General Hall jumped into the front passenger seat of the jeep. General Hawkins climbed into the back seat. The driver shifted into gear and drove away, as the photographers pointed their cameras at the jeep receding into the distance, taking more pictures.

"Sir," said Private Randolph Worthington, "may I have a word with you?"

Lieutenant Breckenridge looked up and raised his hand be-

47

cause the sun was shining into his eyes. He was sitting in a foxhole and had been writing a letter to his mother in Richmond.

"What's on your mind?" Lieutenant Breckenridge said.

Private Worthington squatted beside the foxhole. He had a forward-thrusting jaw that looked as though it could bite through a block of concrete. "I've just been assigned to this platoon, and I thought I should tell you a little something about myself."

"What's your name?" Lieutenant Breckenridge asked.

"Private Randolph Worthington, and I—"

Lieutenant Breckenridge interrupted him. "Don't I know you from someplace?"

Private Worthington was taken aback. "I . . . ah . . . I don't know, sir."

"You look familiar to me. Do I look familiar to you?"

"I can't say that you do, sir."

"Hmmm. Well, go on with what you were telling me."

"It's just this," Private Worthington said. "I used to do a lot of hunting before the war, and I'm an excellent shot. If you ever need an excellent shot for any purpose, I just thought you ought to know you've got one here in this platoon."

Lieutenant Breckenridge squinted and looked Private Worthington over. "Did you ever play college football?" he asked.

"As a matter of fact I did."

"I think I played against you," Lieutenant Breckenridge said. "What team did you play for?"

"I played one year for Georgia Tech, and two years for the University of Connecticut."

"I played for the University of Virginia, and we played Georgia Tech a few times. Were you on the line?"

"I played right tackle."

Lieutenant Breckenridge knitted his eyebrows together, then loosened them up. *"Worthington!"* he said. "I remember you now! You nearly broke my fucking back!"

"Breckenridge!" Worthington shouted. "You stiff-armed me in the face and nearly put my eye out!"

The two men stared at each other. The last time they'd seen each other was on the playing field of Georgia Tech. They'd been young college students wearing colorful uniforms, and beautiful cheerleaders had jumped up and down on the side-

48

lines. The crowd had cheered and it had been a beautiful autumn day that neither of them would ever forget.

Now they were dressed in Army fatigues. Both needed shaves and Lieutenant Breckenridge's uniform was torn and bloody. He wore a bloody bandage on his left leg, and his eyes were bloodshot. Lieutenant Breckenridge looked ten years older, but Private Worthington still had a youthful appearance.

Lieutenant Breckenridge held out his hand and grinned. "Welcome to New Guinea. Good to see you again."

Private Worthington shook Lieutenant Breckenridge's hand. "Good to see you too, but I wish it could be under more pleasant circumstances. Why did you become an officer?"

"Because I like to have some control over what I'm doing. If you're an enlisted man you have to put up with a lot of shit. You ought to think about becoming an officer."

Worthington shook his head. "I don't want to be responsible for other men's lives. I don't want to give the orders that could cause the deaths of other men."

"I understand how you feel," Lieutenant Breckenridge said. "I don't like that part either. But the Army needs officers with brains, otherwise all the idiots will be officers, and there are too many of them around as it is. People like us have a responsibility to our country. We can't let our educations and our brains go to waste."

"In a way you're right," Worthington replied, "but I still don't want anybody to die because of me. I don't want it on my conscience."

Lieutenant Breckenridge shrugged. "That's up to you, I guess. We all have to live with the decisions we make."

Lieutenant Breckenridge wanted to say more, but was interrupted by a commotion on the other side of the clearing. Men from the recon platoon shouted and jumped up and down, waving their arms in the air.

"What the hell's going on over there?" Lieutenant Breckenridge asked.

"I really don't know," Private Worthington said.

"Sir," said Lieutenant Breckenridge.

"I really don't know, sir."

"Don't get lax about that," Lieutenant Breckenridge said, "just because we played football against each other in college. I'm telling you for your sake, not mine. If the men think I'm

49

favoring you in any way, they might kill you."

"Kill me?" asked Private Worthington, making a face. "They'd actually *kill* me?"

"They might," said Lieutenant Breckenridge, getting to his feet. "They're a rough bunch of boys."

"They'd *kill* me?" Private Worthington muttered, disbelief in his voice.

Lieutenant Breckenridge gazed in the direction of the commotion. He saw the men from the recon platoon making a fuss around somebody, and Lieutenant Breckenridge walked closer to see who it was, with Private Worthington trailing him. The men hollered and slammed somebody on the back. They hoisted him up in the air, and now Lieutenant Breckenridge could see who they were cheering.

It was Corporal Bannon, the cowboy from Texas who'd been wounded severely on Bougainville, and the men were happy to see him again. They called him a son of a bitch, a bastard, and a motherfucker. Bannon saw Lieutenant Breckenridge and took off his helmet, waving it in the air the way a cowboy waves his ten-gallon hat when riding a Brahma bull.

"How're you doing, Lieutenant!" Bannon shouted.

"When'd you get back?" Lieutenant Breckenridge replied.

"Last night."

"How're you feeling?"

"Okay."

"Welcome home!" Lieutenant Breckenridge said. "You're the new acting platoon sergeant until further notice!"

The smile vanished from Bannon's face. "I am!"

"You're damn right you are!" Lieutenant Breckenridge replied, laughing at the dismay and terror on Bannon's face.

The documents containing Japanese characters lay on General Hall's desk. General Hall stood and leaned over the papers, examining them. Beside him were General Hawkins, Major Rainey, and several other staff officers. Major Rainey wore his glasses on the end of his long pointy nose, and the corners of his mouth turned down as he shuffled through the documents.

"Unless I'm mistaken, these documents are battle orders," Major Rainey said. "They're ordering the recipient, a Colonel Katsumata, to attack on the night of July ninth."

"My God!" said General Hall. "That's only six days away!"

"That it is," agreed Major Rainey.

"You're sure that's what it says?" General Hall asked him.

"I'm sure as I can be."

General Hall wiped his mouth thoughtfully with the palm of his hand and sat back in his chair. His brow was furrowed in thought. "The question in my mind is whether or not this signifies just an attack by a regiment, or whether it's part of a full-scale attack."

Nobody said anything, because nobody knew the answer to that. The officers looked at each other, and they were worried. What if the Japs mounted an all-out attack in only six days? Could the Persecution Task Force hold them?

Finally General Hall reached a decision. "All we can do is forward this information to higher headquarters," he said. "And we have to get ready for the worst. Captain Parker!"

"Yes sir!"

"Take down this order!"

Captain Parker was one of General Hall's aides, and he got out his pen. "I'm ready, sir."

"Double our patrols and our guard. Make certain adequate ammunition and supplies are close to the front, but not too close because we don't want everything blown up in an artillery bombardment. Place all units on a twenty-four-hour alert." General Hall took a deep breath. "That'll be it for now. I want a meeting of all staff officers and division commanders in this office at,"—he looked at his watch—"fifteen hundred hours. Have you got all that?"

"Yes sir," said Captain Parker.

"Good. That will be all for now. Major Rainey—make certain a copy of those documents is transmitted to General Krueger without delay. The rest of you follow through on the orders I just gave Captain Parker. Are there any questions?"

Nobody said anything.

"That's all for now," General Hall said. "This meeting is dismissed."

FOUR . . .

"What's things like back in the States?" the Reverend Billie Jones asked.

"Things've changed a lot since I was there last," Bannon replied. He sat cross-legged on the ground, smoking a cigarette, and the rest of the recon platoon formed a circle around him. "Everybody, even little kids, have got ration books, and nobody can buy things unless they use the coupons in the ration books. Gas for cars is real scarce. There's collections for paper, tin cans, rags, and you name it. I can't say things are real tough, but in a lotta ways they're tougher than they were before the war, because before the war you could buy anything you wanted if you had the money, but now money don't matter so much. You gotta have them coupons in the ration books."

"I bet there's a lot of black-market shit going on," Frankie La Barbara said.

"I suppose there is," Bannon replied. "I never really saw any of it firsthand."

"Are the folks at home getting mad at us?" Yabalonka asked.

Bannon was surprised by the question. "What for?"

"Because we haven't won the war yet, and they have to make sacrifices."

"Naw," said Bannon. "The folks at home are behind us one hundred percent. They're proud of us and most of them feel guilty that they're not doing more for the war effort. Even old men wanna join up and fight. Teenage kids lie about their ages to join up. Women are working in the factories. In fact, in a certain way things are better than when I left the States, because the Depression's over. Everybody's got a job, and lotsa them jobs pay big money with overtime and all."

"They's lucky," said McGurk. "Wish I had a good job with overtime."

Lieutenant Breckenridge chortled. "You got the overtime. You just haven't got the good job."

The men snickered. They thought that was kind of funny. Private Bisbee leaned forward, and he didn't have a baby face anymore. His face looked like it'd been through a meat grinder.

"How're the women back there?" he asked.

"Same as usual," Bannon replied. "No fucking good." He was thinking of Ginger, but then realized he'd better say something else so the men wouldn't think their wives and girlfriends were stepping out on them. "Waal," he said, "only some of them are no damn good, I guess. Most of the women are behaving themselves."

Frankie spat at the ground. "Yeah, sure."

"They are."

"Bullshit," Frankie said. "As soon as they start getting hot pants they'll run off with somebody else."

Bannon didn't think this was a very good topic of conversation, and he decided to change the subject. "I saw Butsko this morning," he said.

"How was the old son of a bitch?" Frankie asked.

"Full of piss and vinegar as usual."

Lieutenant Breckenridge took a drag from his cigarette. "He's up for the DSC," he said.

"He is?" Bannon replied. "I didn't know that. He didn't mention it."

"He wouldn't," said the Reverend Billie Jones.

"He shoulda got it a long time ago," Lieutenant Breckenridge said.

"You think they'll give it to him?" Frankie La Barbara asked.

"I don't know," Lieutenant Breckenridge replied. "Depends on what criteria they use when they pass out the DSC."

A stubborn expression came over Frankie's face. "I hope they give it to him, because if they do they'll ship him out and I won't have to look at the son of a bitch anymore."

Lieutenant Breckenridge smiled. "Why don't you like Butsko, Frankie?"

"Because of that time on Bougainville when we were on patrol and he wanted to leave me behind enemy lines when I got sick."

Bannon said, "That's because you fight with him every time he tells you something to do."

"Fuck him and fuck his mother," Frankie replied.

"You gotta understand Butsko," Bannon said. "He's very bitter about life, and he's not sentimental at all. He's seen too much. He doesn't have any patience, but he's a great man anyway because he's usually right about things."

"Bullshit," said Frankie. "He's just another asshole as far as I'm concerned."

"Everybody's an asshole as far as you're concerned, Frankie."

"That's right, and that includes you, cowboy."

"You're not that different from Butsko," Bannon said, "because that's the way he thinks too. If he'd been the one who'd been sick behind enemy lines, you'd be the first who'd want to leave him behind."

"Fuck you," Frankie said. "Who asked you anyway?"

"Well," said Lieutenant Breckenridge, "we've probably seen the last of Butsko for a long time. If he gets the DSC they'll probably send him back to the States for a war-bond tour."

McGurk nodded his head eagerly. "With movie actresses and shit like that!"

"That lucky bastard," Frankie said. "Every time he falls into a pile of shit he comes up smelling like a rose."

"You're just jealous," said Bisbee.

"Shaddup before I fuck up your face again, scumbag."

"Oh yeah?" Bisbee said. "Well let me tell you something, buddy. Next time I'm not going to walk up to you and just stand there like last time. Next time I'm gonna stick a knife in your ass."

"Try it and see what happens to you," Frankie growled. "I'll make you eat the fucking knife."

Lieutenant Breckenridge stood up and wheezed. "I get so sick of you guys arguing," he said. "I wish I could leave you all behind someplace, and start out clean with a new platoon." Lieutenant Breckenridge turned and walked away, putting on his steel pot, adjusting his submachine gun slung over his shoulder.

"Fuck him too," Frankie said underneath his breath. "He's just another dipshit officer around here, and he'd better watch his step. Them silver bars on his collar don't mean a fucking thing to me."

Bannon stubbed out his cigarette on the ground, then field-stripped it, tearing off the paper, scattering the crumbs of tobacco on the ground. He rolled the paper into a tiny ball and threw it over his shoulder. "Okay," he said, glancing at his watch. "It's nearly time for chow. Let's police up this area and get ready to go. Let's hit it—on your feet!"

"Shit," Frankie said. "Everybody wants to be a boss."

"Let's go," Bannon said. "We ain't got all fucking day." Bannon got to his feet, and so did the other men, although they took their time. Bannon led them to the edge of the clearing and lined them up, as they grumbled and complained.

"Let's move it out!" Bannon told them. "If God didn't put it there, pick it up!"

The men advanced across the clearing, their faces surly, bending over to pick up empty C-ration cans, scraps of paper, and other bits of debris that were strewn around their bivouac.

Lieutenant Betty Crawford walked from the surgical tent to the tent where she and the other nurses lived. She was on a twisting jungle trail, and she moved over it with her hands in her pockets and her GI fatigue cap askew on her head. She'd piled her curly blond hair underneath the cap, but her hair was unruly and much of it peeked out. Her fatigue pants were baggy and made her look like Charlie Chaplin. Often she missed the pretty dresses she'd worn when she was a civilian, but her mind wasn't on pretty dresses just then.

She was thinking about Master Sergeant John Butsko, and she was greatly disturbed. She thought there must be something wrong with her for having such strong sexual feelings for a man who was so much older than she—twelve years—and who was brutal, crude, and even quite vulgar at times.

Yet she also knew he could be soft and tender. His harsh voice could become gentle and husky, and it really turned her on when it got that way. He was a creature of extremes and contradictions. From a certain point of view he was ugly and even monstrous, but yet she had to admit she found him extremely exciting sexually. She wasn't engaged to him. She hardly knew him. And yet she lusted after him, although her ex-fiancé was barely cold in his grave.

That was an exaggeration, but people in emotional crises often exaggerate. Her ex-fiancé had been a Navy pilot, missing in action for a year. He'd been shot down in some minor air battle in the South Pacific, a decent young man from the Midwest, which was where Betty Crawford was from. They'd been right for each other in every way, but while he still was alive she'd met Butsko on New Caledonia and gone to bed with him in that cheesy hotel, betraying Bob, her fiancé, and causing her to realize she wasn't the sweet young thing she'd always thought she was.

Now she was wondering why she was getting mixed up with Butsko again. They certainly weren't going to get married, and in fact he was married already, She'd committed adultery with him once, and wasn't sure she wanted to do it again. There was no future for her and Butsko, and she was sure he didn't love her, so why had she been behaving as though all she wanted in the world was to get alone with him someplace and tear off her clothes?

I've really got to get hold of myself, she said to herself. *I'm behaving like those silly promiscuous nurses I disapprove of so much, who sleep with all the officers, and Butsko isn't even an officer.*

She reached into her shirt pocket and took out a Philip Morris cigarette, lighting it with her trusty Ronson. She took a puff and turned a bend in the trail. Monkeys chattered in the trees above her, jumping from branch to branch, eating fruits and nuts, spitting the seeds and shells to the ground below.

She walked past a tree with a thick trunk, thinking about Butsko, when suddenly a figure lurched in front of her from behind the tree.

"Hi there," said Butsko.

There he was, standing in front of her. She blinked and did a double take, not knowing what to say.

"You look like you just had a death in your family," Butsko said, leaning on the cane Bannon had made for him. "Why so glum, chum?"

"What're you doing here?" she asked. "You shouldn't creep up on people this way."

"Why not?" he replied. "It's good practice. Keeps me in shape."

She recovered her composure and recalled the gripe she had with him. "What'd your wife have to say in her letter?" she asked.

"None of your fucking business."

"You can't talk to me like that," Betty said, pushing him out of her way so she could continue her walk.

But just because she pushed him, that didn't mean he moved. She weighed 105 pounds, and he weighed nearly two-and-a-half times that much. He didn't budge at all. She pushed him again. "Get out of my way!" she said.

"What's the matter with you?" he asked.

"I want to go home."

"What for?"

"Because I want to go home."

"I thought you wanted to go for a little walk in the woods with me."

"I changed my mind." She pushed him again, but it was like pushing the Rock of Gibralter.

"What changed your mind?" he asked.

"None of your fucking business," she replied.

"Nice talk," he said.

"I learned it from you."

"Too bad you didn't learn more from me."

"Get out of my way."

"You sure that's what you want?"

"That's what I want."

"Okay," Butsko said, limping to the side. "Have it your way."

The path was clear in front of her, but she hesitated.

"What are you waiting for?" he asked.

"Nothing."

"I thought you were in a hurry to get going."

"I am."

"I don't see you moving."

Lieutenant Betty Crawford didn't know what to do. On one hand she wanted to walk away from Butsko, but on the other hand she thought if she walked away from him they'd be finished for good, and she wasn't sure she wanted it to be over for good.

"Looks like you're not in the hurry you thought you were," Butsko said.

She looked into his eyes. "Butsko, what'm I gonna do about you?"

He winked. "Do you really want me to say it out loud?"

She shook her head and sighed. "Oh God," she said.

He smiled and placed his big hairy hand on her shoulder, giving it a little squeeze. "Take it easy, kid," he said. "You're getting yourself all worked up over nothing."

"But what am I going to do about you, Butsko?"

"You don't have to do anything about me. I didn't realize I was making you feel bad. Hell, the war's shitty enough without people making each other feel bad. You're a good kid and I never should've got mixed up with you in the first place." He pushed her gently toward the tent where the nurses lived. "Get along now. Stop worrying about old Sergeant Butsko. He ain't worth it."

She looked up at him and was afraid she might cry. "Yes you are worth it."

"I feel rotten," Butsko said. "I think I'm gonna lie down someplace. I'll talk to you later."

Butsko turned away from her, pushing his cane in front of him, placing its tip against the ground. He took a faltering step, moved the cane forward again, and then took another faltering step.

The nurse in Betty Crawford got the best of her. "Let me help you," she said, moving to his right side, grabbing his arm.

"Naw, that's okay," he said, trying to shake her loose. "I can make it myself."

"I'll help you back to your tent."

"I toldja I can make it myself."

"I know you can make it yourself, but it'll be easier if I help you."

They heard the laughter of a woman's voice, and looked up. A group of nurses appeared on the trail in front of them, talking and joking with each other, on their way back to their tent. They saw Betty with Butsko and slowed down.

"Is Sergeant Butsko all right?" asked a red-headed nurse with a bug bust, whose name was Lieutenant Frannie Divers.

"Yeah, I'm all right," growled Butsko.

"What's he doing back here?" asked a short fat nurse with a terrible acne condition, her curly black hair resembling the hair of a French poodle. She was Lieutenant Agnes Shankar. "Is he a Peeping Tom or something?"

Butsko looked at her. "Who in the hell would want to peep at *you*, you ugly bitch."

There was a loud hissing sound as all the women on the path sucked wind through their open mouths.

Lieutenant Shankar's eyes nearly popped out of her skull. "That's no way to talk to a woman!" she screamed.

"Fuck you in your ass," Butsko snarled.

"What!" Lieutenant Shankar screamed.

"I said fuck you in your ass," Butsko told her. "You want me to say it again? Fuck you in your ass."

Tiny red marks appeared on her face underneath her acne zits. She pointed her sausagelike forefinger at Butsko. "I'm gonna have you court-martialed!" she said.

Lieutenant Frannie Divers blew air out the corner of her mouth. "Oh come off it," she said.

Lieutenant Shankar spun around angrily and faced her. "Come off what!" she demanded. "This filthy bastard here just insulted me, and I'm an officer in the United States Army! I'm gonna bring him up on charges!"

"Fuck you," Butsko said to her. "Who gives a shit?"

Butsko maneuvered his cane in front of him, and it wasn't easy for him because he wasn't accustomed to it yet. He hobbled toward the hospital tents, and Betty continued to hold his arm and keep him steady, because she didn't know what else to do.

"What's your name—soldier!" Lieutenant Shankar hollered.

"Fuck you," Butsko replied.

"Calm down," Betty said softly.

"I am calm."

"Stop talking to her that way, because she's a troublemaker. She hates men."

"I'm a troublemaker too," Butsko said, "and I hate her, so that makes us even."

Betty sighed. "Butsko, I don't know what to do with you."

"Then why don't you go take a flying fuck at the moon?" Butsko's temper was riled now, and once his temper was riled it wasn't easy for him to relax. He turned to her and narrowed his eyes. "You're always telling me that you don't know what to do with me, and I'm getting sick of hearing it. If you don't know what to do with me, get the fuck away from me. Who the hell needs you anyway? I don't need you! I don't need anybody!"

Butsko pulled his arm out of her grip, shot her a dirty look, and limped away. She wanted to run after him and help him, but she had her pride, and besides, the other nurses were watching her. She took a deep breath and walked toward the women.

Lieutenant Divers's hands were in her pockets. "He's sure an ornery son of a gun, isn't he?" she asked no one in particular.

"He sure is," Betty agreed.

Lieutenant Shankar was pissed off. "I'm gonna have him court-martialed!" she said, waving her arms around wildly in the air. "You're all my witnesses! We can't let him talk to women like that!"

"Oh, shut your mouth," Betty told her. Betty was so upset she'd lost her cool, and was speaking out in a situation where she ordinarily would keep her mouth shut.

Lieutenant Shankar was shocked by Betty's reply. "What did you say?" she asked.

"I said shut your mouth."

"You can't talk to me that way," Lieutenant Shankar said.

"I just did," Betty replied. She raised her chin and walked past Lieutenant Shankar, heading toward the tents where the nurses lived.

"I'm still going to have that big ogre court-martialed!" Lieutenant Shanker declared, her face purple with rage.

FIVE . . .

It was the next day. General Douglas MacArthur sat in his office in his headquarters building in downtown Brisbane, Australia. A new headquarters was being constructed for him at Hollandia on New Guinea, but wasn't ready for him to move in yet.

General MacArthur was commander of all U.S. Army troops in the Southwest Pacific. He was sixty-four years old and had been in the Army forty-one years. His military record was illustrious, some would say the most illustrious in the history of the U.S. Army, but he had one black mark on his record.

The Japs had kicked his ass off Bataan in 1941. He'd left his whole Army behind, and there's nothing more disgraceful for an Army officer than to leave his soldiers behind, to be killed, wounded, or captured by the enemy, but General MacArthur had done that on direct orders from his commander-in-chief, Franklin Delano Roosevelt, President of the United States.

General MacArthur was a proud man, and also somewhat paranoid. He believed President Roosevelt and General George C. Marshall, the chairman of the joint chiefs of staff, had conspired to humiliate him. He believed they refused to reinforce him on Bataan for personal reasons, because they were jealous of him, and not for sound military reasons.

MacArthur was a brilliant man. Some said he was the greatest military genius America ever had produced. Others said he was vain, myopic, and a ham actor. General Dwight D. Eisenhower, who'd served as General MacArthur's chief of staff for a while in the Philippines, once said he'd studied drama under General MacArthur.

The main criticism of General MacArthur was that he didn't

take into consideration the war raging in Europe, North Africa, Italy, and other parts of the world. President Roosevelt and General Marshall had to make *global* decisions, and they didn't have sufficient men and matériel to give every local commander whatever he needed. Everything had to be rationed in the Army as it was rationed in civilian life. They said General MacArthur didn't understand this because he thought whatever he was doing took precedence over everything else. General MacArthur thought he was the only show in town.

From his point of view he *was* the only show in town. What did he care about Europe or North Africa? His main objective was to defeat the Japanese Empire, and he devoted all his energies and considerable talents toward that end.

General MacArthur had been making his comeback ever since the dismal days on Bataan. His efforts gained momentum in October 1942, when the Americans first took it to the Japs on Guadalcanal. MacArthur had been moving ever closer to the Philippines since then, island by island, battle by battle, bucket of blood after bucket of blood. Now his Sixth Army, nicknamed the *Alamo Task Force,* was on New Guinea conducting operations, and the Philippines comprised the next island chain to the northwest of New Guinea.

The general was anxious to consolidate his victory on New Guinea and then jump off to the Philippines. He'd sworn he'd return and by God he would, no matter what. Roosevelt, Marshall, and the entire Japanese Army wouldn't stop him. History was on the march. General MacArthur had powerful friends in Congress. He hoped to attack the Japanese in the Philippines before the end of the year.

General MacArthur had developed a new strategy of warfare in the South Pacific, and it was so new many people didn't understand it. Some called it "island-hopping" and others called it "hitting 'em where they ain't," but whatever it was, it was working. Basically the strategy worked like this: Instead of attacking strongly held Japanese bases head-on, he captured weakly held objectives to the rear of the strongly held ones, cut the Japanese supply lines, and starved out the strongly held bases, letting them wither away on the vine. MacArthur had employed this strategy throughout the South Pacific, most notably with the massive Japanese base at Rabaul on New Britain Island, which would have cost countless American lives if he'd assaulted it according to conventional rules of strategy and tactics. Instead, all the Japanese soldiers, sailors, marines, and airmen were slowly starving to death at Rabaul, gnashing their teeth and praying the Americans would attack them so they—the Japanese—could die with honor.

General MacArthur had employed this strategy on New Guinea too, landing troops at Aitape and Hollandia, two lightly held objectives, cutting off the Japanese Eighteenth Army deployed in the vicinity of Wewak. Although the Japanese Army at Wewak was cut off, that didn't mean it'd disappeared. The Persecution Task Force, commanded at that time by Brigadier General Jens A. Doe, assaulted Aitape and the Tadji air strips on April 22, signaling victory on April 23. Shortly thereafter intelligence reports from natives and observation aircraft indicated that the Japanese Eighteenth Army was moving westward toward Aitape from Wewak. Since then there had been skirmishes, fights, and even quite serious battles with the Japanese Army, as its various units approached Aitape.

Now battle lines were solidified in the area along the Driniumor River. The Japanese held the east bank, and the GIs held the west bank. General MacArthur was aware that new Japanese units were coming up on the line all the time, and General Adachi would launch an attack to retake Aitape and the Tadji airfields any day now. If the Persecution Task Force couldn't hold Aitape and the Tadji airfields, General MacArthur's plans to assault the Philippines would have to be postponed, and MacArthur didn't want to do that. He'd sworn to return to the Philippines, and people were starting to ask *when?* He couldn't let the Japanese retake Aitape and the Tadji airfields, and that's why he was devoting his fullest attention to that sector of the Pacific War on the morning of July 4, 1944.

He couldn't assault the Philippines if the Japanese Eighteenth Army was attacking his rear, resupplied by American equipment and gasoline they'd have if they recaptured Aitape. He'd also have the Japanese Air Force on his ass too, because Japanese planes would be able to use the Tadji airfields, which Japanese construction crews had built in the first place. The tiny village of Aitape and the dinky Tadji airfields were becoming crucial objectives in the burgeoning Pacific War.

General MacArthur leaned over the documents on his desk, perusing them, shuffling them with his long fingers. A corncob pipe stuck out the corner of his mouth, not the massive corncob pipe he posed with for publicity pictures, but an ordinary corncob that a man could smoke without difficulty. Tobacco smoke billowed up around General MacArthur's head. Sunlight streamed through the windows, illuminating his craggy profile, and below him were the streets of Brisbane, Australia, where he was treated like a hero. General MacArthur wore his old battle hat for publicity pictures because he was bald on the top of his head, and didn't think a bald head looked so nice. He even tried to cover his baldness with the long strands of hair that grew on the sides of his head, but the strands were stringy and never stayed put. General MacArthur somehow didn't look like such a great military leader without his old battle hat on.

Scattered over the top of his desk were letters, documents, communiqués, reports, maps, memoranda, and various other scraps of paper concerning the situation in the vicinity of Aitape, and everything indicated that General Adachi and his Eighteenth Army would assault Aitape and the Tadji airfields on the night of July 9.

The information had come in from radio intercepts, because U.S. intelligence experts had broken the Japanese codes at the beginning of the war. It also came in from reports by observers in the U.S. Army Air Corps, and from reports proffered by friendly natives. A variety of captured Japanese documents stated in black and white that the attack would take place on that night, and one of the documents on General MacArthur's desk was a translation of the orders captured by Lieutenant Breckenridge and the recon platoon during the morning of July 3. Numerous captured Japanese soldiers had stated that an attack would be launched on the night of July 9.

General MacArthur meditated upon the intelligence information, wondering what he should do. It indicated that General Adachi had twenty thousand men in his forward areas, and another eleven thousand in reserve. Could the Persecution Task Force hold them?

General MacArthur decided he didn't want to take any chances with his assault on the Philippines. He realized he'd better reinforce the Aitape area as soon as possible. He picked up a pen and drafted the orders he intended to dispatch to General Krueger at Alamo Task Force headquarters that very day. The 114th Regimental Combat Team would be shipped to

Aitape without delay. General MacArthur also directed an additional 155-mm howitzer battalion to be shipped to Aitape, because there was nothing like those gigantic shells for breaking up an enemy attack. Number Seventy-one Wing on the Army Air Corps was scheduled to leave the Tadji airfields, but General MacArthur countermanded the order. Finally General MacArthur decided that the 845th Regimental Combat Team also should be sent to Aitape.

He looked at the names of the units he'd written on the sheet of paper, and was pleased. Scrawling notes on another piece of paper, he estimated that the Persecution Task Force's total strength would equal three-and-two-thirds divisions. He doubted whether General Adachi and his Eighteenth Army could defeat such a force.

The best form of defense usually was offense. General MacArthur decided it might be a good idea for local commanders to mount an offense against the Japanese, to knock the Japanese off-balance and upset their attack plans. General MacArthur thought he'd recommend this course of action in his message to General Krueger and General Hall.

General MacArthur wrote the last line of his order and leaned back in his chair. His pipe had gone out, and he rested it on his ashtray. He looked out the window at the expanse of blue sky dotted with clouds that looked like cotton puffballs. He hoped to return to the Philippines in October, and when he did return it'd be the fulfillment of his deepest longing and greatest desire. He wanted to rush even more troops and equipment to Aitape, to insure that his attack would take place at the designated time, but he didn't have unlimited resources. He had to ration what he had and not take too much from one sector to strengthen another, Otherwise he might weaken himself someplace and leave himself open to setbacks and defeats. War consisted of tradeoffs and measurements. If you paid too much to win a battle, it wouldn't be worth it, and if you didn't invest enough, you could lose whatever you did invest.

The general didn't want to make costly mistakes, and not just for the sake of his military reputation either. He cared for his men and didn't want to lose any more than was necessary. He didn't want to gamble with their lives, but on the other hand he had to use his men to win the war and save civilization from the Japanese.

He looked at the orders he'd just written and decided they were the best he could do at that time, given the resources he had at his command. Reaching forward, he pressed the button on his telephone, so he could give his chief of staff his new orders for Aitape.

At Hollandia, General Walter Krueger, commanding officer of General MacArthur's Sixth Army, code-named the Alamo Task Force, received the orders via radio transmission that very day. The orders were decoded and placed before him by one of his intelligence officers. General Krueger was sixty-two years old, born in West Prussia, and had emigrated to America with his family when he was only eight years old. He'd enlisted in the Army as a private in 1898 and worked his way up through the ranks. He was a tough old bird and that was just what he looked like.

General MacArthur's orders were clear-cut and concise as always. General Krueger immediately wrote out his own orders, filling in the details that were his responsibility. He added one item of his own to the orders, directing General Hall at Aitape not only to stop the impending Japanese attack, but also to launch a vigorous counterattack of his own, wiping out the Japanese Eighteenth Army for good.

General Krueger's orders arrived at the headquarters of General Hall at Aitape via radio transmission that evening. General Hall was pleased to be receiving reinforcements, but wasn't happy to learn about the impending Japanese attack. General Hall only recently had been appointed to head the Reckless Task Force. He still wasn't thoroughly acquainted with his new command, but couldn't let that stop him. He knew the significance of Aitape to the overall strategic picture. He couldn't lose Aitape to the Japs.

All he could do was prepare for the attack as best he could, and figure out how best to deploy the new units that would arrive soon. Although he'd been advised that the Japanese would attack on the night of July 9, he didn't know where they'd attack, or whether that date might be changed. He had to keep the Japs under constant scrutiny, and his eyes were the patrols that were sent out regularly.

General Hall decided that patrolling should be conducted

more aggressively than ever, and drafted an order on the spot to insure that would take place. To drive the point home to his subordinates, he'd schedule a meeting for tomorrow morning at 0800 hours in his office. They had to understand the importance of keeping tabs on the Japs.

SIX . . .

The next day the recon platoon received notice that they would go out on just such a patrol that evening. They knew nothing about the decisions reached by Generals MacArthur, Krueger, and Hall, and had no idea the Japanese Eighteenth Army was scheduled to attack on the night of July 9, but they'd been told that a Japanese attack was imminent, and their patrol was supposed to elicit as much information about the attack as possible.

It was 1800 hours—six o'clock in the evening—and chow had just ended. The men from the recon platoon cleaned their submachine guns, sharpened their Ka-bar knives, and got their gear in order, each man trying not to think about what might happen to him on the patrol, because it was possible this would be the patrol from which he'd never return.

The sun sank toward the horizon, and the shadows of the jungle lengthened. A few clouds were in the sky and it appeared as though it might rain. The clank of military equipment could be heard along with conversations among soldiers, the rumble of jeep and truck engines, and birds singing good night to each other high in the trees.

A soldier carrying an M 1 rifle appeared on the trail leading to the recon platoon, and he trudged onward, an expression of sorrow and deep concern on his face. The Reverend Billie Jones happened to glance up at this soldier from his dog-eared, weatherbeaten handy pocket edition of the Bible, and his jaw dropped open.

"It's Shilansky!" he said.

Everybody looked at Shilansky, including Frankie La Barbara, who'd been certain Shilansky was on his way back to the States to fuck his wife. A smile broke out on Frankie La Barbara's face, because now he could be sure that his wife Francesca wouldn't be sleeping with Shilansky.

"What the hell are you doing back here!" Frankie said.

"They found out I really didn't have blood poisoning," Shilansky replied, heading toward Lieutenant Breckenridge.

"What was wrong with you?"

"Who the hell knows?"

Shilansky walked up to Lieutenant Breckenridge's foxhole and kneeled at its edge. "I'm back," he said.

"So I see," Lieutenant Breckenridge replied. "You feel all right?"

"No."

"Good. You can join us on tonight's patrol. We're going out at twenty hundred hours. Get a submachine gun from the armorer and report back here when you're finished."

"Yes sir," Shilansky said listlessly.

"Welcome back."

Shilansky shrugged, because he wasn't very happy about being back, risking his life at the front again, but that wasn't his main problem. Something else was bothering him, and he didn't think he could handle it.

He shuffled his feet and made his way to the command post of Headquarters Company, where the armorer was. He couldn't stop thinking about the article he'd read in a newspaper while he'd been languishing at the division medical headquarters.

The newspaper had been the New York *Times*, sent originally to a patient at the hospital. It was mangled and torn by the time Shilansky received it, but he read it hungrily anyway, his first opportunity in a long time to find out what was going on in the world.

Shilansky ran across the news story that was disturbing him so much on one of the back pages of the newspaper. The news story said Jews were being exterminated en masse in German concentration camps in Europe. The Jews evidently were being gassed and then cremated in huge ovens, perhaps hundreds of thousands, even millions of them. World leaders vowed that the Nazis would be punished for this after the war.

Shilansky was a Jew, and the news story had blown his mind. He hadn't been feeling well since he read it, and he wasn't even that much of a Jew. He hardly ever went to the synagogue back in the States, and never attended Jewish services in the Army. He wasn't particularly an atheist, but he didn't believe in God very much either.

Shilansky was the only Jew in the recon platoon, and often

could forget he was a Jew, thinking he was just another one of the boys, which in fact he was as far as they were concerned, but the newspaper article caused him to realize he was different from them, because nobody ever tried to gas or cremate the entire race of Irishmen, Italians, White Anglo-Saxon Protestants, or any other cultural or religious group.

Shilansky walked through the darkening jungle, his hands in his pockets and his face inclined toward the ground. He couldn't understand why anybody would hate Jews enough to kill them all off. He knew Jews were obnoxious sometimes, but so were all other people sometimes. He knew people often were jealous of Jews, and claimed Jews owned everything, but Shilansky never owned anything, and his father had been a house painter before the Depression, working for wages. He knew some Jews owned little corner grocery stores, or sometimes big department stores, but no Jews owned the really huge stuff in America, like the major banks and enormous corporations like General Motors.

Shilansky thought about Jewish women and little children being gassed and cremated. He couldn't understand why the world didn't do something about it, because it seemed that *something* could be done. But maybe nothing could be done, like the newspaper article said, except the promise to punish Nazis when the war was won, if the war was won.

Shilansky also thought about the men like him who were gassed and cremated. Why didn't they fight back? He knew he would've fought back, or at least he thought he would. Maybe Jews like him had fought back but it wasn't reported in the newspapers because nobody knew about it.

The worst part was that Shilansky had no one he could talk with about the concentration camps. He couldn't say something because then everybody would see him as just another Jew who complained all the time, and he didn't want to be thought of that way. So he'd have to keep his mouth shut and pretend it wasn't bothering him, although it was bothering him, festering and seething inside his soul.

Finally he came to Headquarters Company and passed the command post, on his way to the armorer's tent. Pfc. Levinson, the regimental clerk, happened to be outside, inspecting tent stakes for the storm he thought might be brewing, and Levinson happened to notice Shilansky. Levinson and Shilansky knew each other vaguely and were aware that they were Jews, but never mentioned it or even had a conversation that lasted longer than three sentences.

"Hello Shilansky," Pfc. Levinson said. "How're you feeling?"

"Okay," Shilansky replied, and kept on walking.

Shilansky wondered if Pfc. Levinson knew about the death camps, and would've liked to talk with him about them, but if he and Levinson were seen talking privately together everyone else might think two Jews were conspiring to take over the world.

What the fuck, Shilansky said to himself. *I can't save those Jews. I can't even save myself.* He decided to keep his mouth shut and just go on with his life as if nothing happened, but whenever he closed his eyes he saw those little children going up in flames.

It was night in the jungle. Butsko sat in the clearing outside the medical tent, his cane lying on the ground beside him. He raised his cigarette to his mouth and took a drag. The usual trucks and jeeps rolled by on the road. Groups of wounded soldiers sat around shooting the shit. One had a guitar and strummed an old Kentucky bluegrass tune, while a few GIs sang along about doomed love and the suffering endured by hearts on fire. Butsko was thinking about his leg, of how it had improved during the past few days, and how he hoped to get around without the cane in a few more days.

"Hi,' said the voice of Lieutenant Betty Crawford above him.

Butsko looked up and saw her pretty face in the shadows. They hadn't spoken since the big blow-out on the path near the nurses' tent.

"You still mad at me?" she asked.

"No," he replied.

"Mind if I sit down?"

"Go right ahead."

She sat cross-legged on the grass in front of him and their eyes met, but she quickly averted her gaze. She looked as if she was embarrassed. There was something about Butsko that intimidated her, and she didn't think it was just his physical bulk.

71

"That court-martial's not going through," she said to him. He didn't reply.

"Don't you even want to know why?" she asked.

"Why?" he answered.

"Because all the nurses refused to testify for the one who wanted to court-martial you, and without witnesses she's got no case."

Butsko was surprised. "Those nurses won't testify against me?"

"That's what I said."

"Why not?"

"I guess they like you, and they don't like her."

"Who could like her?" Butsko asked.

She took out her package of Chesterfields, and he flicked his Zippo, lighting one up for her.

"Thanks," she said.

"Don't mention it," he replied.

She puffed her cigarette and he puffed his. The faint evening breeze blew the smoke away in long wispy trails. The wounded soldier strumming his guitar sang that old Army song, "The Reenlistment Blues."

Betty turned to Butsko and looked him in the eye. "What're we going to do, Butsko?"

"About what?" he asked. He knew exactly what she was referring to, but was in a rotten mood and didn't feel like cooperating.

"About us," she said.

"Why do we have to do something about us?"

"You wanna just forget about everything?"

"Naw," he said, "I don't wanna forget about everything."

"Then what are we going to do?" she asked.

Butsko winked. "Why don't we go into those woods over there where we can be alone?"

"C'mon Butsko—be serious. We've got to talk things over."

"Why do we always have to talk?"

"Listen to me," she said. "I'm not one of those silly nurses who sleeps with everybody. I'm twenty-four years old and I only slept with four men in my life. One was Bob, and we were going to get married but he's dead now."

"He might not be dead," Butsko replied. "He's missing in action and could turn up again any day now."

"Extremely unlikely," Betty said. "There was another boyfriend I had in college, and another boyfriend I had all the time I was in high school, and then there was you. I don't go to bed with men for the hell of it. I am not a promiscuous woman. When I go to bed with a man it's because I love him, and I fell in love with you, you big lug. But you never fell in love with me. I'm beginning to realize that I'm just another girl to you, just another port in a storm, isn't that so?"

"No," Butsko said. "I love you too, baby."

"You don't sound very sincere about it."

"Well what else am I supposed to do?"

"You're not *supposed* to do anything. Either you're sincere or you're not."

Butsko puffed his cigarette and looked at her. The moonlight dappled her hair, and shadows played across her cheek, but somehow she didn't look so good to him anymore. She was annoying him with her incessant horseshit, and he didn't need any more hassles in his life. He looked her in the eyes again, and they were the eyes of a frightened child, not the smoldering coals he'd thought he'd seen before.

"You're getting to be a pain in the ass, you know that?" he said.

Her hair bristled on her head and her backbone became as straight as the barrel of a rifle. "What!"

"I said you're getting to be a pain in the ass. I don't need all this shit. I got enough on my mind."

She looked at his face and realized how ugly and beat-up he was, and he was so much older than she, with bad manners and a foul mouth. "Well," she said huffily. "I can see you really don't care about me at all."

"Gimme a break, willya kid?" Butsko picked up his cane and planted its end in the ground beside him. He rested his hand on the top part and pushed himself up.

"Where are you going?" she asked.

"To bed."

She stood also and brushed the leaves and twigs off the rear end of her uniform. "You just can't walk away like this," she said.

"Oh no?"

He turned away from her and leaned on his cane, hobbling toward the tent. She didn't know whether to run after him or throw a rock at him. She decided to do neither. He didn't love her as much as she wanted to be loved, so she might as well forget about him.

She put her hands in her pockets and walked toward the area where the nurses lived, passing the soldier strumming his guitar, singing of old battles, undying love, and lost illusions.

SEVEN . . .

It was midnight and the recon platoon moved cautiously through a deep dark part of the New Guinea jungle. McGurk was on the point, about twenty paces ahead of the others, clearing the way, the eyes and ears of the platoon as it advanced through Japanese-held territory on the east side of the Driniumor River.

Lieutenant Breckenridge was farther back, carrying his submachine gun slung barrel-down over his shoulder, looking to the left and right, alert and observant, expecting to run into Japanese soldiers at any moment, and it was imperative that the GIs saw the Japanese soldiers before the Japanese soldiers saw them.

Private Worthington walked behind Lieutenant Breckenridge, carrying the patrol's walkie-talkie; Lieutenant Breckenridge had given Private Worthington the job of being his runner. Worthington also carried an M 1 rifle instead of a submachine gun, because the M 1 rifle was an accurate weapon and Worthington was supposed to be a crack shot.

Worthington wasn't as nervous as he'd thought he'd be. The patrol reminded him of going on safari in an area full of hostile natives, and wild beasts like lions and leopards who'd like to eat you for dinner.

Private Worthington had hunter's eyes and instincts. He examined the trees and bushes all around him, looking above his head periodically to see if anything or anybody was lurking there. He found himself envying Lieutenant Breckenridge, because Lieutenant Breckenridge was in charge. Private Worthington realized he'd like to lead a patrol himself. He was smart and had good instincts in the wilderness. He was sure he could do a good job.

Behind Private Worthington was Corporal Bannon, second

in command in the recon platoon and second in command on that particular patrol. He carried his submachine gun in his hands, and felt the old familiar atmosphere and danger cover him like a cloak. This was his first patrol since Bougainville, and his instincts were rusty. He'd grown accustomed to the soft life in hospitals and the warm arms of Homer Gladley's sister, but now his life was on the line again, and it didn't feel so good. Somehow he'd have to sharpen his senses and combat skills if he wanted to survive the war, and he definitely wanted to survive the war so he could go back to Nebraska and marry Priscilla Gladley.

Suddenly Bannon became aware that everyone around him was scattering into the bushes on the left side of the trail. He was the last one to take cover in the thick foliage, and raised his head, trying to figure out what was going on. Private McGurk crawled back to Lieutenant Breckenridge, and Bannon crept closer to hear McGurk's report.

"Hear Japs," McGurk said.

"Where?"

McGurk pointed ahead on the trail.

"You're sure?" Lieutenant Breckenridge asked, because he didn't hear anything.

McGurk nodded his head, and it was so big his fatigue cap sat on top of it and looked as though it'd fall off at any moment.

"Okay," Lieutenant Breckenridge said. "Stay put here."

McGurk lay down like a big dog and held his submachine gun in his hands, wrinkling his brow, facing the sound he claimed to have heard.

Private Worthington was on the other side of Lieutenant Breckenridge, and he leaned closer to Lieutenant Breckenridge because he wanted to say something softly so that McGurk wouldn't hear. "I don't hear any Japs," Private Worthington whispered.

McGurk turned around and scowled. He'd heard every word. Worthington was embarrassed and smiled stupidly at McGurk.

"I just don't hear anything," Worthington repeated.

"Be still," Lieutenant Breckenridge said.

Worthington became irritated whenever Lieutenant Breckenridge gave him an order. He'd never felt that way when officers gave him orders in basic training, but he'd played football against Lieutenant Breckenridge and thought of him almost like a friend. It was turning into a very perplexing problem for Private Worthington.

Then he heard the sounds. At first it was like an onrush of wind rustling leaves and branches faintly, but then Private Worthington realized a fairly substantial number of soldiers were headed toward the patrol. He had to admit big stupid McGurk had sharper ears than he.

Lieutenant Breckenridge turned his head around and looked at Bisbee, pointing to him. Then he beckoned with his finger, and Bisbee crawled forward.

"Get ready with your knife," Lieutenant Breckenridge said.

Bisbee nodded. He yanked his Ka-bar knife out of its scabbard, and it gleamed in the darkness. It was razor sharp; Bisbee kept it that way. His face still was bruised and battered, but it was healing. He still hated Frankie La Barbara, but that would have to wait for later. Holding the knife by its blade, the ex-carnie got ready to throw it.

The sounds of Japanese soldiers drew closer, and then they came into view on the trail. The GIs saw a long column of Japanese soldiers carrying large crates on their backs, headed toward the Driniumor River. The Japanese soldiers were skinny and bony, and it appeared the crates should be too heavy for them, but the Japanese soldiers carried them anyway, never faltering or complaining, moving along the trail only a few feet away from the GIs.

Lieutenant Breckenridge took out his notepad and wrote down what he saw. It confirmed what he'd been told already, that the Japanese Army on New Guinea had no transport and carried supplies around by hand. It also confirmed reports that Japs were moving supplies up to the Driniumor, probably in preparation for their big attack.

The GIs watched the Japanese soldiers pass by. The column was a long one, and Lieutenant Breckenridge counted twenty-eight Japs so far. None of the GIs made a sound. For Bannon, these were the first Japs he'd seen since Bougainville, and he couldn't help recalling past battles where he'd shot Japanese soldiers with his rifle, stabbed them with his bayonet, fried them with flamethrowers, and blown them to shit with hand grenades. Now there they were again, and he hated them as before. They were the ones who'd started the war. They were the ones who sneak-attacked Pearl Harbor and butchered American soldiers on the Bataan Death March. They were the ones who were keeping him from Priscilla Gladley back in Nebraska. The old rage came back to Bannon. He wanted to raise his submachine gun and mow the bastards down.

But he didn't raise his submachine gun and mow them down. His patrol wasn't supposed to start wars. It was out to gather information, and if it got into trouble it'd have to fight, but otherwise it was supposed to be invisible and silent.

The column of Japanese soldiers continued to pass by. The Japanese soldiers wore soft caps and had Arisaka rifles slung crossways over their backs. Their uniforms were ragged and they wore leggings above their battered combat shoes. A Japanese soldier approached, having difficulty with his load. This Japanese soldier was even smaller and skinnier than the others, and his legs were buckling under the weight of the crate he carried on his shoulders. He staggered to one side of the trail and then to the other side. Another Japanese soldier said something to him, and when the skinny Jap replied his voice was weak and broken.

A boulder jutted up from the ground on the trail, and the Japanese soldier tripped over it. He fell to the ground, the crate landing nearby. He tried to get up but didn't have the strength. Other Japanese soldiers shouted to someone else. The column continued to move forward, leaving the Japanese soldier behind.

Another Japanese soldier ran back to the skinny one lying on the ground. This Japanese soldier carried a samurai sword in a scabbard attached to his belt and evidently was a sergeant. He shouted and screamed at the Japanese soldier on the ground, but the fallen soldier couldn't get up. He was on his back and dug his elbows into the ground, but was devoid of energy.

The Japanese sergeant got pissed off. His column marched out of sight around the bend, and this scrawny soldier at his feet was holding up the production. The Japanese sergeant screamed at the Japanese soldier and kicked him in the ass. Bending over, he slapped him across both cheeks, because it was acceptable and quite common for sergeants to beat up enlisted men in the Japanese Army. The sergeant hollered louder and kicked the soldier in the ribs. He smacked him across the mouth again.

Lieutenant Breckenridge decided to take a prisoner. He turned

78

to Bisbee and said, "When I say the word, kill that sergeant."

Bisbee nodded and gripped his knife more firmly. Lieutenant Breckenridge looked at McGurk. "You pick up the little Jap lying on his ass when I say so, got it?"

McGurk nodded. The Japanese sergeant continued to shout and beat the soldier on the ground, who tried to get up.

"Do it," Lieutenant Breckenridge whispered to Bisbee.

Bisbee reared back his arm, took aim, and threw the knife. It flew silently through the air, its blade flashing instantaneously, and then *chung*—it slammed into the heart of the Japanese sergeant.

The Japanese sergeant didn't know what hit him, and collapsed onto his back. The Japanese soldier lying nearby raised his head, because the sergeant suddenly had disappeared from his line of vision.

"Go!" said Lieutenant Breckenridge.

He and McGurk charged through the bushes and jumped onto the trail. Lieutenant Breckenridge swung down with his Ka-bar knife, slashing the throat of the officer to make sure he was dead, and McGurk swept the diminutive Japanese soldier up in his arms.

The Japanese soldier didn't know what was going on. One second his sergeant was kicking the shit out of him, and the next second a giant was carrying him into the jungle. The Japanese soldier was weak and sick, and couldn't handle it. He passed out in McGurk's arms.

Lieutenant Breckenridge yanked the Nambu pistol out of the Japanese sergeant's holster and stuffed it into the space between his cartridge belt and shirt. Spinning around, he followed McGurk into the jungle. The other GIs joined the rush to get as far away from the trail as possible. They ran around trees and jumped over fallen logs, dodging bushes, bending under low-hanging vines, while behind them on the trail there was silence; the Japanese soldiers carrying crates didn't yet know what had happened.

The little Japanese soldier opened his eyes. The jungle was dark around him, because clouds obscured the moon. He lay on leaves on the jungle floor, and glanced to his left and right, his heart nearly stopping as a result of what he saw.

He was surrounded by big burly American soldiers, and

opened his mouth to scream. A hand clamped over his mouth, and the head of an American soldier appeared in front of him. The American soldier had a kindly face, and placed his finger in front of his mouth, indicating that the little Japanese soldier should be quiet.

The little Japanese soldier's name was Hirokoshi, and he realized he was a prisoner of war. This frightened him, because he knew how the Japanese Army treated prisoners of war, but the Americans weren't beating him up or threatening him in any way. Hirokoshi hated being a soldier, because he was a weak sickly person who simply didn't have the strength to do all the things a Japanese soldier was supposed to do. This made him a punching bag for Japanese sergeants. Now he realized that his military career was over, and he was safe, with friendly American soldiers.

The hand was removed from Hirokoshi's mouth. Hirokoshi smiled and bowed. One of the American soldiers handed him a cracker to eat, and Hirokoshi accepted it with another little bow, trying to eat it slowly although he was starved to death and tempted to gobble it down like a maniac.

"Friendly little feller, ain't he?" asked the Reverend Billie Jones, who always tried to see the best in people.

"I wouldn't turn my back on him," Frankie La Barbara said. "A good Jap is a dead Jap."

Lieutenant Breckenridge turned to Frankie. "Be nice to him. He can tell us a lot, and he probably will because he must be mad at his own people since that sergeant was beating him up before we saved him."

"I still don't trust him," Frankie said. "If he makes one funny move, I'm gonna kill the little slant-eyed son of a bitch."

"You'd better stay away from him. I want to bring him back alive."

The Reverend Billie Jones handed Hirokoshi another cracker, and Hirokoshi ate it daintily. Hirokoshi was feeling better, realizing he didn't have to worry anymore about getting shot or stabbed in combat. He never thought he'd live long if he ever got into a bayonet fight with an American, because Americans were so much bigger and stronger than he. He'd thought for sure he'd be dead soon after the big offensive began, but now he was going to live.

Hirokoshi was overjoyed. He'd never believed much in the war anyway, and on top of that he was a Buddhist, and Buddhists were discriminated against by the Shintoists, the majority religion in Japan. Hirokoshi had been an accountant in a bookkeeper's office before the war, working with an abacus, writing neat columns of figures on pieces of paper. He'd been a bachelor living with his mother, never paid much attention to the news, and then one day he'd been drafted. He'd worked as a bookkeeper and clerk in the army, but General Adachi was mobilizing as many soldiers as possible for his upcoming offensive. Hirokoshi had been given a rifle and transferred to the infantry.

Hirokoshi hated the Army and had no special loyalty to the Emperor. He was a dissident in the Japanese Army, although he always kept his mouth shut.

Now he was free, and the big American soldier was giving him another cracker. Hirokoshi bowed again and accepted it, raising it to his quivering lips, wondering if he was dreaming or if the war really was over for him as it appeared. He smiled happily at his American captors and said, *"Arigato,"* thanking them for saving his life.

"Watch out," Frankie La Barbara uttered. "When a Jap smiles at you, that's when you'd better start reaching for your gun."

"Leave him alone," Lieutenant Breckenridge told him. "Get away from him. I don't want you scaring him."

"I'll scare him all right," Frankie La Barbara said. "I'll blow his fucking Jap brains out."

"I said get away from him, and I mean it."

Frankie walked on his hands and knees to the outer periphery of the circle around Hirokoshi, and it was a good thing because Hirokoshi could detect the hostility in Frankie's voice. But the strong sensible sound of Lieutenant Breckenridge's voice reassured him. Hirokoshi munched his cracker, still believing he was safe. He hoped the Americans would give him a cigarette after they took him to safety behind their lines. He was sure they would, because they appeared to be decent fellows, except for the one with the threatening voice, and even he seemed nicer than Hirokoshi's platoon sergeant, who used to beat him up with terrible regularity.

They gave Private Hirokoshi all the cigarettes he wanted while he was at the headquarters of the Twenty-third Regiment, and he got more cigarettes plus breakfast by the time he got to the headquarters of the Eighty-first Division. His cuts and bruises were treated by doctors and pretty nurses at the Eighty-first Division Medical Headquarters, and his next stop was the headquarters of the Persecution Task Force. He felt like a movie star or a celebrity, because everybody made a fuss over him, giving him anything he wanted. He thought Americans were kind people, exactly the opposite of the monsters depicted in Japanese Army propoganda. He believed it had been wrong for the Japanese High Command to go to war against such a friendly people, and meanwhile the American officers figured he was going to sing like a bird.

At the headquarters of the Persecution Task Force, Hirokoshi was brought to a tent where an American officer sat behind a desk, and to Hirokoshi's surprise and delight, the American officer greeted him in Japanese!

Hirokoshi regained his composure and bowed. "How do you do, sir," he said to the officer.

The officer was Major Rainey, the former overseas rep for General Electric, who now worked for General Hall. "Have a seat," Major Rainey said.

Hirokoshi sat on a wooden chair. Armed American MPs were on either side of him. Major Rainey lifted a package of Camels from his desk and held them out to Hirokoshi.

"Cigarette?" asked Major Rainey.

"If you please," replied Hirokoshi, although he'd smoked more cigarettes during the past few hours than he'd smoked during the past month in the Japanese Army.

Major Rainey leaned forward and lit the cigarette. Hirokoshi took a few puffs and returned to his chair. He savored the cigarette, thinking that American cigarettes were superior to Japanese cigarettes. He wondered what it would be like to live in America, among such decent people.

"How are you feeling?" Major Rainey asked.

"Very well, thank you," Hirokoshi replied, puffing the Camel cigarette.

"I hope you've received adequate medical attention."

"Oh yes, thank you, I have."

"Good, because we want you to be comfortable."

"You speak excellent Japanese," Hirokoshi said. "Where did you learn?"

"I lived in your country for a while before the war."

"Did you really?"

The conversation continued in this unimportant vein for several more minutes, as Major Rainey worked to put Hirokoshi at ease. He wouldn't have tried so hard if he'd known Hirokoshi already was at ease and had been ever since the recon platoon took him prisoner. Hirokoshi loved to sit around and talk with people, and he wasn't stupid, he knew Major Rainey wanted information, but Hirokoshi was prepared to answer all questions. He wasn't happy about the way he'd been treated in the Japanese Army, and didn't like the military dictatorship that ruled his country.

Finally Major Rainey decided the time had come to get down to business. He continued smiling as he steeled himself for his assault on Hirokoshi's loyalties, little realizing that Hirokoshi had few left.

"I wonder if you could give us some information?" Major Rainey asked.

"What exactly would you like to know?" Hirokoshi asked.

"We understand General Adachi is planning a major attack soon. Is that correct?"

"Quite correct," Private Hirokoshi replied. "Until recently I worked in the headquarters of the Eighteenth Army, and I was aware that the attack was being planned."

Major Rainey was thunderstruck. He couldn't believe his good luck. He had before him not an ordinary infantry private as he'd thought, but a clerk who'd worked in the headquarters of General Adachi himself!

Major Rainey leaned forward. "Tell me," he said, "is the attack really going to take place on the night of July ninth?"

Now it was Private Hirokoshi's turn to be surprised. "How do you know that?"

Major Rainey smiled knowingly. "We have our ways. Will the attack take place on that night?"

"It will as far as I know," Private Hirokoshi said, "but I haven't been in General Adachi's headquarters for several days now, and the plans might've changed."

"Have you ever actually seen the plans?"

"Yes I have, sir."

Major Rainey nearly fell off his chair. "You've seen the plans!"

"Parts of them, sir."

"What parts?"

"The parts concerned with logistics, and some of the overall plans for operations."

Major Rainey swallowed hard. It was his lucky day. "What are the overall plans for the attack, Private Hirokoshi?" he asked politely.

"As I said," Private Hirokoshi began, "the plans might've been changed since I left General Adachi's headquarters, but as I recall, the attack was scheduled to proceed along two axes, the first toward the northern seacoast and the second across the Driniumor River midway between Afua and the point where the Driniumor empties into the sea."

Major Rainey looked down at his map. The sector near the coast was held by the Thirty-fifth Division, and the sector midway between Afua and the mouth of the Driniumor was held by the Eight-first Division. Major Rainey wrinkled his brow and looked up at Private Hirokoshi.

"This is very interesting information," he said.

Private Hirokoshi smiled. "I thought you'd think so, sir," he replied.

EIGHT . . .

At 1400 a meeting was held in the office of General Hall. All his staff officers were in attendance, as well as division commanders, regimental commanders, and their staffs. It was a huge assembly of officers, and if a Japanese artillery shell happened to land on that wooden shack, the entire U.S. Army leadership in the Aitape area would be wiped out.

The officers gathered around a map table six feet wide and six feet long, with various American units represented by squares of wood, while Japanese units were represented by round pieces of wood. It was raining torrents outside, with lightning streaking across the sky and thunderclaps sounding like bomb explosions. Three tin pails had been placed on the floor to catch water dripping through the roof.

General Hall stood behind the map table, holding a long pointer in his right hand. "This meeting has been called," he said, "because of important intelligence that has been obtained this morning. The intelligence arrived in the form of an enemy soldier captured by a patrol from the Eighty-first Division, and I believe the information will give us a leg up on the Japs if they attack as scheduled on the night of July ninth."

Everyone glanced at General Hawkins, and he stiffened his spine, puffing out his chest with pride, because a patrol from his division had brought in the prisoner, although he didn't have anything to do with it.

If anyone in the room should've received credit, it was Colonel Hutchins, because he was the one who'd organized his recon platoon, hand-picking many of its members, and the recon platoon furnished the patrol that captured Private Hirokoshi. But no one paid any attention to Colonel Hutchins, who stood near the rear wall of the tent, behind all the generals, because although he was head honcho at the Twenty-third Regiment, he was just another bird colonel among a conglomeration of one- and two-star generals at Persecution Task Headquarters.

"According to this captured Japanese soldier," General Hall continued, "who was a clerk in General Adachi's headquarters, by the way, the Japanese attack will consist of two main elements. One will be a thrust along the seacoast here"—General Hall pointed to that sector of the map—"and the second will be an attempt to force the Driniumor here." He pointed to the area midway between Afua and the mouth of the Driniumor. "Our informant reports that General Adachi is determined to win this battle and will give it all he has. Although General Adachi is short on supplies, and his men have been poorly fed and cared for, he still thinks he can overcome us. From what our informant tells us, we can expect the same numbers of Japanese soldiers that we've been expecting. Our intelligence up until now has been accurate, I'm pleased to say. The attack itself will come on the night of July ninth, which we've also known for some time, but this new information confirms it."

A hand shot up. It belonged to Colonel Daniel MacKenzie, an intelligence expert on General Hall's staff. "Sir," he said, "may I suggest that this might very well be stale information. It's quite possible that we'll gear up for an attack on the night of July ninth, and the attack itself will come sometime before that date or after it. We know ourselves how often plans are changed, sometimes at the last moment. I don't think we should concentrate unduly on July ninth. I think we should be prepared for an attack at all times. If we exert all our efforts to the night of July ninth, we just might let the Japs trick us. For all we know, this prisoner might be part of an elaborate plan of deception. He might be a Japanese intelligence agent himself. I think we should take what he told us with a grain of salt, and make our own preparations based on our own knowledge. Even the description of the two-pronged attack might be completely erroneous. I think we must exercise extreme caution in this matter, and prepare for all possible contigencies."

Colonel MacKenzie closed his mouth. He'd said what was on his mind and felt relieved. General Hall and the others reflected upon what he'd said. They thought perhaps he was right.

General Hall cleared his throat. "I think we ought to give

very serious consideration to what Colonel MacKenzie has just said. We can't let ourselves be deceived by the Japs. There's too much at stake here. Perhaps we shouldn't give undue weight to the night of July ninth. Perhaps we should maintain a general state of readiness, as Colonel MacKenzie suggests."

Another hand shot up, and this time it was Major Rainey who wanted to speak. "Sir," he said, "I'm the one who interrogated the Japanese prisoner, and I believe his story completely. Moreover, I think it's unlikely that he's an intelligence agent in disguise, because he was captured under the most unusual circumstances. He was being beaten physically by his platoon sergeant when he was rescued by the patrol from the Eighty-first Division, and he's most grateful for being rescued. This particular prisoner has never believed in the war, and always has been opposed to the military men who've taken over the government of his country. On top of all that, he's a Buddhist, and Buddhists have been persecuted by the Shinto majority in Japan. The prisoner might indeed have provided stale information, but it was provided in good faith, in my opinion."

Colonel MacKenzie raised his hand again. "I respect Major Rainey's opinion, and always have admired his facility with the Japanese language, but I still think it's possible this prisoner is a cleverly disguised intelligence agent. His whole story is too pat. His allegation that he worked in General Adachi's headquarters is simply too good to be true. I don't believe it."

The room was silent. A simple straightforward briefing had become a controversy. Everybody looked to General Hall for direction.

"Does anyone have any more thoughts on this matter?" General Hall said, throwing the ball back into their court.

A lively discussion ensued, with some officers taking Colonel MacKenzie's side and other officers on Major Rainey's side. Some officers tried to steer into the middle of the road, always the safest way to go. General Hawkins was one of these, trying to sound reasonable and conciliatory, like a diplomat or a United States senator.

Colonel Hutchins leaned against the rear wall, his thumbs hooked into his cartridge belt. He hated big meetings because they brought out the ham actor and tinhorn politician in some Army officers. Those with something significant to say invariably were drowned out by the phonies. Colonel Hutchins was tempted to mention that he was the only person in the room who'd actually spoken with the officer who'd led the patrol—Lieutenant Breckenridge—and was convinced that the capture of the Jap prisoner hadn't been set up by the Japs. Colonel Hutchins was on the verge of raising his hand, but if he did he knew he'd get into an argument with somebody, and he'd probably punch the son of a bitch out. He didn't want that to happen in General Hall's headquarters, because there could be very serious repercussions, such as Colonel Hutchins being relieved of command.

The discussion continued, boring many of the officers, but providing others a platform on which they could express their ideas and advance their careers. The mood of the room shifted back and forth from believing Private Hirokoshi to not believing him. Colonel Hutchins thought perhaps he could provide important information that would help the other officers make up their minds. On top of that, he was one of the few officers in the room who hadn't spoken out yet, and sometimes it was very bad careerwise to be quiet at meetings, because your superiors might start thinking you were dumb and had no opinions about anything.

Colonel Hutchins took a deep breath and with great reluctance raised his hand.

General Hall aimed his pointer at him and said, "Yes?"

All eyes turned on Colonel Hutchins, and he felt ill at ease because he hated to be the center of attention, where any error he made would fall under the close scrutiny of his superiors. Now, with all those eyes on him, he wished he hadn't raised his hand, but it was too late.

General Hawkins groaned audibly, because he hated Colonel Hutchins and was sure he'd make a fool of himself. Other officers in the room knew of Colonel Hutchins's reputation as a drunk and troublemaker. Many officers knew nothing at all about him, and one of these was General Hall, who thought Colonel Hutchins looked like an old bulldog, the kind of officer whom enlisted men respected and followed because he spoke their language.

"Sir," said Colonel Hutchins, jutting his bulldog jaw forward, "I think I might have some information that might be of use to y'all." Colonel Hutchins sniffed and wiped his nose with the back of his hand. "As far as I know, I'm the only man here who actually talked with the officer who led the patrol that captured the little Jap, and I think it's impossible that the whole thing could've been a setup. In the first place, my patrol was about a mile behind enemy lines, and if the Japs knew they were there they would've killed them and not put on this little show for them. Second, the Japs didn't know where my patrol was going, so they could set up the play, because my patrol didn't even know where they were going themselves—they were just roaming around looking for whatever they could find back there. Third, I doubt whether Japs would deliberately expose themselves to an American patrol, since the American patrol might be tempted to kill them all. Fourth, the officer who led the patrol indicated to me that the little Jap who was getting beat up really looked like he was getting beat up. Fifth, the little Jap would've been killed by his sergeant if my patrol hadn't killed the sergeant. Sixth, I don't want to say that the whole thing couldn't've been a setup, but I think it would've been damn near impossible for the Japs to organize all those factors the way they did, and have everything turn out as they'd planned. It's just not logical, and if we could have the officer here who led the patrol, I'm sure he could give you a more convincing explanation than I have. That's all I got to say."

All the officers stared at Colonel Hutchins, making him feel self-conscious. He wished they'd look away but they kept looking at him as if he were a sewer rat who just crawled out from beneath a manhole cover.

Most of this was the product of his overheated alcoholic imagination. In fact, the majority of officers in the room thought what he'd said was relevant. His voice had been gruff and he spoke with a Southern accent—he was from Arkansas originally—but many of their voices were gruff and some of them were Southerners too.

Colonel MacKenzie decided the time had come to defend his position again. "I appreciate what the colonel just told us," he said, "and I have no doubts as to his sincerity, but I'd like to suggest that he might be mistaken, and our Japanese informer really might be part of an elaborate plot to lead us astray. I realize this might seem unlikely to the colonel, and again I respect his judgment and experience, but let me remind everyone here that the disaster at Pearl Harbor was considered impossible too, but it happened against all the odds, and we must always be prepared for the unexpected in this war."

Colonel Hutchins couldn't help admiring what Colonel MacKenzie had just said, even though Colonel MacKenzie had just put him down. It sounded so logical and right, even though Colonel Hutchins knew it was wrong. *I don't have a chance against these fancy staff officers,* Colonel Hutchins thought. *They're all like a bunch of Philadelphia lawyers.*

Meanwhile the discussion went on, as lightning rent the skies and thunder made the walls of the wooden building tremble. Some officers agreed with Colonel MacKenzie, and others sided with Major Rainey and Colonel Hutchins. Talk was cheap, and only one officer was charged with the responsibility of actually making the final decision. This was General Hall, and he decided to play it safe. He believed the attack probably would come on the night of July 9, but on the other hand it might not. Therefore the Reckless Task Force would remain in a state of readiness for the attack, and continue to patrol aggressively in order to keep track of what the Japs were up to on their side of the Driniumor.

General Hall squared his shoulders and related his decision to the officers assembled in front of him. He spoke specifically of the kinds of patrols he wanted to be sent out, and where they should go. He also shifted some units around, in case the attack did come as Hirokoshi had reported.

Finally the meeting was dismissed and the officers ran to their jeeps through the pouring rain, holding their ponchos over their heads. Their jeep drivers drove them to their respective headquarters through puddles full of water and over roads that had become muck. Each officer still held the opinion he'd formed during the meeting. Some thought the July 9 information was either a hoax or unreliable, since plans often were changed during the final days before an offensive. Others felt certain the Japanese attack was coming on the night of July 9, and were frustrated because so many of their fellow officers didn't take that probability more seriously.

Sitting on the passenger seat of his jeep as it chugged through the jungle, Colonel Hutchins was alarmed that so many officers refused to believe the attack would come on the night of July 9. It was his impression that General Hawkins was one of those who doubted. Colonel Hutchins resolved to visit General Hawkins as soon as possible and try to convince him, because the Eighty-first Division sat directly in the sector between Afua and the mouth of the Driniumor, and the Twenty-third Regiment was in the middle of the Eighty-first Division line.

If the division wasn't ready when the attack came, the Twenty-third would bear the brunt of the attack, and if the attack was major, as all indications predicted, the Twenty-third would take a helluva beating. Colonel Hutchins may have been a drunkard and a buffoon, but he knew disaster had to be avoided at all costs.

"I just changed my mind," Colonel Hutchins said to Pfc. Bombasino, his driver. "Take me straight to General Hawkins's headquarters, instead of my own headquarters."

"Yes sir!" replied Pfc. Bombasino, his nose nearly touching the front windshield so he'd have a better chance of seeing the road through the torrential downpour.

The rain fell heavily on the Japanese side of the Driniumor also, but that didn't keep General Adachi home. As Colonel Hutchins was being driven to Eighty-first Division Headquarters by Pfc. Nick Bombasino, General Adachi inspected a battalion of field artillery.

The battalion was deployed a mile east of the Driniumor, deep in the jungle, and its Type 94 mountains guns, firing 75-mm shells, were covered with netting and canvas painted in camouflage colors to avoid detection from the air.

General Adachi approached one of these guns, accompanied by his executive officer, General Tatsunari Kimura; his aide, Lieutenant Ono; and various officers from the local artillery battalion.

The crew of the gun stood at attention beside it. The gun was one of the workhorses of the Japanese Army, developed in 1934 and proven in all campaigns since the invasion of Manchuria. The maximum range of its shells was 9,080 yards and it was light enough to be maneuvered around in the field by its gun crew.

Water dripped from the tarpaulin overhead, and a drop fell on General Adachi's helmet, making a *ping* sound as he leaned closer to the weapon. It was wiped clean and covered with a thin film of oil to protect it from rust. Ammunition was in crates stacked nearby, ready for action.

"Open the breech," General Adachi said to the sergeant in charge of the gun crew.

"Yes sir," replied the sergeant.

He pulled the lever backwards and twisted it to the side, revealing the empty breech. It too was spotless, covered with oil, shiny and smooth. This was no accident, because everybody knew General Adachi would inspect the battalion on that day, and the soldiers had been cleaning and polishing the guns for twenty-four hours.

"Excellent," said General Adachi, peering inside the breech. "A very fine job of maintenance has been performed here."

The sergeant was so terrified he didn't know what to say. His company commander shot him a dirty look, and the sergeant managed to stutter, "Thank you, sir!"

General Adachi straightened up and looked the sergeant in the eye. "The success of my attack will depend on men like you," he said, "because the attack cannot succeed unless your artillery bombardment prepares the way for the infantry. When the order comes down, fire as quickly as you can, and make your aim accurate, because I and the Emperor will be relying on you. Do you understand?"

"Yes sir!"

"Good."

General Adachi turned and walked away, heading toward the next gun emplacement. He passed another pile of crates full of 75-mm artillery shells, and ground his teeth in frustration, because he had so little artillery ammunition left. His entire artillery bombardment would last only five minutes, due to the shortage of shells. He would've preferred at least fifteen minutes, or better yet a half hour, but American military forces had cut all his supply lines and he had to make do with what he had.

General Adachi had 20,000 combat effectives in his command, but only 13,142 rifles, 726 machine guns, 561 grenade launchers, 22 light mortars, 36 mountain guns (75-mm) of the type he'd just inspected, and 42 70-mm guns. His communications equipment was nearly all ruined by the humidity, and a shortage of mosquito netting for the troops had resulted in a high incidence of malaria. His final supplies had arrived via submarine in May, and there'd been nothing since. Food was running out, and some of his forward units were eating only sago palm starch.

But General Adachi thought he could win the battle. The five-minute artillery barrage would be ferocious, and would soften up the Americans for the infantry attacks. If the men fought hard and kept advancing, they could win. It was all a matter of which side wanted the victory the most. General Adachi visited his troops regularly to raise their morale and give them the will to win.

He approached the next artillery emplacement, and all the soldiers snapped to attention. The sergeant in charge of the gun saluted the famous General Adachi, and General Adachi returned the salute smartly, smiling confidently as he stepped forward to inspect the weapon more closely.

Pfc. Nick Bombasino drove the jeep through the swamp that'd formed in front of Eighty-first Division Headquarters, and stopped in front of the command post tent. Colonel Hutchins was pleased to see General Hawkins's jeep already there.

"Get a cup of coffee for yourself if you can find one around here," Colonel Hutchins said to Pfc. Bombasino, "but don't stray too far, understand?"

"Yes sir."

Colonel Hutchins jumped out of the jeep and ran through the shin-deep muck into the tent, where Master Sergeant Abner Somerall sat behind his desk, and the division clerk, Pfc. Gottfried, pounded away on his typewriter.

"I gotta talk to the general," Colonel Hutchins said.

Sergeant Somerall raised his hand. "Wait a minute!"

Colonel Hutchins already was gone, dashing through the next office, diving past the tent flap and entering the office of General Hawkins, who sat on his cot, changing from wet socks into dry socks, the nasty odor of dirty feet filling the dank humid area.

"What are you doing here!" demanded General Hawkins, who felt naked without his socks on.

"I have to talk with you!" Colonel Hutchins said.

"I'm tired of you barging in here like this!"

"It's important, and I'm not kidding."

General Hawkins sighed. Colonel Hutchins was impossible and nothing could be done about it, otherwise General Hawkins would've done it long ago.

"Have a seat," General Hawkins said. "I'll be with you in a few moments."

"Mind if I smoke?"

"Just don't set the tent on fire."

Colonel Hutchins sat on a chair in front of the desk and lit a Camel cigarette. He blew smoke into the air and picked up the framed photograph of Mrs. Hawkins that sat on the desk, turning it around and looking at it. The photograph depicted an attractive middle-aged woman with short brown hair curled inward at the bottom. She looked as though she came from one of those old-line Yankee families with pots of money and centuries of traditions. Mrs. Hawkins probably had a proper finishing-school education and was an expert at entertaining senior officers. She surely helped General Hawkins with his career advancement and Colonel Hutchins couldn't help wishing he had a wife like that, but most of the women in his life had been barflies just like him.

"Nice-looking wife you've got here," Colonel Hutchins said.

"Thank you," General Hawkins muttered. He laced on a dry pair of combat boots and wondered what problem Colonel Hutchins was about to make for him. Rain pelted the roof of the tent and dripped through in several places. The floor was the ground and it was damp, having absorbed moisture from the rainfall outside.

General Hawkins arose form his cot and walked behind his desk. He was six feet one inch tall, with a rangy build and lively intelligent eyes. He stroked his blond mustache as he sat down, and inserted a Chesterfield cigarette into his ivory cigarette holder, lighting it and leaning back in his chair.

"What's the problem?" he asked.

Colonel Hutchins leaned forward in his chair. "Do you think the Japs are gonna attack on July ninth or don't you?"

"I don't know when they're going to attack," General Hawkins replied. "I'm not a mind reader or a crystal ball gazer."

"You don't believe the Jap prisoner's story?"

"I don't believe it and I don't disbelieve it. I simply don't know what to believe, because I can't verify his story."

"So in other words," said Colonel Hutchins, "you're not gonna prepare for an attack on July ninth."

General Hawkins turned down the corners of his mouth and looked Colonel Hutchins in the eye. "This division stays ready for an attack," he said in his firmest command tone of voice.

"Horseshit," replied Colonel Hutchins. "Save that baloney for the people who kiss your ass. We've been whipped by the

94

Japs before and we'll get whipped again on July ninth if we don't get ready. I'm right in the middle of the line and I'm gonna have a massacre on my hands if the division doesn't back me up. I can't hold off the entire Jap Eighteenth Army on my own."

General Hawkins was getting annoyed, but continued to present an unruffled appearance. "What makes you so sure the attack will take place on the night of July ninth."

"Because I don't think that Jap was lying."

"Maybe he wasn't lying, but that doesn't mean General Adachi hasn't changed his plans."

"If General Adachi changed his plans, so what? I'd rather be wrong than dead!"

"I can understand your concern," General Hawkins said, "but I don't agree with you. I want this division to be prepared for an attack at all times, and you might think that's horseshit, but I don't. I don't know when that attack will come, and I resent the implication that you're more concerned about the men out there than I am. We'll be ready when the attack comes, and we'll be especially watchful on the night of July ninth, but beyond that I'm not going to make a fool of myself by getting the men all worked up about an attack that might never come."

Colonel Hutchins's eyes widened. "So that's it!" he shouted triumphantly, pounding his fist on General Hawkins's desk so hard the desk shook. "I knew it all along! You don't wanna do anything because you don't want people to think you're a fool!" Colonel Hutchins pointed his finger at General Hawkins. "You're too worried about what people think of you! You're a fucking tin soldier—that's what you are!"

It took all of General Hawkins's self-control to stay seated behind his desk, and not leap into the air at Colonel Hutchins's throat. His blond mustache bristled and sparks shot out of his eyes. "I think you'd better calm down, Colonel," he said in a quavering voice, and he knew the advice applied equally well to himself.

"Why should I be calm?" asked Colonel Hutchins. "What in the hell is the use of being calm? I don't wanna be calm! I don't wanna be a tin soldier like you!"

"The value of being calm," General Hawkins said calmly, "is that calm people are in a better position to make clear, rational decisions."

"Is that so?" Colonel Hutchins asked. "Well you're calm

right now, and I'm not, and you're making the wrong decision right now, and I'm making the right one. So what's the good of being calm?"

General Hawkins puffed casually on his ivory cigarette holder. "How do you know you're making the right decision?"

"Any decision that protects men's lives is the right decision."

"You think we're not ready for an attack right now?"

"Not as ready as we could be or should be, since we have pretty solid information that a real definite attack is coming in only five goddamned nights."

"Well," said General Hawkins, with a wave of his cigarette holder, "no one can ever be one hundred percent ready, but I think we're as ready as we need to be."

Colonel Hutchins groaned, because he was getting tired of arguing. "That's crap and you know it. We'd be much better off on July ninth if the men were in their foxholes armed to the teeth, alert and ready to counterattack as soon as the Japs jump off. Just stop and think of what this division could do to the Japs if we were ready like that, and while you're at it, think about how good you'd look if you led the division that threw back General Adachi's spearhead, which is supposed to come right through this sector. You'd probably get a fucking medal, and if the Japs don't attack on those nights, what've you lost? Nothing! If anybody from General Hall's headquarters criticizes you for getting ready for an attack that never came, you just say you'd rather be wrong than dead."

General Hawkins changed position in his chair and inhaled smoke from his cigarette, while cogitating upon what Colonel Hutchins had said, because Colonel Hutchins made sense to him for the first time. It was true: If he erred by being more ready than he needed to be, what was wrong with that? And if he did stop General Adachi's attack, he'd become the hero of the Driniumor. General MacArthur might even hear about it. Major General Hawkins could become Lieutenant General Hawkins, and perhaps even get a job on General MacArthur's staff. He could get the Silver Star, the DSC, possibly the Congressional Medal of Honor! It was a glowing thought, but there was just one problem.

"Tell me something, Hutchins," General Hawkins said. "Assuming you're right about everything, how in hell can this division stop General Adachi's entire army even if we are one hundred percent ready? We couldn't do it alone even under the best of circumstances."

"You'll have to convince General Hall," Colonel Hutchins replied.

"I can't go up there and harass him the way you harass me. He'll relieve me of command."

"I'll talk to him."

"Oh no you won't. You stay the hell away from him, and that's a direct unequivocal order, do you understand?"

"Yes sir, but it sure would be nice if you had the guts to talk to him."

Now General Hawkins got mad. "It's not a matter of guts. It's a matter of good sense."

"It's a matter of being afraid to make waves," Colonel Hutchins said.

General Hawkins leaned forward and gazed at Colonel Hutchins's bulldog face. "Hutchins, I really don't like you," he said. "I've been wanting to tell you that for a long time, and now I'm telling you."

"That's okay General," Colonel Hutchins replied, "because I've always hated your fucking guts too."

Both men stared at each other for a few moments. General Hawkins thought Colonel Hutchins incredibly ugly, with his puffy features and red bulbous nose, while Colonel Hutchins saw weakness and indecision on General Hawkins's face, and thought his mustache a ridiculous affectation. The moments passed and neither man averted his eyes. It was a test of will, but General Hawkins realized he had work to do and couldn't play the game indefinitely. He tore his eyes off Colonel Hutchins's face and looked at his watch.

"I've got a meeting to attend," he said. "You're dismissed."

"What about the Jap attack?" Colonel Hutchins asked. "We haven't decided anything."

"Maybe you haven't, but I have. The division will go on full-scale ready alert as of today, and we'll be especially ready on the night of July ninth. I'll do what I can to convince General Hall to take the same measures. That's it. I believe I just told you you're dismissed."

Colonel Hutchins rose to his feet. "Glad you finally came to see things my way," he said, stiffening into the position of attention.

He saluted, did an about-face, and marched out of the office. General Hawkins puffed his cigarette and looked at his desk calendar. July 9 was only four nights away. He'd have sufficient time to get his division ready, but his division couldn't stop the Japanese Eighteenth Army alone. Somehow General Hall would have to be convinced, and General Hawkins didn't look forward to going to Persecution Task Force Headquarters and trying to convince him. It was never a good idea to argue with your superior officers, because they tended to remember when it came time to fill out efficiency reports, and promotions were based to a large extent on efficiency reports.

Well, General Hawkins thought, *I'll give it a try, but I won't push too far. For all I know the attack won't come on the night of July ninth, and I don't want to look too bad if it doesn't.*

NINE . . .

It was the next morning. Master Sergeant John Butsko sat with his back against a tree and smoked a cigarette, his cane lying on the ground beside him. He watched Lieutenant Frannie Divers walking toward him, carrying her tray of medication.

"Morning Sergeant," she said with a friendly smile.

"Morning," Butsko replied.

She stopped in front of him. "How're you feeling?"

"Better."

She held out a little paper cup. "Your medication."

"Thanks."

He took the cup and upended it, spilling the pills into his mouth. She poured water from a pitcher into the same cup and he raised it to his lips, washing the pills down. He handed her the cup back and she placed it on the tray with the other used cups. Their eyes met for a moment. She looked away quickly, but he didn't. He checked her out carefully and could see that she was a healthy big-boned woman with large breasts, taller than most women, probably strong as a horse. Her face didn't have the neatly sculpted features of Lieutenant Betty Crawford's face, but Lieutenant Divers was pretty in her own raw-boned, tough-looking way.

"See you later," she said.

"I hope so," he replied.

She walked away and he measured her from behind. It was difficult to see exactly what a woman had when she wore fatigue pants and a shirt that had been manufactured to fit men, but it appeared that she had a nice big ass and long healthy legs, not skinny beanpoles. Butsko felt an erection stir in his pants. He'd like to get his hands on Lieutenant Divers, and wondered how he could do it.

99

"How're you doing there, you fucking goldbrick!"

Butsko turned in the direction of the voice and saw Colonel Hutchins walking toward him.

"Morning sir!" Butsko said.

Colonel Hutchins kneeled in front of Butsko and looked furtively from side to side. "I brought you a present."

Butsko looked down at Colonel Hutchins's hands, and they were empty. Colonel Hutchins unfastened his cartridge belt, and Butsko could see that Colonel Hutchins was wearing two cartridge belts, one over the other.

Colonel Hutchins handed him the outer cartridge belt, to which was fastened a canteen in a case made of thick canvas dyed o.d. green.

"There's good likker in there," Colonel Hutchins said with a wink. "Ought to speed up your recovery."

"Thank you sir," Butsko replied. "Good likker's the best medicine in the world."

"It's Sergeant Snider's old recipe, so you know it's the best."

"God bless that dirty old son of a bitch."

The cigarette dangled out of Butsko's mouth as he fastened the cartridge belt around his waist. Colonel Hutchins looked around and spat at the ground. The heat of the sun came on strong and big globules of perspiration clung to his forehead.

"Heard the news?" Colonel Hutchins asked.

"I hear lots of news," Butsko replied. "What news are you talking about?"

"The news about the big Jap attack."

"You mean the one that's supposed to come on the ninth?"

"You heard about it! Who told you?"

"Lieutenant Breckenridge stopped by last night. He said the regiment's getting ready."

"We are, and so's the division, but we don't know about the rest of the units out here."

"That's what the lieutenant told me."

Colonel Hutchins wrinkled his brow. "Where did he hear about all this stuff?"

"Word gets around," Butsko said.

"I guess there ain't no secrets around here."

"Not about something like that."

Colonel Hutchins looked at the ground around Butsko. "You got a weapon?"

100

"Only that hunk of wood I use for a cane."

"I'd better send you something."

Butsko sat straighter. "You think the Japs'll get this far back?"

"They might. According to what we know so far, the entire Japanese Eighteenth Army is coming through here on the night of July ninth, and we can't be sure the Eighty-first can stop them alone."

"The Eighty-first shouldn't have to stop them alone. What about all the other outfits in the area?"

"There's a problem," Colonel Hutchins replied. "The top brass doesn't believe the Japs're really gonna attack on July ninth."

"Why not?"

"They just don't believe it." Colonel Hutchins shrugged. "You know how some people are. If an elephant walked into this clearing right now, and you said, 'Look at that elephant over there,' there'd be somebody around here who'd tell you you're making an assumption. Some people don't believe what's standing right in front of them until it's too late."

Butsko's cigarette was smoked down to the last three-quarters of an inch. He pushed the lit end against the ground until it was out, then tore the paper off and field-stripped the butt.

"I hate this fucking Army," Butsko said, "and I hate this fucking war. There are too many dumb bastards around. It wouldn't be so bad if there weren't so many dumb bastards around. Can't somebody go have a talk with General Hall and tell him what we gotta do?"

"General Hawkins is supposed to do that this morning, but I don't give him much of a chance. He's got no guts. If General Hall says no, General Hawkins'll just turn around and walk out of his office with his tail between his legs."

"Dumb fuck."

"You shouldn't talk about your commanding officer that way, but he is a dumb fuck and there ain't no two ways about it."

Butsko looked at Colonel Hutchins. "Why don't *you* go speak to General Hall?"

Colonel Hutchins snorted. "Hey Butsko, this is the U.S. Army, remember? Colonels don't go over the heads of their division commanders to talk to the commander of something like the Persecution Task Force."

Butsko continued to look Colonel Hutchins in the eye. "Why not?"

"You know why not."

"Yeah, I know why not," Butsko said, "but sometimes you gotta do what you're not supposed to do if you wanna get what you want."

Colonel Hutchins shrugged. "Maybe you're right. If General Hawkins doesn't do any good with General Hall, maybe I'll go have a talk with him myself. It might cost my job, but so what?"

"It won't cost your job if you handle it right. You've been in the Army long enough to know how to handle things."

"We'll see," Colonel Hutchins said.

General Hawkins walked into General Hall's command post and saw Sergeant-Major Seymour Bunberry seated behind one of the desks.

"General Hall in?" General Hawkins asked.

"No sir," replied Master Sergeant Bunberry, who had a weight problem because rear-echelon headquarters always got the best food. "He's out inspecting the Hundred Fourteenth RCT."

"Where are they?"

"Near the airfields."

"Thanks."

General Hawkins turned around and walked swiftly out of the office. He left the tent and made his way to his jeep, jumping into the passenger seat.

"To the airfield!" he said to his driver, Private Lou Grogan, a former Boston cab driver, and they say if you can drive in Boston, you can drive anywhere.

"Yes sir," replied Grogan, shifting into gear and stomping on the gas.

The wheels spun in the soft moist earth, and then grabbed. The jeep shot forward like a bat out of hell. Grogan steered toward the road and turned left, kicking down the accelerator again, shifting into second and speeding toward the Tadji airfields.

• • •

A squadron of P-40 Warhawks took off one by one from the fighter strip at the Tadji airfield area. They rocked and rumbled as they rolled over the runway, made of corrugated steel matting because poor drainage made the ground too mushy to carry the weight of aircraft. The planes hurtled into the sky and headed to sea, to escort transport ships into the port of Aitape.

Near the airfield, General Hall trooped the line. The 114th Regimental Combat Team was arrayed company by company in front of him, with all their equipment, tanks, artillery, and other matériel. They'd arrived by ship only yesterday and many hadn't recovered fully from their sea voyage, but they stood with eyes front as General Hall marched before them, followed by aides and subordinate officers, and at his side was Brigadier General Charles Guthrie, commanding officer of the 114th RCT.

General Hall wore his steel pot on his head and his service Colt .45 strapped to his waist. All the other officers were similarly armed. Individual company commanders saluted as General Hall walked by, and the men presented arms. General Hall and all the other officers saluted as they marched along. It was the first time General Hall saw these new men, and the first time they saw him. The ceremony was the formal introduction between them. It would be followed by a brief parade, with music provided by the Persecution Task Force band.

General Hall scrutinized the men as he trooped the line. They looked healthy and ready for action, some wearing new fatigues and some wearing old ones. A few were a little green around the gills, not fully recovered from their seasickness. They were ready to go to war, but General Hill still didn't know exactly where to put them. He could leave them next to the Tadji fighter strip and use them as a reserve, or put them directly into the line. He had to make up his mind that afternoon, and he was leaning toward leaving them where they were, to deploy them as they were needed, plugging holes after the Japanese attack began.

General Hall came to the last company. He turned to his right and headed toward the spot where he'd review the march-past, his shoulders squared and his chin tucked in, because he knew all the men in the 114th RCT were watching him, sizing him up, wondering what kind of man their new leader was.

General Hall wasn't worried about what they thought. He didn't suffer from lack of self-confidence. He knew what kind of man he was, and believed he was as good as any other officer in the world, if not better.

He reached the spot where he'd review the new men, and performed a snappy about-face. His aides and the officers from the 114th RCT coalesced around him. Nearby stood the band, wearing ordinary Army fatigues, and their conductor raised his baton in the air. The drummers lifted their drumsticks and the trombone players held the mouthpieces of their instruments to their lips. The conductor lowered his baton and the band began the first strains of "El Capitan" by John Philip Sousa. Orders were shouted and the first company of the first battalion from the 114th RCT advanced to begin the parade.

The band wasn't the New York Philharmonic Orchestra conducted by Arturo Toscanini, but it sounded fine to General Hall. The thrilling music caused him to stand straighter and made him glad he was an American. In the distance he saw the companies moving forward and turning left, preparing to circle around and march in front of him. He puffed his chest out and smiled faintly. *We'll stop the goddamn Japs somehow,* he thought. *I don't know exactly how we'll do it, but we'll do it.*

General Adachi sat behind his desk, holding the palm of his right hand over his stomach. He hurt inside and wondered what was wrong with him. The pain began months ago as mild gas pressure, and General Adachi had thought it mere indigestion, but it grew worse every day until now he had a sharp pain in his stomach nearly all the time.

"Lieutenant Ono!" he shouted.

"Yes sir!"

Lieutenant Ono leapt into the office and stood at attention, his arms stiff down his sides.

"Tell Dr. Nojima that I want to speak with him!"

"Are you all right, sir?"

"Of course I'm all right. I just gave you an order. Carry it out."

"Yes sir."

Lieutenant Ono left the office. General Adachi looked down at the documents on his desk. The top one contained a report about American reinforcements arriving in the area, and it bothered General Adachi a great deal. Every new American replacement was an obstacle to the victory he hoped to achieve in only three days. He knew he was outnumbered and the odds against him were growing every day. He felt increasingly desperate about the battle, and the pain in his stomach became sharper. It felt as though something was terribly wrong inside him. The pain was so severe he broke out into a cold sweat, and he bent forward, hoping that would ease the pressure, and in fact it did, but not by much.

He ground his teeth together and swore underneath his breath. He wished the battle would take place that night, so he could get it over with before more American soldiers arrived.

Three more days, he muttered. *Only three more days.*

The parade was over and General Hall walked back to his jeep, followed by his aides. He'd just congratulated General Guthrie on the fine appearance of his men.

A tall rangy figure loomed up in front of him. It was General Hawkins, in the middle of a salute. "I wonder if I could ride back with you, sir," General Hawkins said, snapping off the salute. "There's something important I'd like to discuss with you, and it can't wait."

General Hall returned the salute. "If it's that important, certainly you can ride back with me."

General Hawkins fell in with General Hall's retinue and followed him back to his jeep. The other officers headed toward their respective jeeps, and General Hawkins climbed into the jump seat behind General Hall.

"Back to my headquarters," General Hall said to Private Darrell Sweeny, his driver, a former professional racer who'd competed in the Indianapolis 500 before the war.

"Yes sir!"

Pfc. Sweeny let out the clutch and drove off at breakneck speed. He was a wilder driver than Pfc. Grogan, and took the first corner on two wheels. General Hawkins nearly fell out of the jump seat.

"Slow down!" he yelled.

"Too fast for you?" General Hall asked.

General Hawkins thought twice as he hung on for dear life. He didn't want to appear a coward or sissy in front of General Hall, so he said, "No, I'm all right now."

"We can slow down if this is too fast for you."

"That's okay—I'm used to it now."

But General Hawkins wasn't okay, and he hung on to the sides of the jeep with all his strength. General Hall could see General Hawkins was in trouble, and realized General Hawkins was bullshitting him, trying to be tough when in fact he should've been prudent and insisted the jeep slow down. If General Hawkins wanted to be an ass, General Hall was perfectly willing to let him be one.

"What was it you wanted to speak with me about?" General Hall asked.

At that point Private Sweeny hit a bump in the road, and the jeep flew into the air several feet. It landed on one wheel, bounced around a few times, settled down, and kept going. General Hawkins held on to the sides of the jeep, color draining from his face. General Hall nudged Private Sweeny, the signal for Sweeny to slow down. Sweeny eased off on the accelerator, and General Hawkins took a deep breath, trying to collect his thoughts, because he thought he'd fall out of the jeep at any moment.

"What was that, sir?" he asked.

"I said what was it you wanted to speak to me about?"

General Hawkins took a deep breath and pulled himself together, which wasn't too difficult now that the jeep moved along the jungle road at a reasonable clip. "I wanted to talk with you about the night of July ninth, sir. I don't know whether the Japs're gonna attack on that date or not, but my men'll be ready in their holes with loaded guns, wide awake. If the Japs don't attack, that'll be okay with me. I'd rather be wrong than dead. If the Japs do attack, we'll be ready for them, but we won't be able to stop them by ourselves. I think the rest of the Persecution Task Force should be ready on that night too."

"You attended the meeting in my office the other day, didn't you?" General Hall asked.

"Yes sir."

"Then you heard what Colonel MacKenzie had to say."

"Yes sir."

Trees whizzed past the jeep as General Hall leaned closer to General Hawkins. "I want every unit in my command to be ready for an attack at all times, even right now. Is your division ready right now?"

"Yes sir."

"Good. If you want to make special preparations for the night of July ninth, that's up to you, but what if you keep your men awake for an entire night, and then the Japs attack on the next night. Your men'll be too tired to fight then, won't they?"

"No sir, because they won't all be awake on the night of July ninth. It'll be worked out so that half will sleep and half will stay awake throughout the night. Then the next day the ones who've slept can stay awake and the others can sleep."

"Well," General Hall said, "you're free to command your division as you like, provided you remain within the broad framework of rules and regulations set down by the Department of the Army and your commanding officers. I have no objection to what you're doing, but I don't believe I should make any special arrangements on that night that I wouldn't make on any other night in a combat zone. I cannot afford to place undue reliance on intelligence reports, because they've been wrong before. I cannot gamble with my men."

"What about my men?" General Hawkins asked.

"Your men are my men, General Hawkins. Don't ever forget that. If any of my divisions are attacked, I will reinforce them according to the circumstances, but I cannot favor any one division over another, and I believe that's what you're asking me to do, isn't it?"

General Hawkins realized he'd been put on the defensive by General Hall, and had to think a few moments for an answer. Trees whizzed past his eyes, and he knew he'd look like a dummy if he took too long. He decided maybe it was time to take a step back from his argument. "Perhaps I'm giving undue weight to those intelligence reports, sir," General Hawkins said. "I guess I'm not looking at the big picture the way you are. I apologize for this intrusion."

"That's all right," General Hall said, turning away from General Hawkins and gazing straight ahead at the road, "you've done no harm."

Oh yes I have, General Hawkins thought glumly, bouncing up and down on the jumpseat. *You'll remember this next time you fill out my efficiency report, you son of a bitch.*

"It looks like you've got a peptic ulcer," Dr. Nojima said, removing his stethoscope from his ears. He was short, wearing wire-rimmed glasses, and once he'd been portly, but that had been before the food shortages.

General Adachi stood before him, naked to the waist. "What's a peptic ulcer?" he asked.

"It's a sore on the wall of your upper abdomen, caused by excessive acidity."

"Do you have any medicine for it?"

"No medicine exists for this. All you can do is eat a bland diet. Try not to use so much soy sauce on your rice."

General Adachi took his shirt off the back of his chair and thrust his left arm through a sleeve. "There's nothing I can do for the pain?"

"Other than eating bland food and perhaps taking a vacation, no." Dr. Nojima's little black bag sat on General Adachi's desk, and he stuffed his stethoscope inside.

"How did I get the ulcer?" General Adachi asked.

"It is generally believed that ulcers are caused by anxiety and worry. I imagine the pressures of your position give you a lot of that, no?"

"Yes."

"There you have it." Dr. Nojima showed the palms of his hands to General Adachi and shrugged. "I wish I could do something for you, sir. I would like to prescribe a vacation, but under the circumstances that's impossible."

"You may leave," General Adachi said.

Dr. Nojima bowed. "As you wish, sir."

Alone behind his desk, General Adachi looked at the papers and maps spread before him. The time for his big attack was approaching. Supplies were being carried to the front and soldiers were deploying. General Adachi felt a sharp pain in his stomach and gritted his teeth, sucking in air. He placed the palm of his right hand over the pain, cold sweat covering his body.

General Hawkins's jeep stopped in front of his headquarters, and he climbed out of the front seat, a frown on his face. He believed he'd made a fool out of himself by approaching General Hall the way he did, and thought perhaps he'd damaged his career.

He entered the tent and Master Sergeant Abner Somerall looked up at him. "Colonel Hutchins is waiting for you in your office," he said.

"What!" exploded General Hawkins. "Who let him go in there!"

"I tried to stop him, but he went in anyway."

General Hawkins narrowed his eyes and set his jaw. He strode angrily through the tent network, passing clerks pounding typewriters and staff officers working behind desks. Everybody could see he was rip-roaring mad. He entered his office and saw Colonel Hutchins seated in front of his desk, reading a copy of *Time* Magazine.

Colonel Hutchins looked up from the magazine and turned around. "How'd it go?" he asked.

General Hawkins pointed to the tent flap. "Out!" he shouted.

Colonel Hutchins didn't bother to get up. "It didn't go so well, huh?"

General Hawkins continued to point to the tent flap. "Out!"

"What're you mad at me for?"

General Hawkins stepped toward him as if he was going to rip Colonel Hutchins's head off his shoulders. Colonel Hutchins jumped to his feet. General Hawkins stopped in front of him and his face became exceedingly ugly.

"You son of a bitch!" General Hawkins screamed. "I should've known better than to listen to you."

"You fucked up pretty bad I guess," Colonel Hutchins replied. "Guess I'll have to speak to the old man myself."

"You stay away from him!" General Hawkins replied. "That's a direct order! If I find out you've been talking to him, I'll throw the book at you! You'll be relieved of command so fast you won't know what hit you! And don't *ever* come into this office again without permission!" General Hawkins pointed to the tent flap again. "Now get the hell out of here! I don't want to see you again unless it's absolutely necessary!"

Colonel Hutchins shrugged. "If that's the way you feel about it, okay." He picked his helmet off General Hawkins's desk and headed for the tent flap. "I been thrown out of better places."

It was evening, and chow was finished at the Eighty-first Division Medical Headquarters. The molten copper sun sank toward the horizon, and Butsko practiced walking with his cane in a clearing beside one of the tents. He moved along without much difficulty and his leg felt stronger with every step. The pain had diminished considerably also; it was more than a week since he'd sustained the wound. He raised the cane and took some steps without it, pleased by his success. He hoped he'd be able to walk around without the cane in a few days. He wouldn't be able to walk as well as everybody else, but he'd be able to walk.

Not far away, the GI with the guitar and another GI with a harmonica were playing bluegrass country music. Men around them sang along. It was a quiet night in the area. No guns were fired and no explosions took place. Butsko took a few more steps without his cane, thinking of how peaceful it was in the jungle. The air had become cooler and there were few bugs out that night. New Guinea wasn't so bad without the bugs, heat, and war.

"How're you doing, Big Sergeant?"

Butsko turned his head and saw Lieutenant Breckenridge approaching through the dusk. "Hello there young Lieutenant," Butsko replied.

"I brought you a present," Lieutenant Breckenridge said, holding up a Thompson submachine gun. "It comes with the compliments of Colonel Hutchins."

"Yeah, Butsko said. "He told me I might be needing it. Thanks a lot."

Butsko took the heavy ugly weapon and held it in his hands. It felt right, and Butsko knew how to use it. Lieutenant Breckenridge handed him five bandoliers of ammunition.

"This oughtta hold you for a while," Lieutenant Breckenridge said.

"A few minutes anyway. You in a hurry?"

"Not especially."

"Pull up a chair and sit down."

Lieutenant Breckenridge looked around and saw a spot at the base of a tree with a thick trunk. He walked toward it and sat cross-legged on the ground. Butsko limped behind him without using his cane and sat down facing him. Both men took out cigarettes and lit them up. Butsko offered Lieutenant Breckenridge a drink from his canteen, which Lieutenant Breckenridge accepted.

"You got the good stuff," Lieutenant Breckenridge said after taking a healthy swig.

"The colonel brought it earlier today. How's he getting along without me?"

"The rumor is he's in hot water."

"What he do this time?"

"He convinced General Hawkins to talk to General Hall about reinforcing the division in advance of the big Jap attack, but evidently General Hall didn't go for it. General Hawkins thinks he made a fool out of himself, and blamed Colonel Hutchins for it."

Butsko shook his head. "The fucking Army."

"Anyway, Colonel Hutchins is in the doghouse again."

"He's always in the doghouse." Butsko puffed his cigarette and looked at Lieutenant Breckenridge. "Do you think the attack is going to come on July ninth?"

"Hell yes."

"What're you gonna do about it?"

"We'll be wide awake with our weapons in our hands—what else can we do?"

"The way I heard it, the bulk of the Japanese Eighteenth Army will be coming right through the Eighty-first Division. Is that what you heard?"

"That's what I heard."

Butsko nodded, pinching his lips together. He thought for a few moments and then said, "This is what I think you oughtta do. If the Japs attack in the numbers you said, pull the men the fuck out of there. Don't hang around and get massacred just because General Hall doesn't believe the Japs're gonna attack. Get out and radio for help. That's about all you'll be able to do, the way I see it. What do you think?"

"I can't pull back unless I get orders to pull back."

"Sure you can. You've got to protect your men. That's your job."

"My main job is to fight Japs."

"You can't fight the whole Japanese Army," Butsko said. "Don't get caught up in any losing battles. We've been in enough of them already. Conduct a fighting retreat. That's what the whole regiment should do. That's what the division should do too. Once General Hall sees his airfields threatened, he'll reinforce you. He may be dumb, but he's not that dumb. He'll wake up sooner or later. Understand what I'm saying?"

Lieutenant Breckenridge blew smoke out of the corner of his mouth. "I'll do my best, Butsko. That's about all I can promise you."

"I couldn't ask for more than that," Butsko said.

• • •

The sun had fallen behind the hills, and the western sky glowed red as if the jungle was on fire. General Hall buttoned up his fly in the officers' latrine and pushed open the door, stepping outside. He closed the door behind him and walked over the winding jungle path toward his tent, as crickets chirped around him.

A shadow appeared around a tree, and General Hall went for his service revolver.

"Can I have a few moments of your time?" said a deep resonant voice with a Southern accent.

"Who's there?" General Hall asked.

A heavyset man stepped into the moonlight, and General Hall saw a bulbous nose and fleshy lips. "I'm Colonel Bob Hutchins, sir, and I command the Twenty-third Regiment of the Eighty-first Division. I don't have permission to speak with you, and I know you're a busy man, but you gotta walk back to your tent, and I wonder if you'd let me go just that distance with you and let me speak my mind."

General Hall remembered Colonel Hutchins from the meeting three days ago, and knew what was coming. "I don't encourage officers to break the chain of command," General Hall replied, "but what do you want?"

Colonel Hutchins walked alongside General Hall and opened his big mouth. "Sir, an officer's first responsibility is to his men, isn't that so?"

"It is."

"Well I'm worried about my men, sir. You see, I expect the Japs to attack on the night of July ninth, and I expect them to hit my regiment straight on. If that happens, I'm concerned about casualties. Now I know one regiment doesn't mean a whole lot to you, because you've got lotsa regiments under your command, but this regiment is all I got, and I don't want it to get wiped out, sir. Do you get my drift so far, sir?"

"Are you trying to say I don't care if your regiment gets wiped out?" General Hall asked.

"Oh no, sir. I'd never say that, sir. I know you care about *all* your men, sir, but you gotta look at the big picture, sir, and that includes lotsa regiments, whereas my regiment is the only one I've got." Colonel Hutchins looked ahead and saw General

112

Hall's tent coming closer. He shrugged and wheezed. "I might as well come right to the point, sir. I think you oughtta make more preparations for the attack than you're making. I think you oughtta beef up the center of the line where my regiment and the Eighty-first Division is deployed. If you don't, I'm afraid there's gonna be a helluva mess there. I know General Hawkins asked you about this today, and you turned him down, but I thought I'd give it a try myself, because you see sir, if the Japs get through the Eighty-first Division, you're really gonna have your hands full trying to keep them away from the air strips."

They reached the front of General Hall's tent, and General Hall stopped. He wasn't angry at Colonel Hutchins, because Hutchins had stated his case clearly and General Hall appreciated his concern. But General Hall didn't have much time for Colonel Hutchins, because he still had work to do before going to bed.

"What if the Japs don't attack the Eighty-first Division as you expect?" General Hall asked in front of his tent. "What if they're just trying to make us strengthen one part of our line so they can divert our attention from the sector they really intend to attack?"

"I don't know, sir," Colonel Hutchins replied. "I just think they're really coming through our sector."

"What if you're wrong?"

Colonel Hutchins shrugged. "What if I'm right?"

"If you're right you'll be backed up by my reserves. If you're wrong, the sector that is attacked will be backed up by my reserves. I've got to place my reserves where I can move them about quickly, and not assign them a position they can't leave quickly. Understand?"

"Yes sir."

"I have work to do. Good night, Colonel Hutchins."

"Good night, sir."

General Hall entered his tent, leaving Colonel Hutchins standing outside. Colonel Hutchins took a cigarette out of the pack in his shirt pocket and lit it up. Turning, he walked toward his jeep. *I'll just have to take it as it comes*, he thought. *Whatever will be, will be*.

TEN . . .

Colonel Hutchins stayed awake all night, sitting in his office and working by the light of kerosene lamps. He was assisted by Major Cobb, his G-3 (operations) officer; Lieutenant Harper, his aide; and Pfc. Levinson, who performed typing tasks and ran periodically to the mess hall for coffee.

Colonel Hutchins wanted to reorganize and deploy his regiment so it'd be better prepared to meet the Japanese onslaught he expected on the night of July 9. His men had to be ready, and he had to have a plan for an orderly fighting retreat in case the Japs breeched his line. Colonel Hutchins was an old soldier like Butsko, and tended to think along the same lines.

His first line of defense would be his mortars, because an intense mortar barrage could disrupt an attack. He studied his maps, conferred with Major Cobb, and worked out a plan that would place all his mortars two hundred yards west of the Driniumor, registered on targets and possible staging areas on the east side. The mortars would have overlapping fields of fire and all ammunition available to do the job.

Next he'd lay down physical obstacles to the Japanese attack. All forward positions would be mined and wired, to slow down the Japanese infantry. The next and last line of defense would be his soldiers in their foxholes, armed with rifles, machine guns, hand grenades, and fixed bayonets. If the soldiers couldn't hold, and he already believed they wouldn't, the retreat would begin, first back toward his own headquarters, and if no help arrived by then, back to division headquarters.

The officers worked into the night, calculating every step of the plan, trying to guess what might go wrong and how it could be averted. Colonel Hutchins wished every commander in the task force would do what he was doing. Then they'd have a chance to stop the Japs. He figured some of them might be making plans, but most weren't. Most were like General Hall, holding their cards close to their vests, trying to be ready for everything, but you can never be ready for everything.

Colonel Hutchins understood why most officers weren't taking the measures he was taking. They didn't believe the Japs would attack on the night of July 9, but he believed. He had no hard evidence, but something in his guts told him the Japs weren't faking, and they were going to do what all intelligence reports indicated they were going to do. They'd go for broke on the night or morning of July 9, because it was the only chance they had. They were all played out and had to do something. Colonel Hutchins didn't think the Japs had the time for ruses. A big rumble in the jungle was coming, and the twenty-third Regiment was going to be as ready as possible.

At four in the morning the work was done. The officers looked at each other bleary-eyed, the features on their faces sagging with fatigue. Colonel Hutchins sipped more coffee and lit another cigarette. He looked at the other officers and they looked back at him while in the corner Pfc. Levinson hammered away on his typewriter.

Colonel Hutchins leaned back and blew a cloud of smoke in the air. "Okay," he said, "we can all get some sleep now, but we have to get up real early. Harper, you take a copy of these plans to General Hawkins's headquarters first thing in the morning and mark them *important*. If you can't give them to General Hawkins personally, give them to the highest-ranking officer you can find and tell him to give them to General Hawkins." Colonel Hutchins turned to Major Cobb. "I want you to hold a meeting here at ten hundred hours for all battalion commanders and company commanders and their staffs, and tell them the plans we've worked out tonight."

"You won't be here?" Major Cobb asked.

"No," Colonel Hutchins replied.

"Where will you be?"

"I've got to talk to somebody." Colonel Hutchins looked at Pfc. Levinson typing up orders in the corner. "Levinson!"

Pfc. Levinson shot to his feet and turned around. "Yes sir!"

"Make sure Pfc. Bombasino is in front of this tent at oh-seven hundred hours, with my jeep."

"Yes sir!"

115

"How soon before you'll be finished with that typing?"

"A few more minutes, sir."

"Take your typewriter out to your desk and finish it, becuse I've got to get some sleep."

"Yes sir."

Pfc. Levinson looked like an apostrophe as he carried his typewriter out of Colonel Hutchins's office. A few minutes later Major Cobb and Lieutenant Harper departed, their brief-cases stuffed with papers. Now Colonel Hutchins was alone. He stubbed out his cigarette in his ashtray, drank a bit of white lightning, and stumbled across the ground to his cot, collapsing on top of it without taking off his combat boots; and in minutes he was sound asleep.

In the morning the sky was covered with thick clouds the color of oatmeal. Pfc. Nick Bombasino from South Philly steered his jeep toward the tent of Lieutenant Colonel Rufus Bollinger, commander of the Sixty-third Artillery Battalion. Seated next to Bombasino was Colonel Hutchins, his eyes at half-mast.

Pfc. Bombasino stopped the jeep in front of the tent, and his eyes were half-closed too. He'd had to get up earlier than usual to drive Colonel Hutchins to this destination. Colonel Hutchins jumped down from the jeep and said, "Wait for me here."

"Yes sir."

Colonel Hutchins strode into the tent, the holster and canteen fastened to his cartridge belt bouncing up and down on his hip. He walked past the sergeant major and clerk, and the sergeant major jumped to his feet, about to tell Colonel Hutchins he couldn't go in there, when he realized Colonel Hutchins was a colonel, and sergeants don't talk like that to colonels.

Colonel Hutchins entered Colonel Bollinger's office, which was laid out similarly to his own office, and saw Colonel Bollinger sleeping soundly on his cot, a big smile on his ugly face. Colonel Hutchins looked down at his old friend and saw the big sunburst scar over his right temple where he'd been hit by shrapnel during the battle for the Argonne Forest during the First World War. They'd both been pfcs. in the same outfit, buddies to the end, and they both wound up with battlefield commissions. Now they were field-grade officers and pariahs because neither had graduated from West Point or even an ordinary accredited college. They were roughnecks and outlaws wearing officers' insignia on their collars.

Colonel Hutchins reached down and shook Colonel Bollinger's collar. "Get up you son of a bitch," he said.

In one sudden swift motion Colonel Bollinger rolled over and whipped out the Colt .45 service pistol in his belt, aiming the barrel at Colonel Hutchins's nose.

"Don't shoot," Colonel Hutchins said, taking a step backwards, "it's only me."

Colonel Bollinger blinked his eyes and opened them wide. His sparse red hair was tousled on top of his head and his face looked as though it was made of boiled potatoes pushed together. "What the hell are you doing here!" he bellowed.

"I gotta talk to you."

"What about?"

"Get some coffee and I'll tell you. You need an eye opener?"

Colonel Bollinger grinned, showing snaggled horse teeth. "Sure."

Colonel Hutchins pulled out his canteen and tossed it to Colonel Bollinger, who drank some down.

"Not bad at all," Colonel Bollinger said, wiping his mouth with the back of his hand. He called out to his sergeant major, ordering a pot of coffee. Next he stood and walked barefooted across the ground to his desk, plunking himself down behind it. He had long legs and a short torso, was five feet and eleven inches tall. Bending over, he put on his combat boots and laced them up.

"Must be something important if you come all the way over here this early. What the hell's going on?"

Colonel Hutchins sat on the chair in front of Colonel Bollinger's desk. "You know about the big Jap attack?"

"Yeah," replied Colonel Bollinger. "What about it?"

"You think it's gonna come on July ninth?"

Colonel Bollinger tied a bow on the top of his left combat boot. "How the hell should I know?"

"You making any special preparations?"

"No."

"Why not?"

"I ain't had no orders to do so."

"Would you do me a favor, Rufus?"

"What do you want?"

"I want all your big guns registered on targets in front of my regiment on the ninth of July, because if the Japs do attack, I'm gonna need all the help I can get."

"You got it," Colonel Bollinger said. "Anything else?"

"That's all I wanted to ask you, Rufus."

"Shit," Colonel Bollinger replied, "I thought you wanted something big when you came walking in here so early in the morning." He cupped his hands around his mouth and shouted, "Where's my goddamned coffee!"

"It'll be right there!" said a voice in his outer office.

"Hurry it up, you son of a bitch!" Colonel Bollinger replied. Then he looked at Colonel Hutchins. "I'm not worth a fuck until I have my coffee in the morning," he said.

"I'm the same way," Colonel Hutchins replied.

"This just arrived for you, sir."

General Hawkins looked up. He sat in the Eighty-first Division officers' mess, eating powdered scrambled eggs with toast and coffee. The mess was inside a big walled tent with the walls rolled up. The floor was wide planks of wood, and the officers sat on benches, eating from metal trays on long tables. General Hawkins sat at the head table, and he raised his hand to accept the envelope held out by General Sully, his chief of staff.

"What is it?" asked General Hawkins, laying the envelope beside his metal tray.

"It's from Colonel Hutchins."

"Have you read it?" General Hawkins asked.

"No, because it's addressed to you. One of Colonel Hutchins's aides delivered it to me fifteen minutes ago. He said it was important."

General Hawkins looked at the letter lying beside his tray. He didn't want to open it because he was sure it was trouble, but that was the very reason it should be opened immediately. He picked up the envelope and tore it open. General Sully, a tall lean ramrod of a man, looked over his shoulder.

The document inside the envelope was a simple straightforward report stating the steps Colonel Hutchins was taking to deal with the possibility of the July 9 attack. General Hawkins scanned it quickly and had to admit the measures were prudent. Colonel Hutchins would have his regiment ready to meet the attack if it came. He'd try to enlist the assistance of other units. He suggested General Hawkins try to get whatever help he could, because the more units that were ready, the better the possibility of stopping the Japanese attack.

General Hawkins was surprised by the reasonable tone of the letter, and was enough of a soldier to appreciate the sound tactical decisions Colonel Hutchins had made.

General Hawkins held the letter up to General Sully. "Read this," he said.

"I just did," General Sully replied.

"What do you think?"

"Sounds good to me."

"I want these plans put into effect throughout the division," General Hawkins said, and all the officers in the tent listened intently to what he was saying, although they pretended to be minding their own business. He looked up at General Sully. "After breakfast, prepare orders along these lines for my signature."

"I've already had breakfast," General Sully said. "I'll get to work on it right now."

General Hawkins and Colonel Hutchins, plus their staffs, canvassed the various headquarters of the Persecution Task Force, trying to convince commanders to prepare for the possibility of the attack. Some listened and agreed to make special preparations, and others refused, doubting the attack would take place, suspecting it was a ruse, insisting they always stayed ready for possible attacks.

General Hall learned of the work being done by the officers from the Eighty-first Division, but did nothing to stop them. He'd made his decision; he was going to stand pat and wait. If the Japanese attacked, he'd redeploy his forces to meet the attack. If they didn't, that was okay with him too. He didn't want to get his entire command keyed up for an attack that might never come.

The days passed and July 9 loomed closer. Some units in the Persecution Task Force made elaborate preparations for the attack, while it was business as usual for other units. Patrols were sent across the Driniumor River, and reports were submitted of intensifying enemy activity. General Hall received the reports and mulled them over in his mind. He believed a major Japanese offensive would begin soon, but when and where?

Back at the Eighty-first Division, General Hawkins had a long talk with Brigadier General Thomas Shirrell, commander of his division's artillery. He ordered Shirrell to zero in all his artillery on the opposite side of the Driniumor, to blow the shit out of any Japanese attack that might occur on July 9.

On the other side of the Driniumor River, the Japanese Eighteenth Army was in the midst of its final deployment. All available ammunition and supplies were carried to forward positions. Every unit prepared to attack. Local commanders gave pep talks to their men, telling of vast food storehouses behind enemy lines, and every Japanese soldier's mouth watered at the thought of the food. They knew they could have it all and become heroes too, if they attacked hard and achieved their strategic objectives.

In his headquarters tent, General Adachi studied and re-studied his plans for the attack, making minute adjustments, fine-tuning to his plans, trying to remove any possibility of failure. He did his best to ignore the wrenching pains in his stomach, but couldn't ignore them completely. Sometimes the pain doubled him over, and often it awakened him in the middle of the night. Dr. Nojima had told him to eat a bland diet, so now he ate his rice and canned fish without soy sauce. Dr. Nojima neglected to tell him that canned fish was bad for a stomach ulcer.

Pain didn't stop General Adachi. He toured his front lines, inspecting men and equipment, exhorting and inspiring his men, telling them they must defeat the Americans for the glory of the Emperor, and for the food and supplies on the other side of the Driniumor. Although General Adachi was in terrific pain, he never let it show. He never flinched when in view of his men. No one knew about his ailment except his doctor.

The night of July 9 drew closer, and tension mounted on both sides of the Driniumor. A titanic struggle was looming, one that could alter the course of the war in the Pacific. One side was ready, and the other side half-ready. Lady Luck shook the dice in her hand and threw them down.

ELEVEN . . .

It was six o'clock on the night of July 9, 1944. Chow was over and Butsko took his evening walk through the clearings and jungle paths near the Eighty-first Division Medical Headquarters. He'd thrown away his cane in an effort to make himself walk on his own, and wasn't doing too badly.

His Thompson submachine gun was slung across his back, and the bandoliers of ammunition hung from his neck. He never went anywhere without them. He too was expecting the big Japanese attack that night. But it could come sooner, or later. Butsko liked to stay ready.

The sun drifted to the horizon. Men sat around on the ground. The GI with the guitar and his partner with the harmonica had returned to duty yesterday, so there was no music. Butsko expected to return to duty in about another five days. He limped past the men on the ground and tried to build up his strength, because a weak man could become a dead man quickly in hand-to-hand combat.

"Hey Sarge—how're you doing?"

Butsko turned around and saw Colonel Hutchins walking toward him, followed by Pfc. Nick Bombasino carrying a backpack radio.

"Hello there Colonel," Butsko said. "What're you doing back here?"

"Just checking the joint out, and I thought I'd bring you some water." Colonel Hutchins removed his canteen from his cartridge belt and gave it to Butsko. "Yours must be empty by now," Colonel Hutchins said.

"It is."

"I wouldn't want you to be without sufficient water back here."

"I appreciate your concern, sir."

"There's something else I want to talk with you about too."

"What's that?"

Colonel Hutchins looked around and spoke in a low voice. "Some M 1 rifles and ammunition have been delivered here today along with some sandbags, so the wounded can defend themselves. Captain Epstein doesn't know what to do with the stuff, because he's a surgeon and all he knows is how to cut, so maybe you should take a walk to his office a little later and look the stuff over. He doesn't believe the Japs're gonna attack tonight, so he's not too worried."

"Do you think they're gonna attack tonight?" Butsko asked.

"I believe they are, and we're as ready as we can be. You'd better be ready too. If the Japs attack, it's unlikely that they'll get this far, but they might."

"The little bastards always do what you don't expect," Butsko said.

"That's right." Colonel Hutchins glanced at the watch on his wrist. "I'd better get back to the regiment. I'll talk to you when I talk to you. Good luck."

"You too, sir."

Colonel Hutchins walked away, followed by Pfc. Nick Bombasino. Butsko pulled out the canteen Colonel Hutchins had given him and took a few swallows of white lightning. It went down smooth as silk and hot as a whore's dream. Butsko returned the canteen to its case and headed toward the office of Captain Epstein, who was in charge of the Eighty-first Division Medical Headquarters.

Butsko passed soldiers lying on the ground and orderlies bustling about. No hard fighting had taken place for more than a week, and the medical headquarters had quieted down considerably. The seriously wounded had been shipped out and the patients still around would be sent back to their units when they recovered from their relatively mild injuries.

Nurses scurried about carrying medicine, making their rounds, and Butsko saw Lieutenant Betty Crawford heading toward him. His heart sank because he didn't want to deal with her anymore. He didn't even want to say hello, but couldn't avoid her now. She slowed up as he approached, and he realized she wanted to talk with him.

"Hello Butsko," she said with a smile. "Still mad at me?"

"No, I'm not mad at you."

"I've been thinking about you," she told him. "I've missed you."

"Oh," he replied.

"I guess you haven't missed me much."

"I miss the Betty I used to know in New Caledonia."

"I'm still her."

"No you're not."

"Yes I am." She glanced around to make sure no one was listening. "I'm going off duty in a little while. Let's get together and talk about it."

Butsko looked her up and down, and she was a beauty; there were no two ways about that. He'd always been attracted to cute little blondes. "Okay," he said, "but I don't want any more shit from you. Life is too short and the war is too long."

She winked. "Okay," she said. "No more shit. It's a deal." She looked at her watch. "I'll meet you behind your tent at twenty-two hundred hours, okay?"

"Okay," he said.

"Ta ta," she told him, walking away.

"Right," he replied.

Butsko took out a cigarette and lit it up. He wouldn't mind getting Betty alone in the bushes someplace, as long as she didn't give him any shit. If she started up again he'd just walk away. He needed pussy, but not that bad.

He made his way to the tent used by Captain Epstein for an office, and saw the pile of sandbags that had been dumped next to it. Hobbling inside, he told the clerk he had to speak with Captain Epstein about something important. The clerk spoke with Captain Epstein on the telephone hook-up, and then told Butsko to go inside.

Butsko entered the office of Captain Epstein, and saw the crates of M 1 rifles and ammunition piled up against one wall of the tent.

"What can I do for you?" Captain Epstein asked.

"I believe Colonel Hutchins told you I'd be over to look at the weapons and ammunition."

Captain Epstein had curly black hair and wore wire-rimmed spectacles with thick lenses. "The colonel thinks the Japs're gonna attack this hospital," Captain Epstein said in a voice that suggested disbelief.

"They might," Butsko said, "and they might not. It's better to be ready."

"Do whatever makes you happy," Captain Epstein said. "I've got to look at some patients."

"I think you should tell your clerk to send around a notification that weapons are here if they're needed."

"Tell him yourself. You're in charge of these rifles, as far as I'm concerned. In fact, I'll tell you what. I'm hereby appointing you commander in chief of the hospital defense unit, so you can send out notifications on your own signature. How does that grab you?"

"Okay."

"Good. Now if you'll excuse me, I've got things to do." Captain Epstein arose and put on his helmet. He walked out of his office. "You can use my desk if you want."

"Thanks," Butsko said.

Butsko was alone in the office. The crates of rifles had been opened, and he looked inside. The Cosmoline was removed from the rifles and the metal covered with a thin film of oil. Butsko moved the crates around and found a different-sized crate full of bayonets. Another crate had hand grenades in it, and Butsko took some out, stuffing them into his pockets and pinning them to his lapels. He affixed a bayonet and its scabbard to his cartridge belt. The bayonet wouldn't fit on the end of his Thompson submachine gun, but it might come in handy as a knife. He pulled the bayonet out of its scabbard and touched his thumb to the blade. It was dull as a bread knife, but that wasn't necessarily bad. Dull knives made ugly wounds, and that's what Butsko wanted to inflict on the Japs: ugly wounds.

"What're you doing?" asked a female voice.

Butsko looked up and saw Lieutenant Frannie Divers, her red hair glowing and her breasts standing out proudly.

"Hi," Butsko said with a grin. "Looking for Captain Epstein?"

"What else would I be doing in his office?"

"I thought maybe you wanted a rifle."

"What the hell do I want a rifle for?"

"In case the Japs attack."

"The Japs'll never get back this far."

"I wouldn't bet on that if I was you."

"Where's Captain Epstein?" she asked.

124

"He's gone."

"Where'd he go?"

"He didn't tell me."

"What're you doing here?"

"I'm the new commander of the hospital defense force, and I'm checking out my weapons. Want a drink?"

She blinked. "A drink? What're you talking about?"

"Don't you know what a drink is, Frannie?"

"I used to know but I think I forgot."

Butsko pulled out his canteen. "Try this."

He tossed her the canteen. She caught it, nearly dropped it, but managed to get it again before it touched the floor. "Is this booze?" she asked.

"Well it ain't pinneapple juice."

"Where'd you get it?" she asked.

"Some people I know make it."

"Then it's jungle juice. I never had any jungle juice that was worth a damn."

"You might like that stuff. You ought to try it to be sure."

He watched her raise the canteen to her lips, and she didn't even bother to wipe its mouth. He figured her for a big girl with big appetites and a big lust for life. She appeared easygoing and friendly, without the neurotic problems Betty had. She was the type that could fuck you to death, but what a way to go.

She sipped the canteen really dainty-like, because she didn't want to drink too much of something she might not like. Letting the booze roll around on her tongue, she looked at the ceiling as she made her evaluation. Then she swallowed it down.

"This stuff isn't half-bad," she said.

"Have some more."

"I can't. I'm still on duty."

"When do you go off duty?"

She looked at her watch. "Another two hours."

"Let's get together and get smashed."

She wrinkled her nose and thought for a few seconds. "We shouldn't."

"Why shouldn't we?"

"Well, you know what's going to happen."

"What?"

"You know."

"So what if it does."

125

"Aren't you having a love affair with Betty?"

"Not really."

"What's that supposed to mean?"

"It's supposed to mean I'm not really having a love affair with her."

"I thought you were."

"Well I'm not, and what do you care anyway? Did I ask you whether you're having a love affair with Dr. Epstein?"

Her jaw dropped open. "How did you know!"

Now it was Butsko's turn to be surprised. He'd thought he was just making a wild remark, but he'd hit the jackpot. So that's what she'd been doing in Dr. Epstein's office. Lieutenant Frannie Divers suddenly became even more appealing to Butsko, because there was nothing sexier to him than the wife or girl friend of an officer.

"You look a little upset, Frannie," he said. "Have another drink."

"How did you find out!" she repeated.

"People talk," Butsko said.

"What people talk!"

"Word gets around."

Horror was in her eyes. "You mean everybody knows about it?"

"Only a few people, and I won't tell anybody. Relax," he said. "Calm down. Have another drink."

"I don't dare. Somebody's liable to smell it on my breath."

"I'll meet you at twenty-two hundred hours behind the pharmacy tent. We can have a little party."

"Who's coming?"

"Just you and me."

"Oh, you mean *that* kind of party."

"Uh-huh.

She wrinkled her nose. "I don't know."

"What is it you don't know?"

"I don't know."

"Forget about it," he said. "Gimme back my canteen."

He reached out his arm for the canteen, and his sleeve was torn off at the shoulder. She saw his bulging muscles and the thick dark hair on his arm. Then she noticed the hair on his chest, and became turned on. She'd always thought Butsko was exciting, and now that she was close to him, with her mind relaxed by a few swallows of white lightning, she could feel his raw sexual energy. She knew she wouldn't have as much in common with him as she did with Dr. Epstein, because Butsko was only an ordinary soldier, but it would do no harm if she got a little drunk with him and had some fun, would it?

She handed him the canteen. "It's a deal," she said. "Behind the pharmacy tent at twenty-two hundred hours."

"You're on," Butsko said.

Darkness fell on the island of New Guinea. On the east side of the Driniumor, Japanese assault units moved into their final attack positions. They were in a state of furious excitement, because their commanders told them the attack was their only chance to stay alive or die with honor. They prayed to the Shinto gods and toasted success with whatever remaining sake could be found and watered down, so everybody could have a sip.

Under the cover of darkness the Japanese soldiers moved toward the banks of the Driniumor and looked across the twinkling waters at the American positions on the other side. The Japanese were expecting to have the element of surprise on their sides. They were sure the Americans had no way of knowing what was in store for them. The Japanese soldiers lay on their stomachs and dreamed of warehouses full of American food, coffee, and cigarettes. They thought about fabulous meals they'd soon devour. No one told them about the huge odds they'd have to face, and no one knew that large numbers of American soldiers on the other side of the Driniumor were waiting with their rifles in their hands for the attack to begin.

General Adachi, in full battle dress, his samurai sword at his side, was ensconced in his new temporary command headquarters behind the line of his main advance. All available communications equipment was set up and wired in, so he could receive information from the front as it happened. All his staff officers were with him, and the headquarters buzzed with excitement. In only a few hours the attack that had been planned for so long would commence with a massive artillery bombardment. The officers were so tense they couldn't sit down. They paced back and forth like wild animals in cages, glancing at their watches, speaking confidently with each other, and no one dared mention the possibility of defeat. They couldn't afford to lose. Their lives and honor depended on victory, and there was no substitute for victory.

General Adachi sat behind a collapsible desk, and his stomach hurt like hell, but he didn't let it show. He grit his teeth and sat stoically, staring ahead into the middle distance. All he could do now was wait for the attack to begin. All his effort and planning for the past several months would come to fruition in only a few hours. He couldn't stop the entire attack now even if he wanted to, because of his poor communications. He wished he could attack behind a massive artillery barrage that would last an hour, supported by bombers and fighter planes, but he had to attack the Americans on a shoestring, and rely on the superior morale of the Japanese soldier to bring him victory.

It's all in the hands of the gods now, he thought as he stared straight ahead. *May they smile on the Eighteenth Army tonight.*

On the west side of the Driniumor, the recon platoon waited in holes eight feet deep, and each hole had a grenade sump dug into the bottom. Two men were stationed in each hole. One was permitted to sleep while the other stood guard, but no one slept in the recon platoon that night because everyone was waiting for the big Japanese attack.

Bannon and Frankie La Barbara shared the same foxhole, and Frankie was too mad to sleep. "The thing I hate most about this fucking army is that the brass always gets us all worked up over nothing," Frankie said.

"Shaddup Frankie," Bannon replied.

"I won't shut up, and you know as well as I do that most people on this island don't think the Japs are gonna attack tonight, but that drunken fucking Colonel Hutchins has got a hair across his ass about it, so everybody's gotta stay awake."

"You don't have to stay awake. You can go to sleep."

"How can I sleep with all this shit going on?"

"Then stop complaining."

"Fuck you."

"Fuck you, too."

"Kiss my ass."

Bannon groaned. He didn't feel like getting into an insult contest with Frankie La Barbara, so he thought he'd climb out and check on the recon platoon. He was the acting platoon sergeant and that gave him the excuse he needed to get away.

"You hold down the fort here," he said to Frankie. "I'm going out for a few minutes."

"Where you headed?"

"None of your fucking business."

Bannon climbed out of the hole and walked down the line. A full moon hung in the sky, providing ample but ghostly illumination. He saw foxhole after foxhole in the jungle, spaced six to ten feet apart. Not far away was the Driniumor River, moonlight sparkling and dancing on its surface. Insects chirped and occasionally a night bird screeched. The next foxhole belonged to Private Victor Yabalonka and the Reverend Billie Jones, two of the biggest men in the recon platoon. They looked up as Bannon approached.

"Everything okay in there?" Bannon asked.

"Yo," said Billie Jones.

Yabalonka grunted, and his grunt could've meant anything. Actually Yabalonka was irritated by Bannon's question, because he thought it stupid. Of course everything was all right in the foxhole. What could go wrong?

"Stay awake," Bannon said. "Keep your eyes open."

Bannon walked past the foxhole and continued on to the next one. It contained Private Joshua McGurk from Skunk Hollow, Maine, and Pfc. Morris Shilansky, the former bank robber from Boston. Between them was a .30-caliber machine gun mounted on its tripod.

"How's it going in there?" Bannon asked.

"Okay sir," McGurk replied, a wide smile on his face. He felt happy to be participating in the big enterprise of preparing for the Japanese offensive. It made him feel useful, and he loved to feel useful.

Bannon bent over and saw Shilansky sitting at the bottom of the foxhole. Shilansky was so still it was difficult to know whether he was sleeping or not.

"You okay, Shilansky?"

"I'm okay," Shilansky replied in a deep gruff voice.

"You sure?"

"Yeah."

Bannon paused for a moment, thinking Shilansky had been acting peculiarly lately, but decided that wasn't the time or place to press Shilansky about it. Bannon turned to his right and walked away, to inspect the next foxhole, leaving McGurk and Shilansky behind.

McGurk slid back into the foxhole and sat opposite Shilan-sky, who was staring at his knees. He'd been staring at his knees for more than an hour, and McGurk thought that strange.

"You sure you're okay?" McGurk asked.

"Yeah."

"You look like sumpin's botherin' you."

"Mind your own business."

McGurk had a mind like a child, and his feelings were hurt. He turned down the corners of his mouth and sulked. Shilansky noticed McGurk's change of mood and was sorry he'd spoken so abruptly.

"I didn't mean it," Shilansky said. "I haven't been feeling so hot lately."

"I din't think so. Whatsa matter?"

"Personal problems."

"Oh," McGurk said. "I'm real sorry to hear that."

"Don't worry 'bout it," Shilansky said. "I'll be all right."

"Everything'll turn out okay in the end," McGurk said.

McGurk's remark irritated Shilansky, but he didn't say any-thing. How could he explain to a man who was practically a moron that things don't always work out in the end, and the wholesale extermination of European Jews would be a disaster which never could be made right? Shilansky still was obsessed by the news story he'd read about the European Jews. He still felt sick in his heart, so sick he didn't even care about the impending Japanese attack. He'd lost his will to fight for his life. He didn't see the point of living in a world where such a catastrophe could take place. The world had become a horrible place in his mind. No longer was he obsessed with easy money, fast cars, and fancy blondes. The events in Europe had shaken the very foundations of his existence.

Shilansky wasn't aware that McGurk was examining his face. McGurk was no intellectual, but he was sensitive and knew something terrible was bothering Shilansky. McGurk wished there was something he could do. He felt stupid and frustrated, not realizing that nobody, not even Sigmund Freud himself, could have helped Shilansky just then.

Meanwhile, Corporal Bannon continued his tour of recon platoon foxholes. Ahead was the foxhole occupied by Private Clement R. Bisbee, the pathological thief, and as Bannon ap-proached he heard a scraping sound coming from the foxhole.

Bannon slowed and dropped to his knees, creeping forward on his belly. He saw the mounds of earth around the foxhole straight ahead in the dim moonlight, and then the scraping stopped and two eyes appeared over the edge of the foxhole, followed by the barrel of a gun.

"It's only me," Bannon said.

"You're lucky I didn't shoot you," Bisbee replied.

"I knew what I was doing."

"That's what she said when the bed broke."

Bannon stood up and jumped into the foxhole. Bisbee was at the bottom alone, because everybody refused to occupy it with him. Nobody wanted to get his pockets picked or his watch stolen while he was asleep.

"How're you doing in here?" Bannon asked.

"Just fine," Bisbee replied, a smile on his baby face.

Bannon looked down and saw Bisbee's Washita stone lying on the earth at the bottom of the foxhole. Bisbee's Ka-bar knife lay beside it. Bisbee had been sharpening the knife, and that was the source of the scraping sound.

"You wouldn't have to be alone if you'd stop stealing stuff," Bannon said.

That's okay," Bisbee replied. "I'd rather be alone."

"It's safer to have somebody with you."

"I can take care of myself."

Bannon shrugged. "If that's the way you want it . . ."

"That's the way I want it."

"If you need anything, just call for help."

"I don't think I'll need anything."

Bannon climbed out of the foxhole and walked away, thinking that Bisbee was one of the strangest people he'd ever met in his life. He wondered if Bisbee really preferred to be alone, or just was saying that to conceal his true loneliness. He also wondered what made Bisbee steal anything that wasn't nailed down.

Meanwhile, back in that foxhole, Bisbee resumed the sharpening of his knife. He stopped every twenty seconds or so to listen and look around, so no Japs would sneak up on him. Bisbee didn't feel lonely inside the foxhole. He was glad no one else was there to stare at him and treat him like a freak. Bisbee liked to talk to himself in a low voice, and he couldn't do that when someone else was around. He always was afraid he'd do something bizarre that a stranger would see.

"I hope the attack comes tonight," he muttered to himself. "I got my pliers in my back pocket and I'll be able to get lots of gold teeth. It'll be worth a lot of money someday. I'll be rich and be able to buy anything I want."

Bisbee had been raised in a broken-down orphanage where they dressed him in rags and he never got enough to eat. Perhaps that was why he'd become a pathological thief, or maybe he was a pathological thief because he was born that way.

Bannon approached the foxhole occupied by Lieutenant Breckenridge and his new runner, Private Worthington, who looked up at him.

"Good evening sir," Bannon said.

"What's the problem?" Lieutenant Breckenridge asked.

"No problem, sir. I'm just checking out the platoon, and I thought I'd tell you that everything's okay so far."

"Good deal," Lieutenant Breckenridge said. "I was going out in a few minutes to check on things myself, but now I guess I won't have to." Lieutenant Breckenridge looked at his watch. "It's nearly twenty-two hundred hours. If the Japs attack, it'll be in a little while. I hope we haven't got ready for nothing."

"It's always good to be ready, sir. It's never for nothing."

Bannon walked away. Lieutenant Breckenridge watched him go. "That's one of the best men in the platoon, if not the best," he said to Private Worthington.

"Isn't he the one from Texas?"

"Yes, he used to be a cowboy before the war. Rode brahma bulls and broncos at rodeos."

"No kidding."

"I'll tell you something," Lieutenant Breckenridge said. "These guys are very interesting once you get to know them. That Bannon'd make a good officer."

"Did he ever go to college?"

"No, but that's not really necessary to be an officer. He's smart enough and has the qualities of a leader. Colonel Hutchins never went to college either, and he's a great combat officer."

"I really don't know what to make of him," Worthington said. "He sounds like a bullshit artist to me."

"He is a bullshit artist," Lieutenant Breckenridge replied. "He's also a drunkard and sometimes he goes nuts. But he's a great soldier. I'd follow him anywhere."

Private Worthington stared at Lieutenant Breckenridge, amazed at what he'd said, because Colonel Hutchins was obviously a loudmouth and a buffoon, and looked like a clown with his big red nose and fat belly hanging over his belt. He wondered how Lieutenant Breckenridge could admire a man like that.

Lieutenant Breckenridge saw the expression of doubt on Private Worthington's face, and figured out what he was thinking.

"You've got a lot to learn about this war," Lieutenant Breckenridge said with a chuckle. "There's much more to it than meets the eye."

Bannon finished his inspection of the recon platoon foxholes, and was on his way back to the foxhole he shared with Frankie La Barbara. He looked up at the full moon and saw a few wisps of clouds pass by its face. An owl hooted in a tree not far away, and Bannon walked around a thick tangled bush, following the trail back to his foxhole.

A short squat figure loomed up at him out of the night. Bannon stopped and pulled the strap of his M 1 rifle slung from his shoulder.

"What're you doing out here, young Corporal?" asked the deep gravelly voice of Colonel Hutchins.

"Checking my men, sir."

Colonel Hutchins stepped forward, bringing a cloud of alcohol fumes with him. Bannon was a six-footer and looked down at Colonel Hutchins, who wore his steel helmet low over his eyes.

"How are they?" Colonel Hutchins asked.

"Ready to roll, sir."

"Care for a drink, young Corporal?"

"Don't mind if I do, sir."

Colonel Hutchins pulled his canteen out of his case and handed it to Bannon, who unscrewed the top and drank some down.

"That'll put some lead in your pencil," Colonel Hutchins said.

The booze burned Bannon's throat, and he coughed. His face turned red and his eyes watered. "It's got a helluva kick,

133

sir," Bannon said, handing the canteen back. "Thanks a lot."

Colonel Hutchins sipped some of the fiery liquid and smacked his lips as he inserted the canteen back into its case.

"Is your platoon ready for the attack?" Colonel Hutchins asked.

"Yes sir—as ready as they'll ever be."

"Do they believe the attack will come?"

"Some do and some don't."

"Do *you* believe the attack will come?"

"I don't know whether it's coming or not."

Colonel Hutchins made a fist, held it tight, and raised it in front of Bannon's face. Colonel Hutchins bared his teeth and his eyes sparkled as though a fire burned inside his head. "They're getting ready right now," Colonel Hutchins said in a hoarse whisper, "and they're coming across that river pretty soon. I can smell them and I can feel them in my bones. You'd better get yourself ready, young Corporal. This is no bum steer. Old General Adachi is over there watching his men move toward their jump-offs. I can see him just as clear as I'm seeing you right now."

Colonel Hutchins stared into Corporal Bannon's eyes with great intensity, and Bannon felt uncomfortable. He didn't know what to do. "As you were," Colonel Hutchins said.

Bannon took a step backwards and saluted. "Yes sir."

Colonel Hutchins returned the salute solemnly, then walked past Bannon and continued down the trail. Bannon watched the night swallow him up, then took off his helmet and scratched his head. Returning his helmet to his head, he squared his shoulders and made his way back to his foxhole.

Less than one thousand yards away, General Adachi watched soldiers from his Seventy-eighth Infantry Regiment march by on the trail that led past his bunker. The soldiers carried their Arisaka rifles slung over their shoulders and their long bayonets in scabbards affixed to their belts. Their packs were nearly empty, for there was little food to give them, and their backs were straight because they knew General Adachi was looking at them.

General Adachi stood outside his tent, his hands clasped behind his back. Dots of sweat were on his forehead, caused by sharp gnawing pains inside his stomach, but his face was immobile. He couldn't let his soldiers see he was flawed in any way. Aides stood to the left and right of him, also watching the soldiers.

"The men are ready for this fight," said General Tatsunari Kimura, General Adachi's executive officer, standing to his right. "They will not fail."

General Adachi turned to him. "They *will not* fail because they *can not* fail," he replied. "Everything depends on the outcome of this assault."

Officers nearby heard what he said and knew what he meant. If the assault failed, the Eighteenth Army was doomed and all the officers would have to commit hara-kiri, because the responsibility for the failure would be theirs. That was the long and the short of it. Their lives hung in the balance, and the attack was scheduled to begin in only two-and-a-half hours.

TWELVE . . .

Lieutenant Frannie Divers rushed along the jungle path, glancing at her watch. It was a few minutes after twenty-two hundred hours, and she was late for her appointment with Butsko.

Frannie was all hot and bothered, and it wasn't just because of the tropical heat. She'd been thinking about Butsko ever since she saw him last, of his hairy chest and arms, his big broad shoulders, and the roguish smile on his face.

The truth of the matter was that Frannie needed a good fuck. Captain Epstein was wonderfully interesting intellectually, and had a nice poetic personality, but he wasn't very thrilling from a sexual point of view, with his soft white flabby body that sometimes reminded her of a beached whale.

Butsko was another matter. To her eyes and mind he was positively dripping with sex, bulging with muscles, and she just knew he had a big dick. She realized how sexually barren her love affair with Dr. Epstein had been.

She'd lied to Dr. Epstein, and her conscience bothered her. She'd told him she was going to bed early, and he believed her because he trusted her completely, as she trusted him. She felt terrible about betraying him, but she craved Butsko. She wanted him to screw her all night long and make her come a hundred times.

Finally she came to the rear of the pharmacy tent, where she was supposed to meet Butsko, but he wasn't there. She looked around and saw only bushes and trees, then glanced at her watch. She was nearly ten minutes late for the meeting. Maybe he'd left when she didn't show up on time. "Damn," she muttered, glancing to her left and right. What if Captain Epstein walked by and saw her? What if somebody else noticed her there and mentioned it to Captain Epstein. *What am I doing?* she asked herself. *Have I gone insane?*

Butsko lay only a few feet away in the bushes behind her, watching the show. She shuffled from foot to foot, checked her watch numerous times, crossed and uncrossed her arms nervously, and he couldn't help admiring how pretty and strong she was, with her big tits and hefty physical structure. Lieutenant Frannie was no delicate little flower. She was sturdy as many men, but with the soft flowing curves of a beautiful woman.

"Hiya," Butsko said, inside the bush.

She spun around. "Where are you!"

Butsko stood up. "Right here."

"What are you doing hiding in there?"

"Because I didn't want anybody to see me hanging around. That bitch Agnes Shankar might see me and call the MPs."

"Well," Frannie said, "you shouldn't have made me wait so long."

"You didn't wait so long, and you were late anyway." Butsko walked toward her. "Let's go."

"Let's go where?"

"Come with me, and watch your eyes." He turned around and bent low, pushing his way through the bushes. She followed him, holding her arms up to protect her eyes.

"Where are you taking me?" she asked.

"To the El Morocco nightclub," he replied.

He trudged through the dense foliage, and she followed him, ducking low, branches scraping across her uniform and scratching her arms.

"Do we have to go this way?" she asked.

"Stop complaining."

A few minutes later they came to a small clearing. The moon shone overhead and palm trees leaned all around them. A bird chirped in a tree and the sounds of the medical headquarters were far away.

Butsko threw out his arms. "It's the El Morocco!" he said.

She looked around and smiled. "It's very nice."

Butsko bowed and angled his arm toward the ground. "Have a seat."

"Thank you," she replied, dropping down to her fanny, crossing her legs.

Butsko lowered himself to his knees and reached for his canteen. "Let's get drunk," he said.

"Drunk?" she replied. "I'm not sure I want to get drunk."

Butsko leaned toward her and winked. "Why not? Afraid you'll get crazy and do things you'd never do if you were sober?"

"Maybe."

"You're probably afraid I'd take advantage of you if you was drunk, right?"

"Maybe."

"Well don't worry about it. If I wanted to take advantage of you, it wouldn't matter to me if you was drunk or not."

A chill passed over her. She felt a little afraid, but also turned on somewhat by what he'd said. She thought about how she was all alone in the jungle with a big hairy man, with no one to save her, and that turned her on even more. Butsko took off his helmet, revealing his thick straight black hair. He needed a shave and shower, and Frannie could smell him. That, too, turned her on.

He held out the canteen to her. "Ladies first," he said.

"That's okay," she replied. "You can go first."

He unscrewed the top of the canteen, raised it to his lips, and threw his head back. She watched his Adam's apple bob up and down as he drank the white lightning. His shirt was unbuttoned nearly to his waist and he'd torn the sleeves off for air-conditioning. She looked at his big barrel chest, and then glanced down to his muscular thighs straining against his pants. He was so different from Captain Epstein that she thought they could belong to a different species of human being.

He lowered the canteen and said, "Aaaahhhhh!" Wiping his mouth with the back of his hand, he held the canteen out to her. "Goddamn this is good stuff. Here—have some."

She held the canteen in both her hands and raised it to her mouth. Tilting it upwards, she took a swallow. Butsko could see her nipples against the material of her fatigue shirt, and felt raunchy. He wanted to grab her, throw her down to the ground, and wrestle with her, but didn't want to make any fast moves too quickly, because women were skittish until you got to know them well, and then they threw you down and wrestled with you. He was glad he was with her and not Lieutenant Betty Crawford, whom he'd stood up. He hadn't met her when he was supposed to, and she probably was wondering what happened to him. She could wonder all she wanted to. He wanted to roll around on the ground with Frannie Divers, and

138

he'd deal with Betty Crawford and all her baloney some other time.

"It's awfully strong," Frannie said. "Where did you say you got it?"

"A cook makes it."

"It tastes almost like the real thing. The jungle juice I've drunk up till now tasted like rotten garbage juice."

"This ain't jungle juice," Butsko said. "This is real Kentucky white lightning made from a special recipe. Pass it over when you're finished with it."

"I'm not finished with it."

She raised the canteen and drank more, while he watched greedily and hoped she'd get drunk enough to tear off her clothes and go crazy. He was anxious to hug that strong supple body against him and press his mouth to hers. He couldn't wait to stick his dick into that soft sweet spot between her legs.

She drank more and passed the canteen to him. He swallowed some down and handed it back to her. The canteen went back and forth a few times, and Frannie felt woozy. She hadn't drunk alcoholic beverages for over a month, and the white lightning was 150 proof. She thought about Captain Epstein all alone in his tent, probably reading a book before going to bed, and felt guilty.

"I really shouldn't be here with you," she said, holding out the canteen to Butsko.

"Why not?"

"Because I've got a boyfriend."

"So what."

"I feel guilty being here with you."

Butsko placed the canteen on the ground in front of him and sighed, "Here we go again."

"What are you talking about?" she asked.

"All you women've got the same line of bullshit."

"What line of bullshit?"

"You're always feeling guilty about something. You're always worried that you're gonna do something you shouldn't." He looked into her big brown eyes. "I could understand it if we were back in the States and there was no war on, and you were married to somebody, but you're not married to anybody and there *is* a war on, and we might get killed tonight or tomorrow or who knows when. The war is a nightmare, and if people have a chance to have a little fun, they should take it. Why not?"

"I don't know," she said. "It would be terrible if my boy-friend found out.".

"He's not gonna find out."

"What if he does?"

"If he loves you so much, why doesn't he marry you?"

His question surprised her. Marriage to Dr. Epstein had never occurred to her. "I don't know," she said. "We've never talked about marriage."

"If he doesn't love you enough to marry you, and you don't love him enough to even talk about it, what the hell are you worrying about?"

She wrinkled her nose and looked up at the moon floating across the sky. "I never thought of it that way."

"What way did you think about it?"

"I thought Dr. Epstein and I were having a very serious love affair."

"How serious could it be if marriage never came up?"

She thought for a few moments. "I don't know."

Butsko reached for the canteen again. "Some people make mountains out of molehills. They screw around with each other and try to convince themselves they're in love."

Is that what I'm doing? Frannie asked herself. *Am I just trying to convince myself that I'm in love with Dr. Epstein?* "Hand me that canteen, will you?" she said to Butsko.

Butsko passed it to her and she drank some down, questioning what had been going on for the past month between her and Captain Epstein. Then she looked at Butsko and raised her bushy eyebrows.

"What am I doing here with *you?*" she asked.

"You just want to fuck me," he replied, taking the canteen out of her hands.

He raised it to his lips and drank some down, while she looked at him, mildly shocked by what he just said. She wasn't *too* shocked because she'd been raised in a household of brothers who cursed all the time. Butsko screwed the top back onto the canteen and placed it to his side.

"Guess what I'm going to do now?" he asked.

"What?"

"I'm going to grab you," he said, "so get ready."

She didn't know how to get ready, but he leaned forward

and was all over her anyway. He took her in his arms, pushed her to the ground, and rolled on top of her, feeling her strong firm body underneath him, her breasts pressing against his chest, and then he touched his lips to hers, gently at first, but he hadn't had a woman for a long time and his passions got the better of him. She opened her mouth and he thrust his tongue inside, tasting her saliva tinged with white lightning. They squirmed against each other and Frannie decided to stop worrying and let go. Butsko was so powerful, so different from Dr. Epstein, just what she needed.

He rolled off her and unbuttoned the front of her fatigue shirt. She wore a khaki GI brassiere underneath it, and he reached around to unsnap the hooks. The brassiere came apart and he pulled it away, revealing her size-forty breasts.

"My God," Butsko muttered, burying his face in those fabulous breasts, licking them, sucking her nipples, grunting and breathing hard, while she hugged his head tightly against her and writhed, grinding her teeth together, looking up at the moon.

Bannon raised his head and peered over the top of his foxhole. Ahead through openings between trees he could see the Driniumor River churning and rushing toward the sea. Only darkness and the fuzzy outlines of the jungle could be seen on the other side.

"Anything going on?" Frankie asked.

"I can't see anything."

"I bet the Japs don't attack tonight. I think this alert is just another way to harass the troops."

Bannon dropped back into the foxhole. "You wanna bet?"

"I'll bet you twenty dollars," Frankie said.

"It's a deal."

They shook hands solemnly in the darkness of the foxhole.

"What makes you so sure the Japs're gonna attack?" Frankie asked.

"Colonel Hutchins told me they're gonna attack."

"How does he know?"

"He can tell."

"How can he tell?"

"He's an old soldier and I guess he's got a special instinct about these things."

Frankie laughed. "He's an old drunk—that's what he is.

What's so special about that?"

"I believe him," Bannon said.

"You're just a fucking cowboy," Frankie replied. "What do you know? You just lost twenty dollars."

"We'll see," Bannon said.

"You're a fucking asshole and that's all you'll ever be no matter how many stripes you got on your shoulder," Frankie told him.

"We'll see."

Lieutenant Betty Crawford wondered what happened to Butsko. She'd waited for an hour at the place she was supposed to meet him, and he never showed. She couldn't believe he'd stand her up, not after all they'd been through together. She thought something must have happened to him, and now entered his tent to see if he'd fallen asleep in his sack.

It was dark inside the tent, and many of the cots were empty. Some of the men snored, and a few read newspapers and magazines by the light of kerosene lamps. She walked down the rows of cots and finally came to the one Butsko slept on, but it was empty.

"Anybody know where Sergeant Butsko is?" she asked in a whisper.

"I saw him going into Captain Epstein's office an hour ago," somebody replied on the other side of the tent.

Betty wondered why Butsko had gone to see Captain Epstein. It must have been something important if he'd broken the date he'd made with her. She decided to go to Captain Epstein's office and see if Butsko still was there. Turning, she headed toward the tent flap. She was worried that perhaps Butsko had become ill suddenly with blood poisoning or some other serious medical problem.

Butsko was flat on his back, but it wasn't due to any medical problem. All his clothes were off and Lieutenant Frannie Divers was naked too, sitting on top of his erection, holding on to his shoulders and bouncing up and down.

Frannie was right—Butsko did have a big one, nearly twice as big as Dr. Epstein's, and it felt magnificent inside her as she raised herself up and lowered herself down rapidly on top of it. Her boobs bounced around and she licked her lips as she looked down at Butsko, lying with his head resting on his hands, a cigarette dangling out the corner of his mouth, his eyes half-closed.

Frannie leaned forward and pressed her lips against his ear. "Oh you big bastard—I love you," she murmured.

Butsko smiled and puffed his cigarette. "I love you too, kid," he replied.

Private Victor Yabalonka raised his head over the edge of the foxhole and gazed at the Driniumor River. He couldn't see any Japs coming across, or hear any unusual sounds. Dropping back into the foxhole, he got onto his hands and knees and lowered his face almost into the grenade sump. Then he took out a cigarette and lit it quickly. If he stayed low inside the foxhole the lit end of the cigarette couldn't be seen.

Yabalonka needed a cigarette because he was getting nervous. He didn't know whether the Japs would attack or not, but the constant tension was wearing down his nerves. He puffed the cigarette, crouching low in the foxhole, and looked at the Reverend Billie Jones, squinting and trying to read his handy pocket Bible in the moonlight.

It annoyed Yabalonka to see Billie Jones so calm. Yabalonka was an atheist and supposedly a smart guy, yet he was nervous as a bedbug while Billie Jones, with his stupid superstitious belief in God, was relaxed. "Billie?" Yabalonka said.

The Reverend Billie Jones looked up from his Bible. "Yuh?"

"Can I ask you a question?"

"Go right ahead."

"How can you believe in God, Billie?"

Billie blinked. "Because He exists."

"Where is he? I don't see him."

"Just because you can't see Him, that don't mean He ain't here. You can't see Lieutenant Breckenridge either, but that don't mean he don't exist."

"But we've all seen Lieutenant Breckenridge. None of us has seen God."

"I have," the Reverend Billie Jones said. "I've seen the great living God many times, and I can even see Him in you, Yabalonka, although you don't believe in Him."

"What does he look like?" Yabalonka asked.

"Depends on how He reveals Himself."

Yabalonka realized he wasn't getting anywhere with that line of questioning. He decided to try a new angle. "If there's a God, how could he let things like wars happen?"

"Men make wars, not God. Men cause their suffering, not God."

"He can't be a very good god if he lets wars happen."

"He lets us do what we want, and it's up to us to seek Him out. It's up to us to lead a righteous life. God wants us to choose Him. He wants us to come to Him. If a father gives everything to a child, the child becomes spoiled. God, our Father in heaven, doesn't want to spoil us. He wants us to be strong and choose the path of righteousness over the path of evil."

Yabalonka shook his head. "I don't know how you can believe all that stuff. People like you need religion because you're afraid to face the truth of the world."

"Jesus is the truth of the world," the Reverend Billie Jones replied. "People like you don't believe in Him because you're too high and mighty, and afraid to admit there's something greater than you. It's all explained right here in Paul's First Letter to the Colossians. Let me read it to you." Billie thumbed quickly through his handy pocket Bible.

Yabalonka held out his hand. "Please, not now," he said. "I don't think I could handle it right now."

"Okay Yabalonka," Billie said, "but you really oughtta read this book sometime. I got an extra one right here in my pack. Lemme give it to you."

"Naw, that's all right."

But Billie already was rustling through his pack, and pulled out another handy pocket Bible identical to the one he'd been reading. "Here—take it," he said.

Yabalonka pressed his back against the wall of the foxhole, to get as far away from it as he could. "No thanks—I don't want it."

"Go ahead and take it—it won't bite you."

"Naw—give it to somebody who'll appreciate it."

"C'mon—put it in your shirt pocket. You can take a look at it when you don't have anything better to read, and even if you don't read it, it'll give you good luck."

Billie tossed the Bible to Victor Yabalonka, and it landed in his lap. Yabalonka looked down at it, horrified. He'd been

144

an atheist almost for as long as he could walk, and there was a Bible, that fount of superstition, lying in his lap.

The Reverend Billie Jones had gone back to reading his own Bible. Victor Yabalonka picked up the Bible and held it out to Billie.

"Hey Billie," he said, "I don't want this."

Billie didn't move a muscle or respond in any way. Yabalonka didn't want to throw the Bible back at him, because he didn't want to offend Billie, whom he basically liked. *I know what I'll do*, Yabalonka thought. *I'll just hang on to it until I get a chance to throw it away. If Billie ever asks where it is, I'll just say I lost it someplace.*

Yabalonka picked up the Bible and dropped it into his shirt pocket, buttoning it up. Then he lowered his head and puffed his cigarette, remembering the big Jap attack that was supposed to take place.

He began to worry again.

Butsko lay naked on his back, his head resting on his hands, looking down through heavy-lidded eyes at Lieutenant Frannie Divers on her knees, bending over and sucking his banana.

Her head bobbed up and down as she held his banana in her fist, squeezing it hard, drooling and slobbering. She huffed and puffed and her big rear end wiggled with pleasure. Butsko looked at it, thinking that a woman's ass had to be the most beautiful thing in the world, and he thought maybe he'd do it to her doggie fashion after she finished blowing him.

Frannie pulled her mouth off his banana. "Oh God—I needed this!" she said.

"We all need it every once in a while," Butsko replied, "but don't stop now, kid. I was just gonna come."

Lieutenant Betty Crawford walked into Captain Epstein's tent and saw the C.Q. (Charge of Quarters) Corporal Raymond Dinkens, sitting behind the desk. "Is Captain Epstein in?" she asked.

"Not right now," Dinkens said.

"Have you seen Sergeant Butsko here recently?"

"He was here a while ago."

"Do you know where he went?"

"No ma'am."

"Was he all right?"

"He seemed all right, ma'am."

Betty's brow became furrowed with thought. If Butsko was all right, why hadn't he kept his date with her? Where in hell was the big ugly son of a bitch?

Just then Captain Epstein burst through the tent flap. He saw Betty and stopped cold. His face was flushed with exertion and he appeared worried. "Have you seen Frannie around?" he asked Betty.

"No, I haven't."

Now Captain Epstein's brow became furrowed with thought. Frannie had told him she didn't feel well and was going to bed early, but when he called the nurses' residence tent to see how she was, Lieutenant Agnes Shankar told him she wasn't there.

Captain Epstein turned to Corporal Dinkens. "Have you seen Lieutenant Divers around?" he asked.

"She was here shortly after you left earlier, sir. She was talking with Sergeant Butsko in your office."

Betty's jaw dropped open. Captain Epstein wrinkled his nose and raised his upper lip. Both of them came to the same conclusion at the same moment.

That rotten bastard, Captain Epstein thought.

That dirty bitch, Betty thought.

"What were they talking about?" Captain Epstein asked.

"I don't know, sir," Corporal Dinkens replied. "They were talking awful quiet."

Now Captain Epstein's worst suspicions were confirmed, and so were Betty Crawford's.

"Excuse me," Betty said. "There's something I've got to do."

She turned and stormed out of the tent. Captain Epstein stood in front of Corporal Dinkens's desk and reconstructed recent events in his mind. Evidently Frannie and Butsko had made a date while talking in his office. Then Frannie had come to him and said she was sick. After that she must have gone to meet Butsko.

Captain Epstein was furious. He considered Frannie a dumb broad, but how dare she be unfaithful to him! He wondered where they could be, and realized it had to be fairly close by. Butsko couldn't walk well and Captain Epstein doubted whether they'd stolen a jeep. Somebody must have seen them going wherever they were now. All Captain Epstein would have to do was ask around.

He looked down at Corporal Dinkens. "If anybody wants me, I'll be in the area," he said.

"Yes sir," replied Corporal Dinkens.

Captain Epstein charged out of his tent, to track down Lieutenant Frannie Divers and Sergeant Butsko.

Private Joshua McGurk from Skunk Hollow, Maine, stood in his foxhole and stared at the Japanese side of the Driniumor River. He saw soldiers moving around, but there was no point telling anyone. No one would believe him because they couldn't see what he saw.

Private McGurk had been a lumberjack before the war, and in the off season he used to hunt and trap animals. He was wise in the ways of forests, and the jungles of New Guinea differed from the Maine woodlands only in temperature and the types of creatures indigenous to the area. A man who was accustomed to the black flies of Maine would have little difficulty with the mosquitoes of New Guinea.

McGurk dropped down into the foxhole, where Pfc. Morris Shilansky sat glumly, looking at the ground. Shilansky said nothing as McGurk kneeled in front of him. McGurk was getting worried about Shilansky. "You okay, Shilansky?" McGurk asked.

"Yeah, I'm okay," Shilansky replied.

"You sure?"

"Yeah, I'm sure."

"Well you're sure actin' strange."

"Look who's calling somebody strange."

"I ain't strange."

"Neither am I."

"Somethin's bothering you, Shilansky. Somebody die in yore fambly?"

"As a matter of fact, somebody did."

"Well, worryin' about it won't do nobody no good. Everybody dies sooner or later. There ain't nothin' you can do about it."

"I think there is."

"You can't bring back the dead, Shilansky."

"That's right," Shilansky muttered, "but you can stop more

147

of them from being killed."

"They was killed?" McGurk asked, shocked.

"That's right."

"How many was killed?"

"Millions."

McGurk thought Shilansky was joking with him, because everybody always joked with him, but then he saw Shilansky was serious. McGurk wondered if Shilansky was going crazy. How could somebody have millions of kinfolk, and how could anybody murder millions of somebody's kinfolk?

"I think you'd better get some sleep," McGurk said. "You sound awful tired to me."

"Fuck sleep," Shilansky replied, spitting into the bottom of the foxhole. "I'm waiting for those Japs to come over here."

McGurk had met many oddballs and loony-tunes since he'd been in the Army, and Shilansky was just another of them. It was best to leave them alone. "Well, if'n you're gonna stay awake, maybe I'll get some shut-eye," McGurk said.

"Okay," Shilansky replied.

McGurk raised his knees and rested his back against the wall of the foxhole, closing his eyes. *Look at him*, Shilansky thought. *He doesn't have a worry in the world*.

Shilansky scratched his nose, which was the nose of a hawk. He bent down and lit a cigarette, thinking about the Japs and hoping they'd attack like some people believed they would.

Shilansky had reached a major decision during the past hour. If he couldn't kill Nazis for what they were doing to the Jews, at least he could kill Japs, because Japs were partners of the Nazis in the war, and as far as Shilansky was concerned they were cut out of the same hunk of shit. He hoped the attack would take place so he could annihilate Japs. He'd mow them down with the machine gun, and he had plenty of ammunition. McGurk would feed it in and he'd shoot Japs to shit.

Shilansky looked at his watch. It was 2330 hours, half-past eleven at night. He sat behind the machine gun and wrapped his fingers around the handles, pressing his thumbs against the trigger mechanism. *Come on you sons of bitches*, he thought. *I'm waiting for you*.

In his tent, General Adachi checked his watch at the same instant Pfc. Shilansky looked at his. *Only ten more minutes*,

General Adachi thought. He lowered his hand and laid it on his desk. He looked at the papers lying there and realized they meant nothing now. Although the first bullet hadn't been fired yet, the attack was underway. All his soldiers were in position, and his artillerymen were preparing to open fire. General Adachi couldn't stop the attack even if he wanted to.

He closed his eyes and imagined artillerymen loading their big shells into the breeches of their guns. Their sergeants and officers glanced at their watches, because everyone was supposed to start firing at the same moment, continuing nonstop for five minutes.

Captain Adachi's guts churned in his stomach as he waited through the final minutes before the attack. He looked up and saw his staff officers standing around in small groups, speaking softly. Everyone was aware of the seriousness of their situation. General Adachi felt a sharp pain like a spear being shoved into his stomach. Sweat poured from his forehead, but he never flinched or changed his expression.

THIRTEEN . . .

Lieutenant Betty Crawford arrived at the pharmacy tent and looked around. An orderly approached the tent along another trail, but no one else was there. It was late and nearly everybody was asleep.

Betty felt foolish. She realized she should be sacked out, resting up for her tour of duty tomorrow, but she was obsessed with Butsko and wanted to track him down to tell him he was a dirty lying bastard.

She'd already searched the medical headquarters area, and somebody told her he'd seen Butsko near the pharmacy tent about an hour ago. Now Betty was on the scene, snooping around.

She walked into the tent and saw an orderly sitting behind a desk, dispensing medication to the orderly who'd just walked in.

"Hello there," Betty said in an offhand way. "You haven't seen Sergeant Butsko around here by any chance, have you?"

"No ma'am," said the orderly behind the desk.

"Me neither," said the other orderly.

"How long have you been on duty?" she asked the orderly behind the desk.

He looked at his watch. "Nearly an hour."

Betty walked out of the tent. On an impulse she decided to walk around it, in case Butsko might be in back. She realized she was being foolish, and it was extremely unlikely that he'd be in back, but she thought she'd take a look anyway.

She walked around the side of the tent, looking into the jungle, wondering if Butsko was out there screwing Lieutenant Frannie Divers. It made Betty's blood boil to think that might be happening. How could Butsko stand her up for a big sloppy cow like Frannie Divers? The very thought of it set Betty's teeth on edge.

She turned the corner and was astonished to see Captain Epstein sitting at the rear of the tent, his arms folded like an Indian, looking off into the jungle. He heard footsteps and turned toward Betty, his face twisting and distorting when he saw who she was.

"What are you doing here!" he said in a loud whisper.

"Nothing," she replied, embarrassed at getting caught, but she was no more embarrassed than he. "What're *you* doing here?"

"Nothing."

She walked toward him, because she didn't know what else to do. He didn't walk away because somebody told him he'd seen Frannie near the pharmacy tent a short while ago. He wanted to catch her in the act if he could.

Captain Epstein sat down again and crossed his arms. Betty sat beside him. Each put two and two together and figured out what the other was doing there.

"I think they're in the jungle straight ahead," Captain Epstein said in a whisper. "Keep your voice down."

"What makes you think they're there?" Betty asked.

"Because somebody saw Frannie around here a while ago, and there are fresh tracks leading into the jungle right there."

Betty leaned forward and saw footprints in the soft mushy ground, plus branches bent and broken. She wouldn't have noticed them if Captain Epstein hadn't pointed them out to her.

"I didn't know you were going out with Frannie," she said.

"I didn't know you were going out with Butsko," he replied. "He doesn't seem like your type at all."

"He isn't anymore," she said. "When I see him I'm really going to give him a piece of my mind, and by the way, Frannie doesn't seem like your type either."

"Well you know how it is out here," Captain Epstein said ruefully. "One has so little to choose from."

Betty was insulted. *She* was there, and he'd never attempted to get anything going with her, although she would've turned him down if he did, because he wasn't her type at all. She didn't like soft flabby men who looked like bookworms. Normally she went for men like the actor Van Johnson, who were blond and wholesome-looking. Her boyfriend, the one who was missing in action, had been that type. Butsko was an aberration in her life, she now believed. He'd taken advantage of her during a weak moment in her life, she wanted to think.

Captain Epstein raised his fingers to his lips. "Ssshhh," he said. "Somebody's coming."

Betty perked up her pretty pink ears. Sure enough, she heard rustling straight ahead in the jungle. Somebody was heading their way, pushing through the dense foliage.

Then she heard a laugh, and realized the person laughing was Frannie Divers. She looked at Captain Epstein, and Captain Epstein looked at her, his face pale as snow.

She heard a man's voice, and she'd know that voice anywhere. She couldn't hear what he was saying, but it was Butsko's voice. She still was looking at Captain Epstein, and Captain Epstein still was looking at her. Captain Epstein scowled, and Betty grit her teeth. Her heart beat faster. That dirty rotten Butsko had stood her up and humilated her. Now she was going to tell him what she thought of him and slap his ugly face as hard as she could.

She heard Butsko's voice more clearly.

"I wish we had a hotel we could go to," Butsko said. "I got more mosquito bites than Captain Epstein's got twitches."

Frannie laughed, and Captain Epstein got to his feet, his right cheek twitching so furiously it was as if someone was pinching it and jerking it up and down. Betty got to her feet too, but didn't know what she was going to do. Somehow she couldn't believe that Butsko really was out there with Frannie. Now Betty wished she'd gone to bed like a good little girl. She'd put herself in a position where she had to do something, but she couldn't imagine what. She imagined she was supposed to be mad, but instead she felt confused and awkward. She was in the wrong place at the right time.

Captain Epstein knew exactly what he was going to do. He stood stiffly, his jaw protruding belligerently, and intended to stare at Frannie, not saying anything, just so she'd know he knew she was a no-good worthless bitch. His arms were straight down at his sides and his fists were balled up. Leaning forward, he looked as though he was off-balance and would fall on his face, but somehow he didn't fall. His cheek continued to twitch and he was determined to play the part of a gentleman wronged.

The rustling in the jungle came closer. Butsko's voice could be heard again. "Let's do this tomorrow night," he said.

"You think you can get more of that white lightning?" she asked.

"I'll try."

"It was awfully good. What do they make it with?"

"I don't think you really want to know that part," Butsko said.

Butsko and Frannie emerged from the jungle, and at first they couldn't believe their eyes. It appeared that Dr. Epstein and Betty Crawford were standing in the darkness behind the pharmacy tent, and Dr. Epstein looked as though he was about to fall on his face. Butsko and Frannie blinked, and then they realized with dismay that Dr. Epstein and Betty Crawford were in fact standing behind the pharmacy tent.

Frannie felt embarrassed, but Butsko didn't give a fuck. He was an old soldier and believed you pushed the hardest when the going got the toughest. He also had a perverse sense of humor.

He stopped in front of them and grinned. "Hello there," he said. "Fancy meeting you here."

Captain Epstein expected apologies and remorse, not a wisecrack, and on top of everything else, Butsko wasn't even an officer. Captain Epstein got mad. His face felt on fire. Although he'd told himself he'd keep his mouth shut and walk away after Frannie saw him, Butsko's manner and remark made his emotions boil over.

Captain Epstein looked at Frannie and said, "How could you do this to me—you bitch!"

Butsko held up the palms of both his hands. "Wait a minute now," he said, still grinning because he was enjoying everybody's discomfort. "That ain't no way to talk to a lady."

Now it was Betty's turn to blow her top. "What lady!" She pointed her forefinger at Frannie. "Do you mean that *tramp* over there?"

Frannie recovered suddenly from her embarrassment at getting caught with Butsko. "Who are you calling a tramp, you little twerp!"

"Twerp!" screamed Betty.

Betty lost her composure completely. She bared her teeth, snarled like a wildcat, and dived onto Frannie, knocking her off-balance, and together they fell to the ground.

"Whore!" hollered Betty, trying to scratch out Frannie's eyes.

"Bitch!" replied Frannie, tearing open the front of Betty's shirt, revealing her Army-issue brassiere to the world.

They punched, scratched, and kicked each other, rolling over and around on the ground, getting filthy and all messed up. Butsko turned to Captain Epstein and shrugged.

"Women," he said, as if that explained everything.

Captain Epstein stared at the two women struggling on the ground. He was fascinated and appalled by what they were doing. Never had he seen two women fight before, and they were really fighting. Frannie, the bigger of the two, was sitting on top of Betty and squeezing her throat with both hands. Betty, turning green, clawed red lines onto Frannie's face. Captain Epstein found himself becoming sexually aroused. He wanted to take his clothes off and dive on the both of them. He felt the weird desire to have them beat him up. Captain Epstein never realized it before, but he was a kinky son of a bitch.

Butsko decided the fighting had gone on long enough, and he'd better stop it before somebody got hurt. With one hand he grabbed the collar of Frannie's shirt and pulled her into the air, where she dangled, her feet off the ground. "Cut it out!" Butsko snarled.

Betty jumped up off the ground and charged Frannie, but Butsko held out his hand and her breastbone collided into it. Butsko tighted his fist around the front of her shirt. "I said cut it out!"

His booming no-nonsense voice sent chills up the backs of both the women. They stopped struggling. Butsko eased Frannie to the ground and removed his hand from the front of Betty's shirt. "Calm down you two," he said. "Enough is enough."

The two women stared at each other, hatred in their eyes, their faces red with anger. Frannie pursed her lips and blew her red hair out of her eyes. Then she raised her hands and wiped the rest of it away. She had black-and-blue marks and scratches all over her face. Betty had a bloody nose and a loose tooth, as well as a black eye.

"Slut," Betty said to Frannie.

"Shitpot," Frannie replied.

Butsko couldn't help laughing. Captain Epstein's eyebrows were knitted together. He still had a hard-on and wondered whether he should see a psychologist.

"I don't know about all of you," Butsko said, "but I'm hitting the sack." He looked at Frannie. "I'll see you tomorrow night, same time, same station."

She nodded. Butsko adjusted his submachine gun on his shoulder and took three steps, when suddenly he heard thunder far off in the distance. He stopped cold and looked toward the Driniumor.

"Oh-oh," he said.

On the east side of the Driniumor, Japanese artillerymen, stripped to their waists, shoved shells into their guns as fast as they could, while other artillerymen pulled the strings that fired the shells. Volley after volley blew out the barrels of the big guns and flew in long murderous arcs through the sky. Every Japanese artillery piece fired constantly, one shell after the other again and again, while the artillerymen sweat profusely in the humid night air.

The muzzles of the guns flashed yellow and orange, illuminating the gun crews and crates of artillery shells piled up next to the guns. The shells were passed from man to man and stuffed into the breeches of the guns. The loud constant roar of the explosions numbed the men's hearing, but still they loaded.

The fire was concentrated in the center of the American line, where the main assault would be launched, and also on the beach, where the diversionary attack would take place. The Japanese artillerymen could see the sky light up in the distance where the shells landed. They knew the Americans were getting blown to shit over there, and the Japanese artillerymen were glad. They'd been training for this bombardment for weeks, and now at last they were able to vent their spleen against the Americans.

Their bodies glistening with sweat, they loaded, fired, and reloaded their guns, which blasted and recoiled again and again, while on the American side of the Driniumor the jungle exploded and burned.

The shells spread devastation all across the Eighty-first Division line. Tents were blown into the air, motor pools set aflame, and soldiers who happened to get caught on open ground when the bombardment commenced were mutilated by flying shrapnel.

155

Bannon and Frankie La Barbara crouched low in their deep foxhole. The explosions made their ears ring, and the ground shook so violently it made clods of earth break off from the walls of the hole and fall into the grenade sump. The two GIs covered their ears with their hands and shivered with fear, because they knew one of those shells could fall into their hole and wipe them off the face of the earth.

"You owe me twenty bucks!" Bannon shouted above the roar.

"I'll give it to you on payday!" Frankie replied.

The ground shook and heaved. An explosion nearby blew down trees, and one of them fell a few feet from the foxhole, sending up a cloud of dust and smoke. Another shell hit the dirt only twenty yards away, blowing dirt and rocks into the air.

The dirt and rocks fell onto Frankie and Bannon. One rock the size of a baseball landed on Frankie's helmet, and for a moment he thought he'd been hit by shrapnel. He screamed in imaginary pain, but then felt the rock roll off his head and fall onto his shoulder, finally dropping into his lap.

Bannon clicked his teeth nervously. He took out a cigarette and lit it up, taking a deep puff, seeing flashes and pulsations of light against the night sky.

"I think it's time to fix bayonets," he said to Frankie. "The Japs'll be coming soon."

Frankie nodded. He pulled his bayonet out of its scabbard and affixed it to the end of his M 1 rifle. Bannon did the same. They ducked low in the foxhole and hoped they'd be alive when the bombardment ended.

In his command post bunker, Colonel Hutchins tried to raise his old buddy Lieutenant Colonel Rufus Bollinger, commander of the Sixty-third Field Artillery Battalion, on the telephone, but the lines were dead and he surmised the bombardment must have cut the wires.

Colonel Hutchins looked around and saw his staff assembled around him, looking at him for direction. The ground beneath their feet heaved as if an earthquake was taking place, while huge craters were blown into the ground by Japanese shells.

"Bombasino!" Colonel Hutchins said. "Get over here!"

"Yes sir."

Pfc. Nick Bombasino from South Philly strode toward him,

wearing the big backpack radio.

"Turn around," Colonel Hutchins said.

Bombasino turned around and Colonel Hutchins unhooked the transmitter, holding it against his face. He spoke the call letters of Lieutenant Colonel Bollinger's headquarters into the mouthpiece, but heard only static and whistles through the earphones. He couldn't get through by radio either. His headquarters was cut off from the rest of the world.

He returned the transmitter to the backpack radio and pushed Pfc. Bombasino away. Wiping his nose with the back of his hand, he looked down at the map table spread next to him. The big question now was when the bombardment would end. Colonel Hutchins didn't think it'd last too long, because he knew from intelligence reports and his own common sense that the Japs didn't have much artillery ammunition, since they were cut off from their sources of supply.

When the artillery bombardment ended, the Japs would come. Then all Colonel Hutchins's skill as a combat commander would come into play. It was easy to be a winner when your side outnumbered the other side, but the shoe would be on the other foot this time.

I've been with this regiment too long to let it get wiped out, Colonel Hutchins thought. *If the going gets too tough, I'm just going to pull my men the fuck out of here.*

In his command post dug into the ground, General Adachi raised his hand and looked at his watch. The bombardment had been going on for approximately four-and-a-half minutes. It would end in only a few more seconds. Then the main attack would begin. He looked at his officers and they looked at him. No one said a word. Everyone knew what the stakes were. They'd done all they could do, and the artillery was completing its job. Then the battle would be turned over to the ordinary foot soldiers who ultimately would win or lose the battle. Everything depended on them now, those ragged tired hungry soldiers out there in the trenches, holding on to their rifles and bayonets, waiting for the order to attack.

"How're you doing?" Lieutenant Breckenridge asked Private Worthington, who was undergoing the first bombardment of his life.

Worthington huddled at the bottom of the foxhole, his face

drained of color, his eyes wide open and staring as if he'd seen a ghost. "I knew it'd be bad," he said, "but I never knew it'd be *this* bad."

Lieutenant Breckenridge laughed. "Hell—you haven't seen anything yet. You should've seen some of the bombardments we took on Bougainville. Now that was a *real* war." Private Worthington looked at Lieutenant Breckenridge.

He couldn't imagine anything worse than what he was going through just then. The bombardment seemed as though it'd never end. The explosions hurt his ears and he could feel the concussion waves in his guts. He imagined one of the shells falling on him and blowing him to bits. He found it hard to believe his life could end so suddenly, for no good reason at all.

Lieutenant Breckenridge calmly lit a cigarette. "Don't worry," he told Worthington, "the old soldiers say you never hear the one that lands on you."

Twenty-five yards away, Pfc. Morris Shilansky sat stolidly behind his .30-caliber machine gun, his hands on the grips and his thumbs on the triggers, waiting for the Japs to come. Incoming shells whistled all around him, explosions took place everywhere, huge trees were blasted into tiny toothpicks, but he didn't move a muscle. His mouth was set in a grim line and his eyes glinted like tiny chips of ice. When the Japs attacked, he wanted a piece of them. He hoped the bombardment would end so they'd start coming. They were going to pay for the Jews of Europe who'd gone up in smoke.

McGurk lay behind the sandbags, looking up at him. "I think you'd better get down, Shilansky."

Shilansky didn't even hear him. Shilansky was in another place. Through the holocaust of explosions and flames he looked toward the far bank of the Driniumor, hoping to see a Jap. But he didn't see anything, not yet. But soon they'd come, and he'd be ready.

"C'mon you little yellow bastards," he muttered. "Let's get this show on the road."

"General Hawkins wants to speak with you, sir," said Master Sergeant Seymour Bunberry, the sergeant major of the Persecution Task Force, standing beside the bank of shortwave radios.

"Tell him I can't talk to him right now," General Hall replied.

"Yes sir."

General Hall stood at his map table and looked down at it. He already knew what was going on and didn't need to waste time talking with General Hawkins. The big attack by the Japanese Eighteenth Army was taking place on schedule, and the full weight of the bombardment was hitting the Eighty-first Division. A smaller bombardment fell on the beach where the Thirty-fifth Division was deployed, but that appeared diversionary. General Hall had the main situation figured out. He wished he'd stationed the 114th Regimental Combat Team closer to the front, but that was just hindsight. At the time he'd been sure he was making the right decision, and despite everything, he still believed it was the right decision.

"Colonel MacKenzie!" he said.

"Yes sir!" replied Colonel MacKenzie, rushing toward the map table.

"Order the Hundred Fourteenth RCT to move up here." General Hall drew a line over the map with his finger, and it covered the area behind the Eighty-first Division front line. "Direct all available artillery to open fire here." He pointed to the east bank of the Driniumor opposite the Eighty-first Division. "Then call General Hawkins and tell him to hold on until help arrives."

"Yes sir!"

Colonel MacKenzie dashed to the telephones and transmitted the first two orders easily. The third call, to General Hawkins, didn't go through. Colonel MacKenzie correctly surmised that the telephone wires had been cut by the bombardment. He crossed the room and at the bank of radios told an operator to get General Hawkins for him, but after several attempts the operator still couldn't get through.

Colonel MacKenzie returned to General Hall, who looked down thoughtfully at the map. "Sir?" said Colonel MacKenzie.

General Hall looked up. "What is it?"

"I couldn't reach General Hawkins, sir. Evidently his communications are out."

"Then he'll have to figure out what to do on his own," General Hall said.

159

FOURTEEN . . .

At approximately 2355 hours, the artillery bombardment stopped. The first Japanese unit to come out of their holes was the First Battalion of the Seventy-eighth Infantry Regiment. It was followed by the rest of the Seventy-eighth Regiment, then the Eightieth Regiment, and finally the bulk of the Japanese Eighteenth Army.

The Japanese soldiers attacked in three waves, running down toward the Driniumor River, jumping in and dashing across, splashing and kicking, holding their rifles with fixed bayonets in their hands, screaming bloody blue murder. Their officers waved their samurai swords in the air, exhorting the men on. Every Japanese soldier knew it would be all-out and winner-take-all until the bloody end of the battle.

Morris Shilansky was the first GI to open fire. He sat behind his .30-caliber machine gun and pushed the thumb triggers. The machine gun barked viciously, dancing around on its tripod legs, shooting sparks and hot lead out of the barrel.

The bullets streamed down toward the Driniumor River and cut down a bunch of Japs, but the rest of the Japs kept charging. The belt of ammunition feeding into the machine gun snaked around wildly in the air as Shilansky moved the weapon from side to side on its transverse mechanism, mowing down Japs. "Grab that fucking belt!" Shilansky hollered.

McGurk jumped up and dived on the belt, holding it steadily in his hands so it would feed smoothly into the chamber of the gun. Meanwhile, all around them, the other GIs in the recon platoon raised themselves and perched their weapons on the rims of their foxholes. They fired M 1 rifles, carbines, Thompson submachine guns, and Browning Automatic Rifles, raking the attacking Japanese soldiers with a hail of bullets, but the

Japanese soldiers were all hyped up and the ones who weren't killed or wounded maintained the momentum of their frantic banzai charge, baring their teeth at the Americans, anxious to get close and engage them hand-to-hand.

The Japanese Eighteenth Army spread out and swarmed across the roaring swirling river. American bullets cut many of them down, and Japanese heads sank beneath the surface, but hordes of Japanese soldiers kept coming in jagged skirmish lines, howling at the tops of their lungs.

They got halfway across, and then the American artillery opened fire. The first unit to send the shells flying was the Sixty-third Field Artillery Battalion, commanded by old Lieutenant Colonel Rufus Bollinger, who laid down a carpet of shells on the Driniumor River and jungle behind it.

The artillery fire was devastating. Japanese soldiers moving toward the river were blown into the air along with trees and tons of earth. Then the other artillery units in the Eighty-first Division opened fire on previously prepared concentrations along the bed and east side of the Driniumor. Despite their zeal, a few Japanese soldiers faltered. In the terrible explosive horror, some turned tail and ran, but most kept charging, thinking of the food and supplies on the other side of the river, and willing to die for their Emperor, the most noble death of all.

Not all the regiments along the Driniumor were as ready for the attack as the units of the Eighty-first Division. Some of those officers hadn't believed the attack would come on July 9, and it took them a while to get their artillery firing. Meanwhile, multitudes of Japanese soldiers rampaged ever closer to their positions.

The Japanese units in front of the Eighty-first Division took a terrible beating from the artillery bombardment, but continued to push forward anyway. They were two-thirds of the way across the Driniumor and only had a little way to go. Leaping through the water, dreaming of exalted death or the glory of victory, they lunged toward the American side of the river.

Meanwhile, back in his bunker, General Adachi received word that the center of his attack, its most crucial element, was receiving a severe artillery bombardment. Standing at his map table, General Adachi knew exactly what to do. He'd run all the possibilities through his mind long before this day, and had alternatives ready for everything.

Without any hesitation he ordered two regiments from his reserve to follow the units hitting the center of the American line. They were to push through the American artillery barrage no matter what.

"Once they're on the other side," he told General Kimura, "they won't have to worry about the artillery barrage anymore! Just tell them to keep moving forward for the Emperor!"

Private Worthington rested his M 1 rifle on the edge of his foxhole and took aim at a Japanese soldier near the riverbank below. Centering the Japanese soldier in his sights, he squeezed the trigger.

Blam! The rifle fired and Private Worthington watched with morbid fascination as the Japanese soldier collapsed onto his face in the shallow water. Worthington moved his rifle an inch to the right and lined up his sights on another Japanese soldier, this one an officer or a sergeant with a samurai sword in his hand. *Blam!* That one dropped to his knees, letting the sword fall from his hands, and then he toppled forward into the water. Worthington moved the rifle two inches to the left and aimed at a short skinny Japanese soldier, reminding Worthington of an insect. *Blam!* The impact of the bullet knocked the Japanese soldier onto his ass, and he didn't get up again.

Worthington moved his rifle and aimed, firing again and again. He was a crack shot and never missed. He'd shot big game in Africa, but it'd never been anything like this. Shooting animals had been sport, but he didn't see much sport to this. He realized that shooting for sport and shooting in a war were entirely different things.

He fired the last bullet in the clip and the clip clanged into the air, landing on the ground beside him. Reaching into a bandolier, he pulled out another clip and stuffed it into the chamber of the M 1, closed the bolt, and took aim again at a Japanese soldier charging up the riverbank in front of him. *Blam!* The Japanese soldier tripped over his feet and fell to the ground, landing head first and not moving; he was dead before he landed.

All alone in his foxhole, Pfc. Bisbee fired his M 1 rifle at the wave of Japs assaulting the barbed-wire barricades. He heard rifle- and machine-gunfire all around him, while on the other side of the river the American artillery bombardment continued to blow up Japanese soldiers and destroy the jungle.

But the bombardment didn't fire at the Japanese soldiers on the American side of the Driniumor. Those Japanese soldiers were too close, and their shattered skirmish lines rushed forward to the barbed-wire barricades, most of which had been decimated by the Japanese artillery bombardment. Japanese soldiers shrieked for joy as they jumped over the torn barbed wire. A few land mines exploded, blowing Japanese soldiers to bits, but the Japanese artillery bombardment had destroyed most of the mines also.

Japanese soldiers poured through openings in the barbed wire, and Private Bisbee fired his M 1 rifle as quickly as he could. He shot down Japanese soldier after Japanese soldier, but there were too many Japanese soldiers and the American fire in the area couldn't stop them. Private Bisbee knew the Japanese soldiers would swarm over the recon platoon area in a matter of minutes, and then it would be hand-to-hand and gruesome as hell until one side or the other gave way.

For once Private Bisbee wasn't thinking about stealing things. He was afraid he might become a casualty very soon. But he gave no thought to running away. He wasn't a coward. He'd stand and fight until he couldn't fight anymore, but what he really hoped for was an order to retreat.

Meanwhile, Japanese soldiers rushed closer, leaping over their dead comrades, seeing the American foxholes straight ahead. *"Banzai!"* they shouted. *"Tenno heika banzai!"*

General Adachi looked down at his map table, as reports from the front were delivered to him by his staff officers. Lieutenant Ono, his aide-de-camp, moved colored pieces of wood around on the map, so General Adachi could have a clear picture of how his big offensive was proceeding.

General Adachi's hands were clasped behind his back and he stood erectly except for the forward tilt of his head. His stomach twisted and wrenched with terrible pain, but he exerted his will and managed to ignore the distraction, as he drew conclusions from what he saw on his map.

His main assault wasn't going well. The center of the American line held fast because it was protected by a fierce artillery bombardment. Others of his units, on the flanks of the American center, were making excellent progress. The only thing to do was wheel around those units on either side of the American center and have them hit it from both sides.

"General Kimura!" he said.

General Kimura stood next to him at the map table. "Yes sir!"

General Adachi pointed to the center of resistance on the map. "Americans in that sector are holding. I want our units on both sides of them to attack their flanks *now*. Is that clear?"

General Kimura looked at the map. "Yes sir!"

"Have it done immediately," General Adachi said.

"Yes sir!"

General Kimura rushed to the telephones, to transmit the order as far forward as possible. Then couriers would be used to carry the orders the rest of the way to the front. Still at the map table looking down, General Adachi took out a cigarette and lit it up, his hand trembling slightly. The attack was in its most crucial phase, and General Adachi was nervous as hell. Acids spilled into his stomach, causing incredible pain and nearly doubling him over. *They must break through now,* he said to himself. *Everything depends on it.*

A stampede of Japanese soldiers made their way through the barbed wire and mine fields, headed straight for the recon platoon. Pfc. Morris Shilansky ground his teeth together as he swung his machine gun from side to side on its transverse mechanism, cutting them down. In his eyes, every Jap was a Nazi who killed Jews. The corners of his mouth turned down and his eyes glittered with hatred as he fired the machine gun in bursts of six, so the barrel wouldn't melt down.

In front of him, Japanese soldiers fell like wheat before a scythe, but more Japanese soldiers kept coming. They were twenty yards away, fifteen yards away, and then ten yards away. Shilansky realized the time had come to grab his rifle and bayonet, but didn't want to let the machine gun go. He could kill more Japs with the machine gun than with his rifle and bayonet.

He heard Lieutenant Breckenridge's voice: *"Pull back! Get the hell out of here!"*

McGurk let go the belt of ammunition and it danced around wildly in the air. He picked up his rifle and bayonet and prepared to follow Lieutenant Breckenridge's orders, when he noticed Shilansky still firing the machine gun, as if he hadn't heard the orders. McGurk glanced at the Japanese soldiers, who now were so close he could see the whites of their eyes. Then he looked at Shilansky. "Let's go!" McGurk said.

Shilansky continued to fire the machine gun in measured bursts of six, the corners of his mouth still turned down, his eyes gleaming with hatred.

"Come on!" McGurk called out, glancing nervously at the approaching Japs.

Shilansky still wouldn't get up. He continued to fire the machine gun, and Japs spun around in front of him, blood spouting from holes in their bodies.

McGurk did the first thing that came to his mind. He didn't want to leave Shilansky behind to get killed, so he grabbed him by the back of his collar and yanked him off his ass.

"Hey!" shouted Shilansky.

McGurk jumped out of the hole, dragging Shilansky behind him. Shilansky lost his grip on the machine gun, and found himself dangling in the air behind McGurk, who retreated at top speed through the jungle, holding his rifle and bayonet with one hand, pulling Shilansky along with his left hand.

"Lemme go!" screamed Shilansky.

But McGurk wouldn't let go. He'd received orders to retreat and couldn't leave Shilansky behind to certain death.

"I said lemme go!"

Shilansky was facing backwards, looking at Japanese soldiers running through the jungle, jumping over empty American foxholes, dodging around trees and bushes. They reminded Shilansky of an army of ants, overwhelming everything in their paths. Then Shilansky noticed one of them raise his rifle and bayonet to his shoulder. This Japanese soldier stopped and appeared to be *taking aim at Shilansky and McGurk!*

"Watch out!" hollered Shilansky.

McGurk didn't pay any attention. McGurk believed the only thing to do was move out as quickly as possible, and not worry about anything else. Shilansky's eyes bulged in horror as he saw the Japanese soldier aiming directly at him. He held out his hands, hoping somehow they'd miraculously stop the bullet.

The Japanese soldier squeezed his trigger, when another Japanese soldier, not noticing him, ran in front of him. The first Japanese soldier eased off his trigger a split second before he would've drilled his comrade. When his vision was clear again, the two American soldiers were gone.

Pfc. Nick Bombasino sat behind the wheel of the jeep, and his accelerator was jammed to the floor. The jeep took a corner on two wheels, sped down a dirt road straightaway, and took the next corner on a wheel and a half.

Seated next to Pfc. Bombasino was Colonel Hutchins, and in the back seat was Major Cobb and Lieutenant Harper. They were on their way to the front lines, because Colonel Hutchins wanted to direct the retreat personally.

Colonel Hutchins had received the bad news over his radio, and wasn't surprised by anything that'd happened. He held on to his helmet with his right hand as the jeep hit a bump and flew into the air. The jeep landed with a sickening crunch, bounced again, and kept going. Colonel Hutchins's submachine gun was cradled in his lap, and his lapels were festooned with hand grenades. Hand grenades were stuffed into his pockets and bandoliers of .45-caliber ammunition hung from his neck. In the distance, above the roar of the jeep's engine, Colonel Hutchins heard shells exploding, automatic weapons firing, and individual gunshots.

Colonel Hutchins was angry, and chewed the butt of the cigarette in his mouth. Everything was happening just the way he'd said it would, and if General Hall had listened to him the Japs would've been stopped cold at the Driniumor. Instead the Japs were advancing steadily into the American side of the river, and Colonel Hutchins couldn't predict where the lines finally would settle down.

Pfc. Bombasino had to lift his foot off the accelerator, because a truck with a white cross painted on the side was coming from the direction of the front, carrying wounded soldiers. Colonel Hutchins looked at the truck and narrowed his eyes. *Fucking bastards,* he thought. *Nobody ever listens to me.*

General Hawkins's command post tent was being dismantled. Soldiers carried typewriters and file cabinets to jeeps and trucks, and General Hawkins took one final look at his map table, to fix in his mind the last known positions of all his units.

"Can I take this now, sir?" asked one of the division clerks.

"Go ahead," said General Hawkins.

The clerk gathered up the maps on the table. Another clerk tipped the table over and folded in the legs. General Hawkins walked out of his tent and made his way toward his emergency bunker. The Japs were getting too close for him to remain in his tent.

General Hawkins walked through the jungle, looking down at the ground, tasting the bitter gall of defeat. General Hawkins didn't like to lose battles, but the battle wasn't completely lost yet. His division was pulling back everywhere and he intended to make a last stand right where he was. He hoped the 114th RCT showed up in time to save him and his men.

If the 114th RCT didn't show up, the Eighty-first would have to retreat again, if that was possible. If it wasn't possible, General Hawkins knew he might die with his men in the very jungle he was walking through then, on that very day.

Butsko stood in a clearing amid the tents of the Eighty-first Division Medical Headquarters, a walkie-talkie pressed against his face, the aerial high in the air.

He was trying to make contact with the front, to find out what was going on. So far he'd been unable to raise the recon platoon, the Twenty-third Regiment's Headquarters Company, or Colonel Hutchins. Now, however, he'd just got through to Captain Philip Mason, commander of George Company.

"What the hell's going on up there!" Butsko shouted into the mouthpiece of the walkie-talkie.

"The shit has hit the fan!" Captain Mason replied. "The Japs keep coming and we can't stop them!"

"Where are you now!"

"About a thousand yards west of the river. We're dug in and we're gonna try to stop 'em here."

"Have you seen the recon platoon?"

"No."

"Have you seen Colonel Hutchins?"

"I can't talk any longer. Over and out."

The connection went dead in Butsko's ear. Butsko looked up and saw orderlies unloading wounded soldiers from a truck. Some of the soldiers were missing arms and legs. Others were covered with blood. Some looked like they were dead already.

Butsko hopped over wounded men lying on the ground and entered the surgical tent. He stepped over more wounded men and pushed aside the tent flap.

Doctors and nurses were operating in earnest. Wounded men lay on the tables, being cut open or sewed up. Butsko spotted Captain Epstein sawing off the shattered leg of a wounded soldier. Captain Epstein wore a bloody white gown, hat, and surgical mask. Assisting him were Lieutenants Frannie Divers, Betty Crawford, and Agnes Shankar.

"Sir," said Butsko, "I've just talked to a friend of mine at the front, and he says it might collapse at any moment. I think I'd better start organizing a defense around here, because we can't evacuate all these wounded, can we?"

Captain Epstein continued to saw off the wounded man's leg. Captain Epstein's forehead was covered with sweat and flecks of blood. The operating area smelled of fresh blood, like a butcher shop.

"No, we can't evacuate," Captain Epstein said. "We're staying right where we are."

"Then I'll have to organize a defense."

"Do whatever you want. Just don't bother me."

"I just want to be sure I've got your authorization to do whatever has to be done."

"You got it," Captain Epstein said. "I thought I put you in charge of the defense force yesterday. Leave me the fuck alone."

"Yes sir."

Butsko turned around and limped out of the tent. He stepped into the clearing outside, stopped, placed his fists on his hips, and looked around at the orderlies and wounded soldiers. Butsko could hear the sounds of a mighty battle in the distance. Some of the wounded were unconscious, others seriously crippled, but some could fight, and so could the orderlies and nurses.

Butsko opened his mouth and hollered, *"The Japs are headed this way! If anybody wants a rifle, follow me! Let's get a move on, because we don't have much time!"*

Butsko turned and headed toward Captain Epstein's tent, where the rifles were stacked in crates. Following him were orderlies, nurses, and the walking wounded like himself.

FIFTEEN . . .

Bannon ran through the jungle in a zigzag line, keeping his head low. He heard Japs hollaring behind him, and Frankie La Barbara was at his side, cursing and snarling.

"Sons of bitches!" Frankie said. "Dirty bastards! Cuntlappers! Shitheads!"

They crashed through bushes and jumped over fallen trees. Bullets whistled over their heads and slammed into the trunks of trees still standing. Frankie tripped on a rock and fell into a shell crater, managing to throw out his arms a split second before his neck would've been broken. Cursing more viciously than ever, Frankie bounded out of the crater and resumed his headlong dash to safety.

He and Bannon were tired. They gulped air down their parched throats and their uniforms were plastered to their bodies with sweat. Other members of the recon platoon were to their right and left, also hurtling through the jungle, trying to save their skins. Never had they been thrown for a loss like this, not even on Bougainville or Guadalcanal, and they wondered where it would end.

Behind them, Japanese soldiers thought they'd won the war. They had the Americans in full rout, but some of the Japanese soldiers dropped back to open the packs of dead American soldiers and eat their food. Other Japanese soldiers ransacked tents and bunkers, taking food and ammunition. Their officers and sergeants tried to stop them, to no avail, and some officers and sergeants participated in the looting too.

But the main body of Japanese soldiers pursued the Americans, hoping to catch up with them and cut them to shit. These Japanese soldiers were aware of the main objective of the attack—the Tadji airfields—and knew they had to capture them before total victory would be theirs.

Bannon dodged around a tree and saw a system of foxholes and dugouts up ahead. His heart jumped for joy and he redoubled his speed, because he could take shelter. Dashing forward, a smile on his face, he saw the GI helmets inside the foxholes. A Japanese bullet whizzed over his left shoulder and he jumped into the air, raising his arms and falling into a trench.

He landed next to Private George Samaltanos from Toledo, Ohio, a husky swarthy man who took aim through the sights of his M 1 rifle.

"What outfit is this?" Bannon asked.

"J Company," replied Private Samaltanos.

Bannon knew J Company was in the Third Battalion, which was the regiment's reserve. It shocked Bannon to realize that Colonel Hutchins was using his reserves, because after the reserves there was nothing left except cooks, bakers, and truck drivers.

Bannon turned around, rested his rifle on the edge of the trench, took aim, and fired. *Blam!* A Japanese soldier's legs collapsed underneath him as he fell down. Private Samaltanos squeezed his trigger, and *Blam!*—a Japanese soldier was hit in the head by the bullet. The Japanese soldier's legs stopped moving and he tumbled asshole over teakettle onto the ground.

Machine guns rattled and their bullets chopped down entire ranks of Japanese soldiers. The soldiers from J Company fired BARs, M 1 rifles, and carbines as quickly as they could, as the soldiers from the recon platoon and Headquarters Company took shelter in the area fortifications.

Lieutenant Breckenridge vaulted into a trench and Private Worthington landed beside him.

"How're you doing?" Lieutenant Brecknenridge asked Worthington.

Worthington's face was beet red and covered with sweat and grime. "It's horrible," he said.

"Cheer up," Lieutenant Breckenridge replied. "Things'll be a lot worse in a little while."

Lieutenant Breckenridge turned around and looked at a soldier aiming an M 1 rifle.

"Who's in charge here?" Lieutenant Breckenridge asked.

"Captain Stanford."

"Where's he at?"

The GI squeezed the trigger of his M 1 rifle. *Blam!* The Japanese soldier he'd been aiming at fell on his face. Then the GI pointed to his right.

"That way," he said.

"Come with me," Lieutenant Breckenridge said to Private Worthington.

Lieutenant Breckenridge lowered his head and walked in the direction the GI had indicated, passing other GIs firing at the advancing howling mass of Japanese soldiers. The intense fire from J Company slowed the Japs down. The Japanese attack appeared to be faltering, but their officers and sergeants urged the men on. The Japanese soldiers surged forward again, and Americans bullets ripped into them, but the Japs kept coming. It looked as though they were going to make it all the way to the trench.

Lieutenant Breckenridge decided to see Captain Stanford some other time. He pulled a grenade off his lapel, yanked out the pin, and hurled it at the wave of attacking Japanese soldiers.

Barrroooommmmm! The grenade exploded with a mighty roar, blowing Japanese soldiers into the air. Lieutenant Breckenridge pulled another grenade from his lapel and threw that one too. *Barrrooooommmmm!* More Japanese soldiers were blasted to smithereens. Private Worthington positioned his M 1 rifle on the edge of the trench, took aim, and fired the rifle as fast as he could. The front wave of Japanese soldiers was thirty yards away, twenty-five yards away, and then twenty yards away. The GIs in the foxholes and trenches fired their weapons nonstop. Some threw hand grenades. A few barbecued Japs with flame throwers, but still the Japs kept coming.

"Hold them!" shouted a deep booming voice that everyone recognized as the voice of Colonel Hutchins. *"Don't let them pass!"*

Colonel Hutchins had just jumped out of his jeep and was running with his submachine gun in his hands toward the trench.

"Nobody retreats until I say so!" Colonel Hutchins hollered. *"Kill them fucking Japs!"*

Colonel Hutchins leapt into the trench and landed beside the Reverend Billie Jones, who was perched behind his BAR firing 600 rounds per minute in its full automatic mode. Colonel Hutchins raised his submachine gun and opened fire, spraying lead at the front rank of Japanese soldiers who now were only twenty yards away.

"Keep firing!" yelled Colonel Hutchins. *"Stop the bastards!"*

The GIs' morale went up when they realized their regimental
commander was fighting alongside them. They'd been fighting
hard, but now fought harder. They pulled their triggers faster,
and threw even more hand grenades. Machine gunners didn't
fire in bursts of six—they fired nonstop. GIs with flame throwers burned huge numbers of Japs into crispy black hunks of
charred meat.

The Japanese front wave came to within fifteen yards of the
GI fortifications, and their assault came to a halt. Heaps of
dead Japanese soldiers were piled everywhere, and attacking
Japanese soldiers couldn't get over them. The ones who tried
got shot. GIs hurled grenades at the Japanese soldiers, blasting
arms and heads off their bodies.

The Japanese soldiers couldn't advance and didn't dare stay
where they were. They were in deep bad trouble and the only
place to go was backwards. Their officers realized they had to
retreat a short distance, regroup, and try again.

"Retreat!" they shouted. *"Move back!"*

Japanese soldiers still alive turned around and ran into the
jungle from whence they'd come, dropping down to their bellies, gasping for breath, wondering what had gone wrong.
Officers and sergeants ran among them calling them cowards
and saying they'd let the Emperor down, but they could redeem
themselves if they tried harder next time and took that American
trench system.

The Japanese soldiers loaded their rifles with fresh ammunition and checked to make sure their bayonets were affixed
properly to their rifles. Some bound their wounds with torn
strips of their shirts. The Americans had stopped them once
but they wouldn't do it again, especially now that more Japanese soldiers were advancing through the jungle to reinforce
them.

"This time you will capture that American position!" an
officer screamed, waving his samurai sword over his head.
"This time you will not fail!"

Colonel Hutchins leaned against the wall of the trench and
looked into the jungle through his binoculars. He couldn't see
many details in the smoke and confusion, and burnt Japanese

bodies stank disgustingly, but he could perceive Japanese reinforcements moving into the jungle ahead. Colonel Hutchins knew discretion was the better part of valor, and it was time to get the hell out of there.

He removed his binoculars from his eyes and turned around, pointing back toward the Eighty-first Division Headquarters. "All right everybody," he bellowed, "we're gonna retreat now! Pull out and move fast! Get the lead out! We don't have much time! The recon platoon will bring up the rear!"

That was the order the GIs were waiting to hear, except for the recon platoon.

Frankie La Barbara turned to Bannon. "Why do we get all the shitty jobs?" he asked.

Bannon didn't reply. He was tired, getting hungry, and didn't feel like dealing with Frankie La Barbara. Meanwhile the other GIs jumped out of their foxholes and trenches and ran west as fast as they could, heading toward the last-ditch defense line General Hawkins had set up.

Medics carried the wounded, those from heavy weapons platoons carried mortars and machine guns, and the recon platoon went last, firing behind them at the Japanese soldiers in the jungle, hoping to discourage them from attacking before everybody got away.

General Kimura walked up to General Adachi and saluted. "The American center has collapsed!" he said, triumph in his voice.

General Adachi was so happy he wanted to jump for joy, but that would have been beneath his dignity. He permitted himself only a faint smile, and looked down at the map. "Show me exactly what you're talking about."

General Kimura pointed at the map. "Initial reports indicate that the Americans are in a headlong rout from here to here. The flank attack you ordered broke the back of their defense. Our soldiers are pursuing them relentlessly."

General Adachi closed his eyes for a few moments, savoring the delicious taste of victory. Then he opened his eyes again and looked down at the map.

"How deep has our penetration been?"

General Kimura pointed at the map. "To here, according to last reports."

"Would you say they've advanced a thousand yards into the American position?"

"More than that, sir. I'd say two thousand yards at least."

General Adachi looked at the map. It was true: The American front line had been shattered, but the Tadji airfields still were a long way off, and the Americans had plenty of reserves to bring up. The battle wasn't won yet by any means, but the initial results were promising.

General Adachi turned to General Kimura. "Transmit this order to as many of the assault units as you can. Tell them I am pleased with their performance, and I expect them to pursue their attack with redoubled effort, because now victory is within our grasp. That is all."

"Yes sir." General Kimura dashed off to relay the message to one of his subordinates, who actually would transmit it.

General Adachi looked down at the map table again. *Can the momentum of this attack carry through all the way to airfields,* he wondered, *or will the American reserves stop it?*

He balled up his fists, resting them on the map table, and closed his eyes, praying to the Shinto gods for the victory he believed was in his grasp.

The Eighty-first Division bore the brunt of the attack, and its front line was torn apart. Troops throughout the division retreated from position to position, falling back toward the final defensive position set down by General Hawkins.

General Hawkins's headquarters was slightly in back of that position, as was the Eighty-first Division Medical Headquarters, the terminus for convoys of trucks delivering soldiers wounded at the front.

Doctors, nurses, and orderlies worked non-stop, removing bullets, sewing up holes, sawing off ruined limbs. Some wounded men were beyond hope and set aside, shot up with morphine so they wouldn't feel pain, left to die in peace.

Meanwhile Butsko built sandbag fortifications with a handful of orderlies and the walking wounded. The sandbags were laid down in a semicircle on the east side of the medical headquarters, and stood two to three feet high.

Butsko was stripped to the waist as he threw sandbag on top of sandbag, building up the fortifications. His helmet and Thompson submachine gun rested against a tree nearby in case he needed them in a hurry.

Butsko had no communications with the front, but knew the battle wasn't going well. He could hear the sounds of fighting coming closer, and believed Japs should be in the area in about an hour, maybe less. He wished his old recon platoon was with him, but he was stuck with a bunch of orderlies who had skinny arms and wore glasses, and the walking wounded, some of whom were so dazed on drugs they walked into each other.

"Hurry up!" he shouted. "Move your fucking asses! The Japs're gonna be here in no time at all!"

The recon platoon continued to retreat, bringing up the rear behind J Company. Lieutenant Breckenridge and his men stopped every ten yards or so, turned around, and fired a wild shot at the Japs behind them, to slow them.

Their bullets made the Japs advance more cautiously, but not too cautiously. They smelled victory and knew they were moving closer to the main American supply depots where all the good stuff was stored. They weren't as close as they thought, but charged like maniacs anyway, pursuing the Americans in front of them, stopping occasionally to take potshots at the Americans whenever they could get a clear view of them through the moonlit jungle.

Japanese bullets whistled around the heads of the men from the recon platoon, and whacked into the ground near their feet. They kept their heads low and sped through the jungle, stopping occasionally to fire a few quick shots at the Japs.

Victor Yabalonka thought for sure he was going to die at any moment, and couldn't understand why he wasn't dead already. He was scared, but not so scared he couldn't think straight. He knew sooner or later he and the others would have to stop and fight it out with the Japs. They couldn't keep running forever.

Yabalonka was between the Reverend Billie Jones and Private Joshua McGurk. Lieutenant Breckenridge was to his left, with Private Worthington. No one was seriously wounded yet, although they all had nicks and cuts. A bullet had grazed Shilansky's cheek and left a red burn mark.

Bullets flew around the men's heads like angry gnats. Ahead they could see the tail end of Company J, with medics carrying the wounded, and other soldiers hauling mortars and machine guns. Yabalonka heard Colonel Hutchins's voice.

"Keep moving!" Colonel Hutchins hollered. "We're almost there!"

Private Yabalonka stopped and turned around to fire a quick shot at the Japs. He raised his rifle to his shoulder, and *Pow!*— he felt as if a truck crashed into his chest.

The Japanese bullet pierced his shirt and spun him around. He fell to the ground stomach down and lay still.

The Reverend Billie Jones didn't see him fall, but thought something was wrong. Still running, he looked back over his shoulder and saw Private Yabalonka lying on the ground motionless. The Reverend Billie Jones stopped, turned around, and galloped back to the place where Yabalonka lay. Jones looked down at Yabalonka and didn't see any blood, but Yabalonka seemed dead as a doornail. Jones couldn't be sure of that, but didn't have time to take Yabalonka's pulse. Jones slung his rifle crossways over his back and bent over, lifting Yabalonka and throwing him over his shoulder. Yabalonka weighed 208 pounds, but the Reverend Billie Jones was a powerhouse. He turned around and ran behind the others, trying to catch up, but they were too far ahead of him. A bullet grazed the top of Billie Jones's helmet as he stretched out his legs and ran like a son of a bitch. "Oh Lord," he muttered, "if you can't help me now, just don't help them Japs!"

SIXTEEN . . .

General Hawkins's bunker was on the crest of a squat hill overlooking the jungle. It was in an area of hills, valleys, and flat ground, pockmarked and scarred with foxholes, trenches, and bunkers set up in a long winding series of lines across the territory the Eighty-first Division was supposed to defend.

The moon drifted across the sky and shone down on the jungle. No birds squawked and no wild dogs howled, because the artillery bombardments had scared them away. The Japanese artillery bombardment had ended nearly two hours ago, but American artillery units still blasted the attacking Japanese, raising their sights steadily to keep up with the advancing Japanese Army, but careful not to rain shells on retreating American soldiers.

Stars twinkled in the sky as General Hawkins stood at the narrow slitted window of his command post bunker, holding his binoculars to his eyes, gazing down at the jungle below. He saw GIs fleeing toward the defensive line he'd established. Random shots were fired as swarms of GIs streamed around trees and boulders, jumping over bushes or barreling through them, carrying their weapons, their wounded, crates of machine gun ammunition, some limping and some bleeding.

General Hawkins was angry at himself and angry at General Hall. He lowered his binoculars and stepped away from the window, looking at his staff officers standing around in the dim light inside the bunker.

"Cover the window and turn on the light," he said.

A black curtain was dropped over the window and a kerosene lamp lit over the map table. Lieutenant Utsler adjusted the wick and General Hawkins looked down at the map of the area. He took out a cigarette, poked it into his ivory cigarette holder, and lit it with his Zippo, inhaling, blowing smoke out his thin lips.

General Hawkins was angry at himself for not paying more attention to Colonel Hutchins, who'd been right about the attack all along. General Hawkins realized he hadn't listened to Colonel Hutchins because Colonel Hutchins was a drunkard and a buffoon, but Colonel Hutchins also was a seasoned old combat veteran, both as an enlisted man and a front-line commander, and in the future General Hawkins would give Colonel Hutchins's opinions more weight.

General Hawkins was angry at General Hall because General Hall hadn't taken seriously the intelligence information that the Japanese Eighteenth Army was going to attack on the morning of July 9. General Hall also hadn't taken General Hawkins seriously during that horrendous jeep ride when General Hawkins asked to be reinforced before July 9.

General Hawkins now was glad he'd taken precautions himself, because those precautions saved most of his division. He knew he'd taken those precautions only because Colonel Hutchins had driven him to it. *I've been such a fool*, General Hawkins thought. *I should've listened to that old drunken son of a bitch.*

General Hawkins's problems weren't over yet by any means. He'd saved most of his division, but the battle wasn't finished. It had barely started. Immense numbers of Japanese soldiers, perhaps two divisions, were pursuing what was left of his division, which had been at half strength when the battle began.

His division fell back toward its final defensive position. It would stand fast and fight it out with the Japanese Eighteenth Army there, and General Hawkins hoped the 114th RCT would arrive in time to save his men. If the 114th RCT didn't arrive soon, his men would be in serious trouble, and General Hawkins might not be able to save them by ordering another retreat. Troops were most vulnerable when retreating, especially now that the Japanese Eighteenth Army was hot on their heels. Those Japs were desperate and they'd show no mercy. General Hawkins was worried about his men. He may have been an ambitious career officer, but his men still came first. "Colonel Jessup!" he shouted.

"Yes sir!"

"Get General Hall for me on the phone."

"Yes sir!"

Colonel Jessup talked to the soldier sitting at the telephone switchboard, and General Hawkins looked down at the map. If the Japs broke through the Eighty-first Division, it would be the end of the Eighty-first Division, but that wasn't the main problem. The main problem was the Japs would have nothing between them and the Tadji airfields except some rear-echelon personnel and the 114th RCT coming up on the line. The 114th RCT wouldn't be much without the Eighty-first Division, and the Eighty-first Division couldn't hold off the Japs alone. Together they might be able to do the job.

Can I retreat back to where the Hundred Fourteenth is? General Hawkins asked himself. *Or am I stuck here?*

General Hawkins puffed the cigarette in his ivory holder and looked down at the map, wondering if there was a way out of the mess he was in.

"Sir," said Colonel Jessup, "Colonel MacKenzie is on the phone."

"I wanted General Hall."

"Colonel MacKenzie says he's not available."

"Give me that phone," General Hawkins muttered. He crossed the room in long strides and plucked the receiver out of Colonel Jessup's hand. "This is General Hawkins!" he said in a loud angry voice. "I want to speak with General Hall immediately!"

"He's not here right now, sir," said Colonel MacKenzie on the other end.

"Where's the Hundred Fourteenth RCT?" General Hawkins asked.

"On the way, sir."

"They've been on the way for the past hour! When are they going to get here!"

"Soon."

"How soon!"

"I can't tell you that exactly, sir."

General Hawkins heard a burst of machine gunfire, and then a volley of rifles went off. "The Japs are here," General Hawkins said calmly into the mouthpiece of the phone. "Can you hear them?"

"No sir."

"Well they're here, and I don't know how long we can hold on. Tell that to General Hall when you see him. Over and out."

"Wait a minute!" Colonel MacKenzie said. "Are you still there?"

"I'm still here," replied General Hawkins.

179

"Do you have any idea of how many Japs are attacking you?"

"I'd say that the whole Eighteenth Army is attacking me, and we're outnumbered about four to one."

"Are you sure the odds are that great?" Colonel MacKenzie asked.

"That is my professional rough estimate. If you think you can do better, come up here and have a look for yourself. Do you have any other questions?"

"No sir."

"Over and out."

Colonel MacKenzie hung up the phone and looked at General Hall at the map table, surrounded by staff officers and aides. Colonel MacKenzie was irritated by General Hawkins's manner, and pinched his lips together in repressed anger. Colonel MacKenzie thought General Hawkins was too ambitious for his own good, although Colonel MacKenzie was just as ambitious himself.

He walked to the map table and tried to get General Hall's attention while General Hall was conferring with Lieutenant Colonel Beane, one of his operations officers. General Hall glanced over Colonel Beane's shoulder and saw Colonel MacKenzie.

"You have something for me, Mac?" General Hall asked.

"I was just speaking with General Hawkins, sir. He said his headquarters is under attack, and inquired about when the Hundred Fourteenth RCT would arrive."

"What did you tell him?"

"I told him they'd arrive in about an hour."

"Did he say whether he could last that long?"

"He expressed his doubts about that matter, sir."

"Did he give any indication about the number of enemy who were attacking him?"

"He said he thought he was outnumbered about four to one, and that means approximately two full Japanese divisions."

"Except the Japs don't have full divisions anymore," General Hall said.

"If I may say so, sir—I think General Hawkins might be exaggerating."

General Hall realized he had to make an important decision.

180

If General Hawkins was facing as many Japs as he said, he'd need more help than the 114th RCT could provide. On the other hand, if General Hawkins was exaggerating, and General Hall provided more help, it might siphon troops from a sector where they might be needed more.

It all boiled down to one consideration: What kind of man was General Hawkins? Would he exaggerate, or was his estimate reasonably accurate? General Hawkins wasn't an easy man to like, because he was so obviously vain. He didn't appear to be particularly intelligent either, but maybe he was, who could say?

General Hall looked down at his map. He decided he'd better not take any chances second-guessing a general in the field. He'd send more help to the Eighty-first Division. Better too much than not enough, and if the help wasn't needed, he'd send it somewhere else where it was needed, and relieve General Hawkins of command.

"General Sully," he said, "where is the Eight Hundred Forty-fifth RCT?"

General Sully pointed to the map. "Here sir."

"They're the closest reserve regiment to the Eighty-first Division, aren't they?"

"No sir—the Hundred Fourteenth is."

"I mean except for the Hundred Fourteenth."

"Then the Eight Hundred Forty-fifth would be the closest, sir."

"Notify their commander to move out immediately and reinforce the Eighty-first Division."

General Sully moved toward the telephones. General Hall looked down at his map. The center of his line had to hold at all costs, otherwise the airfields would be in danger. He'd have to gamble to save the Tadji airfields, but if General Hawkins had exaggerated the strength of the enemy, he'd be in a whole world of trouble. General Hall wouldn't rest until General Hawkins was sitting in an office in the cellar of the Pentagon, pushing pencils around for the rest of his life.

Private Joshua McGurk's chest heaved as he sucked air through his flared nostrils and ran in huge leaping strides toward the trench ahead. He was so gigantic his rifle looked like a toy in his hands, and he vaulted into the air, kicking his feet, screaming at the top of his lungs, finally landing with a crash in the trench.

McGurk turned around and faced the enemy. He was all wound up and strung out. A bullet was lodged in his left shoulder blade, and blood drenched the back of his shirt, but he was so big and strong it barely affected him.

He saw the other members of the recon platoon coming fast, heading toward the trenches and foxholes where they'd make their last stand with the rest of the Eighty-first Division. Lieutenant Breckenridge held his helmet on his head with one hand, and carried his carbine in his other hand. Private Worthington jogged behind him, lugging his M 1 rifle and the platoon's walkie-talkie. Bannon jumped into a foxhole to McGurk's right. Bisbee dived into a shell crater on McGurk's left.

McGurk thought everybody was safe, and then saw the Reverend Billie Jones emerge from the jungle, carrying Private Victor Yabalonka over his left shoulder. Japanese soldiers were in hot pursuit only twenty or thirty yards behind Jones and Yabalonka.

Every GI in the area saw what was happening and trained their guns on the Japanese soldiers, sending out a withering hail of bullets, and the Japanese soldiers staggered and fell, but more kept coming; they always kept coming.

The Reverend Billie Jones had just about had the green weenie. He'd run a half mile with Victor Yabalonka on his back, and Victor Yabalonka was no lightweight. Billie Jones's knees were creaking and his tongue hung out of his mouth but he kept going, while the Japs kept coming. They were gaining on him but then another volley of fire erupted from the American trenches and Billie Jones was free and clear.

He half-ran and half-staggered toward the American lines. A Japanese soldier behind him dropped to one knee, raised his rifle to his shoulder, and lined up his sights.

Blam! The Japanese soldier was knocked over onto his ass as if a mule had kicked him in the face. He'd been struck on the nose by a bullet from the M 1 rifle fired by Private Worthington, the sharpshooter. Billie Jones ran the final yards and leapt into the air. He landed in the bottom of a machine gun nest, and Victor Yabalonka landed on top of him, knocking the wind out of his body.

The men in the machine gun nest were from the Twelfth

Regiment of the Eighty-first Division, and they'd never seen Jones or Yabalonka before. Neither Jones nor Yabalonka moved. Their eyes were closed. They didn't appear to be breathing.

"Are they alive?" asked Staff Sergeant Petros, who was in charge of the machine gun section.

"I don't know," said one of his men.

"Here they come!" somebody shouted.

The men in the hole looked up and saw waves of Japanese soldiers charging toward them through the jungle. Sergeant Petros sat behind the machine gun and pressed the thumb triggers. The machine gun barked and sparks shot out of its barrel along with bullets and smoke that billowed up into the night air.

The Japanese soldiers looked like specters of the night as they ripped through the jungle, hollering and screaming, moonlight glinting on their sharpened bayonets. They were forty yards away, thirty-five yards away, and then thirty yards away.

GIs shoulder to shoulder in the trenches fired rifles and machine guns as quickly as they could pull the triggers. Machine gunners tried to maintain fire discipline and shoot bursts of six, but the Japs were too close and they couldn't do it. They'd worry about machine gun barrels melting down later. They had to stop the Japs first, so they held the triggers down and sprayed the Japanese soldiers with hot lead.

The sound of a machine gun firing next to him woke the Reverend Billie Jones up. He raised his head, looked over the sandbags, and saw Japanese soldiers only twenty yards away. Sergeant Petros held the thumb triggers of the machine gun down, gritting his teeth, and then a Japanese bullet hit him on the forehead, splitting his head apart, spraying everyone in the trench with blood and brains.

The force of the bullet sent Sergeant Petros flying back against the rear wall of the machine gun nest. The other soldiers in the nest were stunned for a moment, then Billie Jones lurched toward the machine gun, sat behind it, worked the bolt, and pressed the trigger down.

Japanese soldiers were only ten yards away, and Billie Jones shot them to bits with the machine gun, swinging it from side to side, and Japs fell on Japs, blood spurting from holes in their bodies. One of the GIs in the nest threw a hand grenade over the pile of bodies, and it exploded with a deafening blast, blowing up Japanese soldiers on the other side of the pile, and Billie saw them flying into the air minus arms, legs, and heads, silhouetted by the orange blast.

GIs sweat and cursed all along the Eighty-first Division line, firing their weapons as quickly as possible at the charging Japanese army. They threw hand grenades and squirted fire from their flame throwers, but still the Japanese Eighteenth Army maintained its forward momentum. Japanese soldiers jumped over their dead and wounded comrades and charged onward, their officers and sergeants screaming at them against a chorus of American rifle- and machine-gunfire, and the endless percussion of hand grenades. American artillery shells exploded behind the Japanese main advance, so the Japanese soldiers couldn't go back. They had to move forward and take the trenches and foxholes directly in front of them.

One of the Japanese soldiers fired a wild shot from the hip, and it whacked the soldier standing beside Private Joshua McGurk from Skunk Hollow, Maine. The bullet hit the soldier in the mouth and blew out the back of his head, and he slumped down into the bottom of the trench, balled up like an infant sleeping.

McGurk looked down at him. He'd barely noticed the soldier before, but he'd been a young man, probably still in his teens, a boy really, and now that McGurk thought of it, the soldier reminded him somewhat of the younger brother of a friend of his.

McGurk wasn't a sophisticated thinker. He didn't know much about what the Second World War was about. All he knew was that a young American had been killed, and it pissed him off.

McGurk looked over the edge of the trench at the charging Japs. They were fifteen yards away, ten yards away, and then five yards away. In another second or two they'd be inside the trench, and McGurk didn't think he'd have enough fighting room in there. He glanced at the young soldier lying in the bottom of the hole, blood pouring out the cavern in the back of his neck, and then raised himself up, leaping out of the trench in one mighty stride.

He stood on the edge of the trench, and now had the fighting room he needed. He snorted through both nostrils like a wild bull and glowered at the Japanese soldiers rushing toward him, murder and destruction in their eyes. He heard rifle fire and grenade explosions all around him, and was aware other GIs were climbing out of their holes too. He raised both his hands high in the air, his rifle and bayonet in his right fist, and screamed, *"Come on! Here I am!"*

Lowering his rifle, he aimed the tip of his bayonet at the Japanese soldiers and charged. The wall of Japanese soldiers rushed toward him and he smashed into it, swinging his rifle and bayonet wildly, stabbing Japanese soldiers, bashing them in their heads, kicking them in the balls. Japanese bayonets nicked his arms, legs, chest, and back, and spit dribbled out of his lips as he lunged and plunged into the Japanese Eighteenth Army. A Japanese rifle butt came out of nowhere and hit him on the head, dazing him momentarily and knocking his helmet off, but it didn't stop him. He was a giant of a man in the full vigor of his youth, and nothing could stop him except a bullet through his heart.

The Japanese soldiers weren't firing bullets. They were too close-packed for that and might hit their own people. Most of them didn't even see Private McGurk, and those who saw him didn't see him for long because he killed every Japanese soldier in his path.

McGurk lunged forward and thrust the bayonet on the end of his M 1 rifle into the chest of a Japanese soldier who tried to kill him first, but McGurk was faster, stronger, and his arms longer. He pulled down on his rifle and bayonet, disengaging from the chest of the Japanese soldier, then swung his rifle butt around and mashed another Japanese soldier in the face. The Japanese soldier went down for the count, and McGurk parried the thrust from a Japanese rifle and bayonet to the side, kicking that Japanese soldier in the balls, the force of the blow raising the Japanese soldier a foot into the air. The Japanese soldier cried out in pain and his eyes rolled up into his head as he grasped his ruptured testicles and dropped to his knees on the ground.

McGurk kicked him to the side and pushed forward, but a swarm of hungry Japanese soldiers was in front of him, row after row of them, and they pushed him back. He retreated, slamming Japs in the head with his rifle butt, stabbing them with his bayonet, kicking their stomachs, and still they continued to cut him up with their bayonets until he was a bloody torn mess.

Some boxers fight harder when they're hurt, and big Private McGurk was that way. Roaring like a lion, he pushed his left foot behind him for leverage and launched himself forward again, punching his rifle and bayonet into the stomach of a Japanese soldier, pulling it out and shoving it forward again, this time into the chest of another Japanese soldier, dislodging it with a mighty pull and ramming it into the chest of the third Japanese soldier.

Japanese soldiers and GIs were locked in close combat on both sides of McGurk. They pushed and heaved, swore and grunted, trying to kill each other by any means possible.

One short Japanese soldier snuck up behind McGurk to stab him in the back, when *Wham!*—the butt of an American rifle struck the Japanese soldier on the back of his head, splitting it wide open, and the Japanese soldier tumbled to the ground.

Pfc. Morris Shilansky was holding the rifle, and he stepped to the side of Private McGurk, a hurricane of mayhem swirling all around them. Shilansky was covered with blood, most of it Japanese. *"You Bastards!"* he screamed at them. *"You fucking pigs!"*

A Japanese officer ran toward Shilansky, aiming his Nambu pistol at him, pulling the trigger. Shilansky saw him coming through the smoke and moonlight, and reflexively raised his rifle to protect himself.

Blam! The pistol fired and the bullet hit the stock of Shilansky's rifle, splintering it. The officer's momentum carried him forward and Shilansky dived for the Nambu pistol. Both men crashed against each other, lost their footing, and fell to the ground. Japanese soldiers and American soldiers stepped on them and didn't even bother looking down to see who was there, so intent were they on murdering each other.

Shilansky and the Japanese officer rolled around on the ground, trying to get leverage against each other, each hoping to gain possession of the Nambu pistol. The Japanese officer elbowed Shilansky in the eye and Shilansky punched the Japanese officer in the mouth, splitting his lip open, blood gushing out. The Japanese officer tried to knee Shilansky in the balls, but Shilansky twisted to the side and avoided the blow.

Shilansky saw something land on the ground nearby. It was

186

McGurk's helmet, kicked in his direction unwittingly by a Japanese soldier, and the helmet rolled within Shilansky's reach. Holding the Japanese officer's wrist with one hand, Shilansky picked up the helmet with his free hand and bopped the Japanese officer on the head with it.

The Japanese officer stopped struggling. He was out cold. Looking down at him, Shilansky wanted to bop him again, to pay him back for the slaughter of the Jews in Europe, but didn't have time to settle that score just then. He yanked the pistol out of the Japanese officer's hands and jumped to his feet.

Japanese and American soldiers stabbed and elbowed each other everywhere he looked. They rammed bayonets into each other's chests and banged each other on the heads with their rifle butts. Japanese officers with swords decapitated American soldiers, and American officers with pistols and carbines shot down Japanese soldiers.

It was a snarled bloody melee. General Hawkins looked down at it from the window of his bunker, and it appeared as though the line was holding, but just barely. *Where's the Hundred Fourteenth RCT?* he wondered. *If they don't get here soon— I don't know what will happen.*

General Hawkins wanted to leave his bunker and join the fight, but he couldn't do that. He had to stay at the nerve center of his division and furnish leadership, although there wasn't a hell of a lot he could do except be a cheerleader at long distance. All his reserves were in the trenches below. Even his truck drivers and cooks were down there. There was nothing else he could do now except watch.

General Hawkins lowered his binoculars and wiped his mouth with the back of his hand. *Where in the hell is the Hundred Fourteenth?* he asked himself. *My men can't hold out much longer.*

Private Victor Yabalonka opened his eyes and looked around. He felt disoriented and didn't know where he was. His chest hurt terribly; he touched his hand to it. He lay on his back next to a machine gun, hearing rifle shots and the clash of bayonet against bayonet.

He wondered if he was dreaming. Glancing around, he realized he wasn't alone. Next to him a soldier was sleeping, but then he realized the soldier wasn't sleeping at all. He was too motionless to be sleeping. He was dead.

Yabalonka felt weird, as if he was losing his mind. *What the hell's going on here?* he wondered. He squinted his eyes and tried to figure out what had happened to him. His chest felt as though somebody had kicked it, and then suddenly he remembered everything.

He'd been retreating with his buddies when he'd stopped to fire his rifle, and then he got hit. Sitting up, he touched the palm of his right hand to his chest and that's where it hurt. Something hard was in there. It was the handy pocket Bible the Reverend Billie Jones had given him. He reached into the pocket and pulled it out, holding it up to the moonlight.

The front of the Bible was smashed in. He touched his finger to the center of the cover, and felt a chunk of lead. "Holy shit," he mumbled. "It's a bullet."

He realized with a jolt of astonishment that the Bible had stopped the bullet! The Bible had saved his life! Yabalonka, the ardent atheist and former Communist sympathizer, had been saved by a Bible!

Yabalonka was dumbfounded. It was so weird. He wasn't a superstitious person and tried to tell himself it was just a coincidence that the Bible was in the right place at the right time, but then he opened the Bible to the page where the Japanese bullet finally stopped, and his eyes fell on Jeremiah, 32:27:

> *Behold, I am the Lord, the God of all flesh:*
> *is there any thing too hard for me?*

Yabalonka's jaw dropped open. His heart thundered in his chest. *What the hell's going on here?* he wondered. He felt eerie and light-headed. Then he heard running footsteps coming closer. He looked up from his handy pocket Bible and saw a Japanese officer running toward him out of the bright moonlight.

"Banzai!" the officer screamed, holding his samurai sword high over his head.

Yabalonka realized the officer was headed straight for him with the intention of chopping off his head. Yabalonka dropped the handy pocket Bible that had just saved his life, and bounded to his feet. He jumped out of the foxhole and dived toward the

Japanese officer just as the Japanese officer began his down-swing.

Yabalonka's big strong longshoreman's hands closed around the slim wrist of the Japanese officer, and Yabalonka yanked to the side, causing the Japanese officer to lose his balance. The Japanese officer fell to the ground, and Yabalonka landed on top of him, jabbing his elbow into the Japanese officer's eye. Yabalonka slammed his forearm against the Japanese officer's head, stunning the Japanese officer mildly, but the Japanese officer struggled to get out from underneath Yabalonka, so he could swing at him again with his samurai sword.

Yabalonka took aim and punched the Japanese officer in the mouth, and that did it. The Japanese officer was stunned, and Yabalonka grabbed the samurai sword, jumping to his feet. Raising the sword over his head, he swung the blade down at the dazed officer, cracking his head open, blood and brains spattering in all directions.

Yabalonka spun around. Three Japanese soldiers charged him, aiming their rifles and bayonets at his chest. Their commanding officer had just been killed by Yabalonka, and they wanted revenge. Yabalonka dodged to his right and swung sideways with the sword, chopping off the head of one Japanese soldier. The others danced around on their toes, trying to get into position for straight bayonet thrusts, and Yabalonka swung from the side again, striking one Japanese soldier on his left biceps muscle, busting through the bone, and the Japanese soldier's arm fell to the ground. The Japanese soldier suffered instant shock and his eyes closed as he dropped on top of his arm.

The third Japanese soldier thrust his rifle and bayonet toward Yabalonka's chest, and Yabalonka jumped backwards, swinging down with the samurai sword, connecting with the top of the rifle, driving it toward the ground, then backswinging quickly, slicing off the Japanese soldier's head. The head flew into the air, and Yabalonka paused to catch his breath.

He looked around and saw GIs and Japanese soldiers fighting hand to hand all around him. The Japanese soldiers obviously outnumbered GIs, but the GIs fought back gallantly in a mad frenzy, trying to save their skins, but every GI knew he could go at any moment.

Yabalonka knew the same thing. He also knew he could

turn tail and run away, but Yabalonka was an American soldier and wouldn't retreat unless ordered to do so.

The only thing to do was fight, and the best form of defense was offense. Yabalonka raised the bloody gory samurai sword over his head and charged into the midst of the melee. Swinging the sword down, he slammed it between the shoulder and neck of a Japanese soldier, busting the Japanese soldier's collarbone and several of his ribs. Pulling the sword loose, Yabalonka grit his teeth and swung sideways, chopping off the head of a Japanese soldier. On the backswing he lopped off the arm of another Japanese soldier. Swinging low, he took off the leg of the next Japanese soldier. He charged into Japanese soldiers, wielding the heavy samurai sword as if it were made of balsa wood, chopping, slicing, severing limbs from bodies, cutting a wide swath through the middle of the battlefield, leaving a trail of mutilated Japanese soldiers behind him.

In the Eighty-first Division command post bunker on top of the hill, General Hawkins had just made a telephone connection with the headquarters of the Persecution Task Force, and found himself speaking with Colonel MacKenzie.

"I demand the right to speak with General Hall!" General Hawkins said.

"He can't come to the phone right now," Colonel MacKenzie replied calmly. "Can I take a message?"

General Hawkins was so angry he thought the top of his head would blow off. "Tell him if the Hundred Fourteenth doesn't get here within the next ten minutes, the Japs will break through! That means all you people back there near the airfields had better arm youselves and prepare for the worst!"

"Hang on a moment," Colonel MacKenzie replied.

General Hawkins stood next to his telephone switchboard, hearing shots and shouts outside the bunker. He also could hear an artillery bombardment in the distance, as American cannons plastered Japanese staging areas, trying to prevent more Japanese soldiers from reinforcing their front line.

General Hall's voice came over the wire. "What's the problem, Hawkins?" he asked in no-nonsense clipped words.

"We can't hold the Japs off much longer," General Hawkins replied. "If the Hundred Fourteenth doesn't arrive soon, and I mean *soon,* we'll be wiped out and you'd better start running for the hills."

"Don't tell me you'll be wiped out!" General Hall said with a hard edge to his voice. "You'd better not get wiped out! You'd better contain those Japs or else I'll hold you personally responsible!"

"Is that so!" General Hawkins shouted angrily. "Well who's responsible for the lack of preparedness of your command prior to this attack, when your command knew it was going to take place!"

"I don't answer your questions," General Hall replied. "You answer my questions, and you follow my orders. I'm ordering you to contain those goddamn Japs until help arrives—is that clear?"

General Hawkins swallowed his rage and pride, and it went down like a big lump of shit. "Yes sir."

"Over and out."

General Hawkins hung up the telephone. All his staff officers and aides were looking at him.

"Our orders are to contain the Japs until help arrives," he told them.

They didn't reply, because what could they say? Not one of them thought they could stop the Japs, but they had to try.

The wooden plank door of the bunker was flung open, and a sergeant covered with dust and filth burst inside. He looked around and saw General Hawkins.

"Sir," he said, "the Japs are on their way up this hill!"

"Everybody out!" General Hawkins shouted.

The officers in the bunker adjusted their helmets on their heads and drew their Colt .45 service pistols. General Hawkins inserted a cigarette into his ivory holder, lit it up, and yanked out his Colt .45. His long legs carried him to the door of the bunker, and everybody got out of his way. He stepped outside and saw the trench network cut into the hill just below the bunker.

"Here they come!" somebody shouted, and General Hawkins heard commotion and consternation on the other side of the hill, the side that faced the front line of fighting.

General Hawkins ran down the hill ten yards and jumped into the trench with his Headquarters Company soldiers and the officers from his staff. Everyone moved toward the side of the trench that faced the front line, and General Hawkins pushed his way through the crowd, the cigarette and ivory holder sticking out the side of his mouth.

"They're coming!" somebody shouted.

"Out of my way!" General Hawkins said.

Machine guns opened fire, and soldiers stepped aside so General Hawkins could see what was going on. He looked down the hill and saw waves of Japanese soldiers charging up its side, having broken through the trench system below. Soldiers and officers fired their rifles and pistols at the Japanese soldiers, and many of the Japanese soldiers bit the dust, but the rest kept coming. Machine gun nests mowed them down, but for every Jap who fell, two more took his place and raced up the hill toward its crest.

"Fix bayonets!" General Hawkins screamed. *"Prepare to repel the bastards!"*

Japanese soldiers rushed toward the top of the hill, and the American soldiers and officers got ready behind their sandbags, firing their weapons as quickly as they could. They shot volley after volley at the advancing Japanese soldiers. General Hawkins held his Colt .45 automatic pistol in both hands and aimed at a Japanese only six feet away. He pulled the trigger, and the pistol kicked violently in his hands. The big fat bullet hit the Japanese soldier in the chest and knocked him backwards onto his ass. The Japanese soldier went flat on the ground. A tiny hole was in the front of his shirt, and a gigantic crater in the center of his back where the bullet had blasted out.

General Hawkins and his men maintained their vicious hail of fire, and Japanese bodies piled up high in front of the trench.

SEVENTEEN . . .

Butsko knelt behind the sandbags and peered through the jungle. He knew the Japs were coming; he could smell them in the humid night air. He also could hear them. A huge number of Japanese soldiers roamed through the jungle, looking for American supplies. They'd broken through sections of the Eighty-first Division line and were on their way to the Tadji airfields and the port of Aitape.

The medical headquarters had been protected by the main fortifications of the Eighty-first Division, but now there were breeches in that defense. An hour ago General Hawkins sent soldiers back to protect the hospital, but the equivalent of a company wouldn't be much against the hordes of Japanese soldiers behind the Eighty-first Division main line of defense.

Butsko thought the situation extremely serious. The soldiers General Hawkins sent were truck drivers and clerks who didn't know much about fighting, but they manned the barricades anyway, their mouths set in grim lines, waiting for the inevitable shoot-out.

Butsko glanced to his left and right and thought, *These are the guys I'm gonna die with*. He wished some men from his recon platoon were there to help him out. The ones he was stuck with were unfit for the infantry, which meant they were in pretty bad shape. Most wore thick glasses, so they weren't exactly crack shots. Others suffered from trick knees, overweight, underweight, asthma, nerve conditions, the shakes and shudders, and numerous other physical and psychological ailments.

And then there were the wounded soldiers with bandages on their arms and legs, some barely able to stand, others barely able to hold rifles, but they were prepared to fight it out with the Japs heading toward them and coming closer with every passing second.

Butsko wasn't in such great shape himself. His leg still wasn't completely healed and he couldn't walk well; he limped everywhere and running was out of the question.

A truck arrived with more wounded soldiers. Inside the tents, doctors and nurses continued to operate on the injured. An atmosphere of doom pervaded the area. Everyone knew the score and figured they'd be lucky if they lived another hour.

The first faint glimmer of dawn was on the horizon. Butsko wondered why the Eighty-first hadn't been reinforced yet. He knew there were thousands of troops in the Persecution Task Force. *Where the fuck are they?*

Sounds of Japanese soldiers in the jungle came closer. Butsko crouched lower behind the sandbags and gazed straight ahead. He saw figures moving behind the leaves and trees on the other side of the road, and knew they had to be Japs.

"There they are," Butsko said to the men near him.

He heard Japanese soldiers chattering in the jungle, making plans. Butsko saw more figures in the jungle as additional Japanese soldiers arrived on the scene. Butsko wanted to smoke his last cigarette, but the lit end of a cigarette could be seen a long way at night, and he didn't want to get shot so early in the game.

Butsko spat a lunger onto the ground and looked into the jungle again. It appeared to be filling up with Japs. Evidently they were massing for a big banzai attack.

"Get ready," he told the men near him.

Their bayonets were fixed and their M 1 rifles were loaded. Some of them gasped for breath. Others' hands trembled. They knew they'd be in some deep shit very soon, and didn't look forward to being stabbed by a Japanese bayonet.

Butsko continued to look at the jungle. It was filling up with more Japs. He figured they were drawn to the area by the lights inside the tents where the doctors and nurses were operating. The Japanese soldiers knew they were behind American lines and wanted to find the tents full of food that they'd heard so much about.

"Banzai!" screamed a Japanese officer in the woods.

A mass of Japanese soldiers debouched from the jungle and crossed the road, charging toward the sandbag barricades, their officers waving their samurai swords over their heads, the men shaking their rifles and bayonets and screaming.

The GIs opened fire, and the first fusillade cut down many of the Japanese soldiers. The rest ran forward, crossing the clearing in front of the tents, the same clearing where wounded GIs sat around and sang songs on nights past.

Volleys of fire tore through the Japs, and they dropped like flies, but the others maintained the charge, and they only had a short distance to go. They closed it rapidly, bullets whistling all around them, many bullets striking down their comrades, and then they were only ten yards from the sandbag barricade.

Butsko jumped to his feet and pulled the trigger of his submachine gun. It bucked and kicked in his hands, and its bullets shredded the head of a Japanese soldier directly in front of him. Another Japanese soldier leapt into the air, soaring over the sandbags, and Butsko leveled a stream of bullets at his chest, mangling the Japanese soldier's lungs, heart, and major arteries.

Butsko dodged to the side so the Japanese soldier wouldn't land on top of him. He fired at another Japanese soldier jumping through the air and tore up his intestines. Pivoting to the right, he pulled the trigger of his submachine gun and shot a Japanese soldier in the shoulder. Pivoting to the left, he mangled the neck and shoulders of another Japanese soldier.

The Japanese infantry companies were too much for American truck drivers, clerks, and medical orderlies. Japanese soldiers poured over the barricades and forced the GIs back. A wounded Japanese soldier lying on the ground tried to grab Butsko's ankle, and Butsko kicked him in the face. Butsko swung his submachine gun from side to side, mowing down Japanese soldiers, and they fell at his feet, blood pouring from holes in their bodies. A whole slew of Japanese soldiers ran toward him and he aimed his submachine at them, pulling the trigger.

Click!

The submachine gun was empty. Butsko reached into his bandolier for another clip, but didn't have time to get it out. The Japanese soldiers were already on top of him, and he couldn't run away because of his bum leg.

Butsko threw the submachine gun at them, then picked up an M 1 rifle and bayonet lying in the arms of a dead American soldier on the ground. Butsko pointed the rifle and bayonet at the Japanese soldiers in front of him and thrust forward. The bayonet plunged into the chest of a Japanese soldier, and Butsko turned the M 1 loose, diving at the next Japanese soldier, grabbing his rifle and bayonet and kneeing him in the balls. He pulled the rifle and bayonet out of his hands, spun around, and bashed the third Japanese soldier in the mouth with the rifle butt. The Japanese soldier dropped to the ground, but another was behind him, and he lunged at Butsko with his rifle and bayonet.

Butsko parried the blow expertly and delivered a vertical buttstroke to the Japanese soldier's jaw, snapping his head back. Butsko raised his rifle and bayonet in the air and slashed downward, the blade glancing off the helmet of a Japanese soldier and slicing open his shoulder. The Japanese soldier bellowed in pain and Butsko kicked him in the balls. The Japanese soldier fell to the ground, blood oozing from the massive gash on his shoulder, clutching his shattered balls, and Butsko stepped over his writhing body, getting low and shoving his rifle and bayonet into the stomach of another Japanese soldier, then pulling back and smashing the next Japanese soldier in the chops with his rifle butt.

For a few brief seconds Butsko found himself without an adversary nearby. Bodies of Japanese soldiers littered the ground all around him, and he saw his submachine gun lying there. He dropped the Japanese rifle and bayonet in his hands, scooped up the submachine gun, and loaded it while glancing around.

The situation was desperate. Japanese soldiers advanced toward the tents. The ground was covered with dead and wounded GIs. Butsko saw a bunch of Japanese soldiers working their way toward the surgery tent, methodically killing the GIs in their path.

Butsko thought he'd pull back and try to defend that tent, when a Japanese soldier nearby spotted him and decided to kill him. The Japanese soldier shouted *"Banzai!"* and charged Butsko, and Butsko turned toward him, pulling the trigger of his Thompson submachine gun.

The submachine gun chattered angrily, and the Japanese soldier backpedaled, tripping over his feet. He fell to the ground, blood spouting from holes in his chest and stomach.

Butsko hopped, hobbled, and limped toward the main tent.

He saw Japanese soldiers going around toward the back of the tent where the operating section was. Two Japanese soldiers near the front of the tent turned toward Butsko as he ran toward them, and Butsko pulled the trigger of the submachine gun, peppering them with holes. They fell to the ground and he jumped over them, plunging into the main tent.

Wounded men lay all over the ground, either unconscious or too feeble to fight Japs. Butsko limped past them swiftly, leaping on his good leg and taking it easy on his bad one. He burst into the operating room, and the doctors and nurses continued to operate on wounded men as shots were fired outside and men screamed when they were sliced open with bayonets.

"The Japs are gonna be in here any moment now!" Butsko said. "You'd better arm yourselves!"

"We're medical personnel," Captain Epstein replied, looking up from a shrapnel wound in the chest of a soldier, "and we'll continue with our work."

"You won't be continuing with it for much longer," Butsko told him.

A Japanese bayonet jabbed through the side of the tent and ripped down. Butsko fired at the slash in the tent, and a Japanese soldier fell through, blood spurting from a hole in his forehead. He landed at the feet of Lieutenant Betty Crawford, who screamed in horror.

Another Japanese soldier jumped through the hole, and Butsko gave him a submachine gun burst in the face. The far wall of the tent was torn open and seconds later a big burly Japanese soldier leapt inside the tent. Butsko spun around and gave him a shower of hot lead, knocking the Japanese soldier back through the hole he'd just made.

A Japanese soldier charged through the first hole, and Butsko aimed the submachine gun at him, pulling the trigger.

Click!

The machine gun was empty. Butsko held it in both his hands and charged the Japanese soldier, parrying the thrust of his bayonet to the side, bashing him in the snout with the submachine gun, knocking the Japanese soldier back through the hole.

Butsko went after him, jumping through the hole. He collided with another Japanese soldier, and the Japanese soldier's bayonet cut open Butsko's left biceps muscle, but Butsko kneed him in the balls and the Japanese soldier stuck out his tongue, reaching for his flattened testicles.

Butsko pushed him out of the way, bashed another Japanese soldier in the mouth with his submachine gun, and then raised it in time to block the downward thrust of a samurai sword in the hand of a Japanese officer.

Sparks flew into the air as the sword collided with the barrel of the submachine gun, and Butsko kicked the Japanese officer in the balls. The Japanese officer let go the sword and Butsko plucked it out of the air, spinning around and swinging sideways, lopping off the head of another Japanese soldier. He swung down and chopped a Japanese soldier's head in two. He swung low and hit another Japanese soldier in the waist, the blade hacking through nearly to the Japanese soldier's spine.

Butsko tugged the sword but it wouldn't come loose. Two more Japanese soldiers ran toward him, and he dived toward the one on the right, his big hands clamping down on the Japanese soldier's rifle and bayonet, and he spun the Japanese soldier to the side, pulling the rifle and bayonet out of his hands.

Bam!

A rifle butt hit Butsko upside his head and sent him stumbling backwards. He fell through a hole in the tent and landed on his ass inside. A shot rang out as Lieutenant Frannie Divers shot a Japanese soldier with a Colt .45. The Japanese soldier had just entered the tent through the other hole, and now another Japanese soldier came in through the same hole. Frannie aimed her Colt .45, fired, and missed the son of a bitch.

Butsko picked up a Japanese Arisaka rifle and bayonet and jumped to his feet. He charged the Japanese soldier and rammed his rifle and bayonet forward. The Japanese soldier parried the blow and tried to bash Butsko in the head with the butt of his rifle, but Butsko reached out, grabbed the Japanese soldier's throat with his big hand, and squeezed, cutting off his supply of air.

The Japanese soldier blacked out, dropping to his knees, but still Butsko didn't let go. The doctors and nurses watched the Japanese soldier turn purple, and then they heard a roar of gunfire outside the tent.

"What the hell's that?" Butsko muttered, dropping the Japanese soldier.

His first thought was that more Japanese soldiers had attacked the beleaguered medical headquarters, but then he heard Bronx cheers, rebel yells, and Indian war-whoops. He rushed to the side of the tent, poked his head outside, and saw American soldiers swarming into the area. The GIs charged past the tents, shooting at Japs, clubbing them with their rifle butts, and sticking them with their bayonets. More GIs followed the ones Butsko was looking at, and then more GIs came after those.

"My God!" Butsko said. "The reinforcements are here!"

He heard the voice of Captain Epstein. "What's going on out there!"

Butsko pulled his head back into the tent and turned around. "We've just been reinforced," he said wearily. "You can go back to work now."

The doctors and nurses returned to their patients, resuming their operating procedures. Exhausted, Butsko sat on the floor, leaning against a tent pole. He took out a bent Lucky Strike and lit it up, taking a deep puff.

An American soldier stuck his head through one of the holes. "Everything okay in here?" he asked.

"It's about time you guys showed up," Butsko snarled.

EIGHTEEN . . .

"Sir?"

General Adachi looked up from the map table and saw General Tatsunari Kimura, his executive officer, standing in front of him.

General Adachi's eyes were bleary with fatigue and his jowls sagged. "What is it?" he asked.

"I'm afraid I have bad news, sir." General Kimura paused. His lower lip trembled.

"Out with it!" General Adachi shouted.

"Our soldiers have been stopped, sir."

"Stopped, you say?"

"Yes sir."

"How can this be? According to the last reports, they were advancing in the crucial center of the American line!"

"American reinforcements arrived and filled the gap. At least a division of them, sir."

"You're sure of that?"

"Yes sir."

"The attack has been stopped *everywhere?*"

"Yes sir."

General Adachi could've been knocked over by a feather. He took a deep breath and saw spots in front of his eyes. He'd been stopped before he captured the Tadji airfields, and he knew what that meant: It was all over for him and the Eighteenth Army. "Excuse me," he said.

He turned and walked through the tent flap into his office, and now that his men couldn't see him anymore, he went limp. His shoulders sagged and he collapsed onto the chair behind his desk.

All is lost, he thought. *The offensive has failed.* He covered his face with his hands. All he could do now was commit harakiri. He felt a terrible sinking sensation in his stomach, and a jackhammer pounded inside his skull. *I've lost.*

He leaned back in his chair, removed his hands from his face, and took a deep breath. A map of the front lay on the desk in front of him and he swept it away; it fell to the ground.

I should've known it wouldn't work, he said to himself. *I didn't have enough troops or supplies.* It was clear to him why he'd failed. He'd been living on hope during the past three months, planning a campaign that deep in his heart he knew wouldn't work, but the gallant old field general knew he couldn't just lie down and die; he had to fight and that's what he did.

It's all over now, he thought. It had been a wild gamble and it hadn't paid off. He thought of all his men out there on the west side of the Driniumor, dead and wounded or alive and waiting for the Americans to counterattack and push them back.

General Adachi pursed his lips and blew air out. Acid spilled into his stomach, burning his ulcer so furiously that he cried out softly and doubled over, clutching his aching guts with both arms.

A sliver of the sun broke over the horizon, making the sky glow a light shade of red. Colonel Hutchins sat on a log and sipped from his canteen, thinking of the events of the night. Nearby a crew of soldiers from his Headquarters Company erected a sandbag bunker that would be his new command post.

Colonel Hutchins was happy and sad at the same time. He was happy because the Japs had been stopped, and that meant they'd shot their wad on New Guinea forever. Their attack had cost them plenty, and they'd never be able to mount one like it again. The battle for New Guinea would become a mopping-up operation from then on.

He was sad because so many men had been lost. His casualties hadn't been as high as they might've been, because his fighting retreat had gone smoothly. The heavy casualties had come when they'd had to stand and fight.

Colonel Hutchins wasn't mad at General Hall. Colonel Hutchins knew that somebody had to stand and fight sooner or later, to hold the Japs until reinforcments arrived, and his regiment was one of those that got the dirty job. That's the way war went. But it could've gone worse. The Japs could've won the battle, and then his casualties would've been much higher.

He heard footsteps and looked around. General Hawkins walked toward him, a cigarette in his ivory holder sticking out the corner of his mouth. "Morning Colonel," General Hawkins said.

"Morning sir."

"Mind if I sit down?"

"This jungle belongs to you sir. Sit wherever you like."

General Hawkins sat on the log next to Colonel Hutchins, and could smell the liquor on his breath. "It's been a helluva night," General Hawkins said.

"Sure was," Colonel Hutchins agreed.

"Looks like we licked the Japs."

"Looks like we did."

General Hawkins turned to Colonel Hutchins. "I figure I owe you an apology. You drink too much and you're insubordinate most of the time, but you were right about everything to do with this attack, and I was wrong. I just thought I ought to tell you that, and in the future I'll try to pay more attention to your views."

There was silence for a few moments. Both men felt awkward. Colonel Hutchins shrugged. "That it?" Colonel Hutchins asked.

"That's it."

"Have a drink," Colonel Hutchins said, holding out the canteen.

General Hawkins hesitated a moment, then reached for the white lightning. He raised it in the air and said, "Here's to victory."

"Right," Colonel Hutchins said.

General Hawkins touched the mouth of the canteen to his lips and leaned his head back, swallowing some down. The white lightning was sweet and intoxicating, but not nearly as sweet and intoxicating as the victory he'd just won. The Japs had been stopped. His division was intact. Tomorrow he'd take it to the Japs and push them back all the way to Tokyo.

"Save some for me," Colonel Hutchins said.

General Hawkins passed the canteen back. Colonel Hutchins raised it in the air. "Here's to good booze," he said.

He held the canteen with his hand and his teeth and guzzled until every drop of white lightning was gone. Burping, he wiped his mouth with the back of his hand. His eyeballs danced around in his head and he heard whistles and bells. "It's empty," he said to General Hawkins. "Let's get some more."

"Where?" General Hawkins asked.

"From my mess hall."

"Lets go."

The two officers stood, hitched up their belts, and walked off side by side.

Look for

SATAN'S CAGE

**next novel in THE RAT BASTARDS series
from Jove**

coming in November!